THE FIELDS OF EDEN

By the same author

Summer Solstice

THE FIELDS
OF EDEN

Michael T. Hinkemeyer

G.P. Putnam's Sons, New York

Copyright © 1977 by Michael T. Hinkemeyer

SBN: 399-12094-7
Library of Congress Cataloging in Publication Data
Hinkemeyer, Michael T.
   The fields of Eden.

   I. Title.
PZ4.H6638Fi   [PS3558.I54]   813'.5'4   77-23754

PRINTED IN THE UNITED STATES OF AMERICA.

Author's Note

I would like to thank my brother, Richard J. Hinkemeyer, for suggesting this story, which is based on a tragedy that occurred in Stearns County, Minnesota, several years ago. Other than that, the story is a fiction. I have taken liberties with the location of certain villages—there is no Lake Eden, for instance—and of course all the characters portrayed herein are fictional creations of my own.

MTH

"At the Scene of the Crime"

I

Sheriff Whippletree said nothing as he watched the guys from the Stearns County Ambulance Service carry out the last of the bodies. This one was a little girl. He could tell by the pathetic little ring on one of the fingers of the tiny hand that extended over the edge of the stretcher, from under the green plastic sheet. Her small, perfect body lay under that sheet but not her face, which had been destroyed by the blast of a shotgun. Whippletree said nothing because he was afraid that his voice would break if he spoke. As appalled by these five murders as he was, he did not want to let his deputy "Bimbo" Bonwit get something on him to use when he ran around the county crowing—as he always did—that the sheriff was "candy-assed" and "unprofessional." Outside the parsonage, he could hear Bimbo bellow at the ambulance

7

guys and the other deputies, calling out unnecessary orders for standard practices that had already been taken care of.

This hurricane of death, however, was far from standard.

They carried the little girl out. Bimbo was bellowing at them. "Get her in the ambulance! Come on, now, move it. Get her in the ambulance." And Whippletree was alone in the house. Still stunned by the horror of what he'd seen, he sat down on the threadbare couch in what the Reverend had always called the "front room." He looked around. He knew that those called to the ministry made a decision to forego many of the material pleasures of life, but the parsimony, the poverty, revealed in this house was close to obscene. Especially because the community, Lake Eden, out here in the resort area of Western Stearns County, was pretty well off. Whippletree was not a man with a formal religion, and he had difficulty understanding why anybody would want to be a minister, but that was an issue of small wonder compared to problems he had now. Why would anybody want to shoot Reverend Matthew Koster? And kill his whole family? And who had done it?

Whippletree sat there in the dingy room, looking from the ravaged wooden floor to the paint-peeled gray walls, wondering where to start. Then Bimbo came barreling in, all officious, and the sheriff started and stood up. Whippletree was a tall man, six-two and broad-shouldered, but Deputy Bonwit still towered over him, huge, ham-handed, his jaw prognathous beneath a blond "butch" cut, his head unnaturally small. He wanted the sheriff's job.

"The ambulances are leavin' now, Whip," he said. "They won't have to break no speed records this trip."

"How about the one carrying Koster? They make it to the hospital yet?"

"Not yet," Bimbo said, giving the room a once-over. "They

give me a call on the radio a minute ago sayin' they was goin' past David's."

David's was a bar and restaurant on the outskirts of the county seat, St. Cloud, where both the hospital and the sheriff's office were located.

"If you'da been able to get that helicopter"—Bimbo pronounced it "hell-ee-copter"—"I suggested, he'da been there already. As it is, he might die, too, now."

Bimbo dropped his head at the tragedy and enormity of the thought.

So, Whippletree thought angrily, *more ammunition for you. I couldn't persuade Melvin Betters to give me county money for a chopper because you and he are both working against me, and now you can run around saying Reverend Koster died because we didn't have one. So you have it both ways.*

"County this big, got to have one," Bimbo was saying piously. "They got one in Meeker. They got one in Kandiyohi. How come we don't have one?"

"Talk to Mel Betters, then, why don't you, Wayne?" Whippletree said, letting the deputy know he knew what was going on. "And, Wayne, run on out to the patrol car and get me a camera and a yellow pad."

He was still the sheriff and he still gave the orders. *At least until the next election, ha!*

"Bimbo," who detested being called by his real name, slouched resentfully out of the house. "You goin' to let me take the pictures this time?" he grunted.

"No," Whippletree shot back, "You never hold the damn camera still and the pictures don't turn out."

II

The whole thing had begun just a little over an hour ago. It was a hot, quiet August night, and a bunch of them were sitting around the office, playing a little poker. Bimbo talked a good game, but he played recklessly, even stupidly, and he was down fifteen bucks. Whippletree watched him keep on losing and was very content. In the background, the radio crackled and barked occasionally, tied into the various wanderings of the St. Cloud police patrol cars and to Jamie Lugosch, a truly spastic deputy, whom Whippletree had sent out to console a Sauk Centre farmer who'd had a cow killed in a hit-and-run. Jamie took things very seriously and he could handle the farmer with a straight face. Although it was no joke: cattle were worth good money on the market in St. Paul.

After a while, a little after midnight, Jamie called in to say there was a local thunderstorm out west there, and he was going to sit it out in Lake Eden.

"Probably wants to get a beer at the Valmar," Deputy Pollock said. He was a short, paunchy kid who had once been a local football hero. The poker players laughed through their noses at the mention of the Valmar, Lake Eden's most active tavern. Their reaction had little to do with the Valmar, which was a tavern much like any other, but rather with Mary Prone, the owner and barmaid, who was pretty active herself. Bimbo was seventeen bucks down now, and starting to realize it, and it was the sheriff's deal. He'd just started flipping out the cards, with a couple of aces totally under his control, when the radio crackled again. Not a man there didn't jump and feel a cold tingle up his back when they heard Jamie Lugosch shrieking breathlessly over the speaker:

"Sheriff! Sheriff! My God, it's . . . it's . . . Oh, *God*! It's

10

murder. The whole . . . the whole Koster family's been
. . . it's some maniac. Jesus, get out here fast
. . . I'm . . . scared!"

Whippletree took in Bimbo's reaction. As soon as the big
guy got his mouth shut and his eyes unbulged, he looked to
see how the sheriff was taking it. Was he still in command?
Was he going to panic? They were sure as hell watching his
every move, hoping to get plenty on him in time for the election in November.

"All right," the sheriff said, standing up and leaving the
cards where they were. "Pollock, tell him we're on our way.
You stay here and monitor the radio. We'll take two cars. I'll
take one. Bimbo, you get the other. And take weapons. We
don't know what's going on, and Jamie is the kind of guy to
panic, but I don't think this is one of those times."

"And get some ambulances out there, too," he yelled to
Pollock as he ran for the parking lot. "Call Jamie and see how
many we're going to need." *Except we probably need hearses,* he
thought, with a sinking feeling.

The Stearns County sheriff's office was in the front section
of the county jail, right across the street from the ornate
gold-domed, marble-staircased courthouse, which had been
built in the twenties in an attempt to imitate the state capitol
in St. Paul. No attempt to imitate anything had been made
when the jail was put up, except maybe a squat brick building. The sheriff and his deputies left on the run, heading for
the parking lot around back. The men leaped into their cars
and wheeled out onto the courthouse square, Bimbo with his
siren wailing away already, although he was fifty miles from
the scene of the crime. Whippletree picked up his radio mike
and told him to shut the damn thing off, since it was after
midnight and why wake up everybody in St. Cloud.

So they sliced through town at high speed, swung west out

11

by the Red Owl, and took the highway out to Lake Eden, with Bimbo in the lead car at about ninety miles per. ("He could hardly keep up with me, the old goat," the sheriff could hear Bimbo saying.)

The county did not have many murders, and a mass murder such as the one Jamie reported was close to unimaginable. In fact, the whole area was usually so quiet that a lot of people called it comatose, although those who did were unaware of a lot of stuff going on beneath the surface. The county was bordered on the eastern end by the Mississippi River, and stretched westward toward the lake region in a geographical shape much like the state of Pennsylvania's, except squarer, being roughly sixty miles square. Not a mean distance after midnight. St. Cloud, the county seat, was where Philadelphia would have been (the green sign on the outskirts read: WELCOME TO ST. CLOUD, THE GRANITE CITY, POP. 42,315. WE LOVE OUR CHILDREN.) Lake Eden would have been near Pittsburgh.

Pollock radioed to report that three ambulances were on the road behind them. Jamie, somewhat calmed down, radioed to say he'd cut Koster down and was trying to stop the bleeding and in God's name where were they and what was keeping them?

"So the Reverend's still alive, anyway," Whippletree muttered. Deputy Axel Vogel, riding beside him, cooking in his own fat in the August heat and fondling the double-barreled shotgun between his knees as if it were his joint, had the wit to deduce, "Maybe he can tell us what happened."

Whippletree nodded, then shook his head, partly for the tragedy toward which he sped, partly in contemplation of the sagacity of his deputies, whose positions were acquired and maintained through a complicated system of patronage over which the sheriff had only a modicum of influence. He intended to make it an election issue.

12

The Fields of Eden

The little towns flashed by, Rockville, Cold Spring, Richmond, St. Alazara, dark and plain and identical. The fieldstone church with the high steeple. The tavern. General Store. Gas station. A cluster of ranch style houses, built by retired farmers and their wives, who moved into town after leaving the farm to their sons or maybe a daughter and a son-in-law. There were about a hundred thousand "souls" in the county, as the St. Cloud Bishop was fond of saying, and Whippletree, who had been in politics for twenty years, knew of most of them. Aside from St. Cloud, it was a rural county, as sober and rugged and inspiring as the dark shafts of the grain elevators in some of the towns.

The Reverend Matthew Koster was somebody Whippletree had only heard of. A couple of years back, Koster and his family had moved to Lake Eden, where the Reverend had been called to serve as pastor of the Seventh Reformed Church of Christ. The sheriff had it all down in the books back in his office, books he used not for any sinister purposes, but simply for electioneering. When fall came and the campaign started up, Whippletree went around the county from one town to another, and when he did the little book would enable him to walk up to the Seventh Reformed parsonage and say, "Reverend, glad to meet you. How's the wife, Bonnie? And the kids? Let's see, Ben and Paul are in the little league, right? And how's little Ruthie and the baby? Named him "Matt" after yourself, I hear. Glad to see it. Keeps a tradition, know what I mean . . ." And so on and so forth. In Stearns County, and elsewhere, such tactics translate into votes.

But not this year, Whippletree thought. *At least I won't have to go checking up on the names of the victims.*

Then the air cooled and the highway turned slick and wet, and even Bimbo slowed down a little. "Yep, looks like there was a little thundershower out this way," Axel Vogel offered,

13

and ahead of them in the western sky they could still see the dark retreating clouds, shattered by jagged reflexive patterns of lightning. "Lake Eden 2 Miles" said the sign, and ahead of them Bimbo slowed down.

"What the . . ." Axel wheezed, leaning forward.

Whippletree shot around the lead car. "I don't suppose he knows where the parsonage is," he said, with no little satisfaction.

But the sheriff did. It was one block off the main street, next to the modest one-story clapboard church, on a green lawn surrounded by box elder trees. The house was directly behind it, and there in his headlights he caught Jamie's patrol car, and Jamie himself bent low over a shape in front of the headlights. Thank God he hadn't put on the red riot light. All they needed was a crowd gathering. Whippletree drove up the gravel drive and stopped. Bimbo followed, without the siren, a move that, for him, qualified as near genius.

Whippletree got out of the car. It would have been a great night. The storm-cooled air was pure delight, carrying a hint of clover and wheat from the prairies beyond. It was a reminder of his boyhood. The grass was thick and wet, and the leaves on the dark shapes of the trees were fresh and dripping. It was very quiet.

Jamie Lugosch stood up. His short-sleeved white shirt with the badge over his breast pocket had a dark, irregular patch across the front that glistened in the headlights. Jamie was near tears. He wiped bloody hands on his trousers.

"God, sheriff. I think he's passed out. And . . . and, sheriff, *please* don't make me go in the house again. *Please!* You can say I'm a coward or anything you want, but please don't make me . . ."

Bimbo, hurrying up, said, "Now, goddam it, Jamie, you'll do . . ."

14

"That's enough," Whippletree said softly. It was a tone he seldom used, but even Bimbo knew what it meant. *Shut up.* "Jamie, you go down to the main street and flag the ambulances over here when they come through. Hurry up, they'll be here any second. Bimbo, you and Axel check the church and the grounds. In case anybody's still here. We'll take the house together in a minute. Farley," he said to the remaining deputy, "let's see if there's anything we can do for the Reverend."

Jamie had done all he could, about all anybody could do under the circumstances. Using a flashlight, Whippletree knelt down on the wet grass and took a look. It looked very bad. Matthew Koster was one of those slender men with regular, almost handsome features. Whippletree had heard people say that he was a verbal person, quick with sympathy and a smile, sensitive, almost diffident. In the big cities of the country, such men are regarded as handsome and attractive, and if they play their cards right, they can get what they want. In Stearns County, however, such men are "pretty," and it is best that they stick to "women's things" like the church, where they won't hurt themselves playing with the men. Whippletree had not heard enough of Koster to know what forces led him to religion, or even Lake Eden, but he had certainly gotten himself hurt, all right.

The young clergyman was out like a light, his face pale and getting paler. Jamie had put him down on a couple of army blankets, which were kept in the trunks of the sheriff's patrol cars for occasions such as this, and had also wrapped another blanket around Koster's body. The front of the blanket was getting darker and darker by the minute and the dark place spread out over the blanket. Gently, Whippletree folded it and took it off. He directed the flashlight carefully. There, in the upper abdomen, was the source of the blood, from a wound that looked as if it had come from a small-caliber rifle,

15

a .22 most likely. The blood came slowly and steadily. There was a good chance, too, that if the bullet had exited, Koster was also bleeding from the back, and that was bad. Thank God the flow was as slow as it was.

"Jesus God," Farley said, bending over, "look at his wrists."

The sheriff did, and saw the knotted cords around them, the ends ragged, and he remembered Jamie's remark about "cutting him down." Down from where? On an impulse, he checked the man's legs and there, too, above the severe black oxfords, the ankles were bound by similar knotted lengths of cord. Whippletree felt sick. They had tied the man and shot him, or shot him and tied him, and left him to die. Where? He would have to ask Jamie Lugosch.

Worried about shock, worried about the steady seepage of blood, he was trying to get a pressure bandage in place when the first of the ambulances turned off the street and came up the drive. In accordance with his previously radioed instructions, they were only showing their fog lights. The big vehicle rocked gently up the drive on its heavy-duty shocks and came to a stop. Two eager interns jumped from the rear of the ambulance and rushed over, and Whippletree felt a great relief. This part of it, anyway, was out of his hands.

"Get him in the ambulance," one of the doctors barked to an attendant, a command that Bimbo Bonwit, coming around the corner of the church, shotgun at the ready, repeated with relish.

"Nothin' there, Whip. Quiet as a mouse. Or as the house." He made a sound somewhere between a chortle and a snarl. "When we goin' in?"

"Get the plasma ready," one of the doctors was saying to the other. "I think he'll make it, but he's lost a lot of blood."

"When can I talk to him?" Whippletree asked.

"I said I *think* he'll make it," the doctor said. "Now, move away, we've got to get back to the hospital in St. Cloud."

16

Jamie held the other two ambulances at the entrance to the parsonage drive, and the first ambulance backed out, turned, and shot away. By the interior lights of the emergency vehicle, Whippletree could see the two doctors bending over the clergyman, working, working.

Now comes the hard part, he thought. He reached inside the glove compartment of his patrol car and took out a pint of Christian Brothers' Brandy. ("Drinking on duty, and encouraging others in same," Bimbo would say, the beer-bellied bastard.) "Jamie," the sheriff called quietly, "come on over here." He led the trembling young deputy to the car and sat him on the hood. "Take a drink of this," he said, handing him the pint, "and tell me what happened."

"But in the house . . ." Jamie began.

"Don't worry about in the house. You take yourself a couple of swallows of this, and tell me as best you can."

Lugosch did, throwing it back. He grimaced but he did not cough. He was grateful for the drink. He took another swallow, and this time he did not grimace. Axel Vogel and Bimbo, still holding their shotguns, gathered around. Farley crouched down next to the car. The attendants from the other ambulances were here now, too, waiting, listening.

"This is the way it was," Jamie said. "I was heading on back from Sauk Centre, after handling that hit-and-run and . . . you want to know about that?"

"Save it for later."

"Yeah, and . . . and anyway, I cut down across county like you told us to do, showing the car and keeping an eye out, down through Padua and Elrosa, and I was just about ready to cut on over to Lake Henry and back to St. Cloud when the storm come up. Looked pretty bad to me, and when it started raining, I could hardly see, so I says to myself, I'll just go on over to Lake Eden and sit it out there. Have myself a beer at the Club Valmar."

17

The deputies nodded sagely.

"Well, hell," Jamie said defensively, "lot of trouble starts in there! I might have been able to head off a fight or somethin'."

"Skip it," Whippletree said.

"And so I hit town in the other direction, goin' real slow, on account of the storm, and just as I'm driving by the Reformed Church, there's a tremendous flash of lightning and thunder, you know, one of them flashes that lights up the whole sky like it was daytime? And that's when I seen him. The Reverend. Of course, I didn't know it was the Reverend then, but in the lightning I saw this man tied spread-eagled to the laundry posts in the backyard. And even in the storm, I could see the blood.

"So it's pouring rain, see, and the lightning is flashing, and I stop the car. Then comes the next flash and I see it again, and I'm scared. There's the guy tied out there in the rain, and nothing and nobody around, and me alone. So I thought, should I give you guys a call or check it out first, and I thought, well, I better check it out first, you know, maybe it's a scarecrow or somethin' . . ."

He broke off, and made a sound like a smothered sob. Whippletree quickly handed him the brandy, and he took a slug.

"Except it wasn't no scarecrow." He shuddered. "It was the Reverend Koster. He was still conscious, just barely. I shine the headlights on him and go over and cut him down."

"Did he say anything?"

"Let me think. He was moaning. He muttered something about God, or something like that. Then I got him some blankets, and the rain let up. Then he said, 'The house. They killed my. . . .' And that was it. He passes out, right there. I didn't know what to do, so I took the flashlight and run for the house . . ."

18

"Stupid move," Bimbo growled. "Somebody still could of been in there."

The sheriff waved away Bonwit's remark.

". . . and the electricity was out," Jamie was saying, "on account of the storm. So I shined the flashlight around, you know? There was nothing downstairs that I could see, but there was somethin' about the place, somethin' . . ."

Whippletree nodded. He was only a country cop, and had seen only a few murders in his time. Death has a smell to it, but Jamie Lugosch was talking about the *feel.* The feel of something monstrous, alien and untouchable, right there in the air around you, soundlessly mocking your powerlessness and mortality, laughing at the very soul of you.

"So?" he prompted.

"So then I went upstairs . . ." Jamie tried. It was all he could tell them just then.

III

"No point waiting until it's light," Whippletree said. "We got to go in now."

Already, to complicate matters, a few sleepy neighbors had come out of their houses, saying, "Howdy, sheriff, what's up?" and not knowing what *was* up, but with expressions on their faces that held simultaneously the dawning realization of, and the conditional acceptance of, something that would turn out to be very bad. He could see it in their faces, and he could see it in the forward-leaning shapes of women in upstairs windows, women in housecoats and curlers, holding emergency lamps. (Out here, the summer storms almost always knocked out the electricity.)

"Nothing that we're sure of yet," Whippletree told the

men. "You can help me out by keeping any women away, though, or kids, if any should happen to wake up this time of night."

Then they went in. Whippletree and Farley from the front, Bimbo and Axel Vogel from around in back of the house. They made a check of the basement and the downstairs, but, as Jamie had reported, nothing was there. It was all upstairs. Whippletree started climbing. A portion of his life passed before him when he saw what he saw. It was that portion he had spent confronting and dealing with the other murders during his tenure as sheriff. There was the time St. Alazara farmer Otto Ronsky shot Father Ripulski, blew off his head with a ten-gauge shotgun in Ronsky's cornfield, for messing with Ronsky's wife. Ronsky not only admitted the shooting, he swore he'd tell the whole damn county. So he not only never spent a night in jail, he was never even booked. The whole thing was covered up. Whippletree figured the bishop was still paying Ronsky off to keep his mouth shut. And there was the time Dick Kufelski, the janitor at the refrigerator plant in St. Cloud, killed his foreman with a blowtorch. And the case of the Shaeffer widow, who had asked for it, most people thought. But when he saw the first body, he knew this was going to be far, far worse, and, for just a second, he thought this might just be the time to quit, and wasn't he too old and too much given to sympathy to look at things like this and keep a level head?

The circled beam of the flashlight found the blood first, and it was everywhere: on the walls, floors, bedclothes, furniture, and there were wispy chunks of debris as well, which would later prove to be pieces of skull and hair. In the bedroom at the top of the stairs, in the bed in an attitude of sleep but with her head shattered, was Bonnie, Mrs. Koster. The baby in the crib in that bedroom was all over, all but blown away at close range. Down the hall, one of the boys was at the doorway of the next bedroom, headless, slumped against the door, and his brother, who looked a few years younger, was lying next to the bed. He had been shot in the back, and shiny purple entrails glistened in the light. But the one that brought tears to Whippletree's eyes—he was glad for the darkness then—was the little girl, Ruthie, shot, apparently, in the back of the head right at the closet door, to which she had most likely been going for shelter. Whippletree and his wife had lost a daughter years ago, and the pain still came back every time he thought about it. It came back now. The deputies, even Bimbo, were quiet, as the feel of horror swirled about the room and withdrew, passing them, passing them *this time,* an angel of death already satiated.

"Okay," the sheriff said, "okay. We got to keep people out of here. Farley, you and Lugosch handle that. Axel, call the lighting company and see what their story is. Bimbo, you and me'll have to do the diagrams of the bodies. Bring the chalk to make the marks on the floor. And black magic marker for the ones in the bed and crib. Jesus, goddamn . . ." he turned his face to the wall and retched. He did not particularly feel like retching: he felt like crying. ". . . we'll take the pictures later. Now, let's go on downstairs."

He prepared the ambulance guys as best he could for what they were about to see. Meantime, Pollock, back in St. Cloud, radioed that Koster was in the emergency room of the St. Cloud hospital, and so far there was no word on his condition or prospects. Whippletree felt a tiny shred of soothing anger take root down in his gut: Koster *had* to pull through, dammit. He *had* to. Koster could tell them what had happened, who had done this, and by God in heaven, Whippletree would find whoever it was, and if he got to them at the right time, before there were a lot of other people around, he would walk all over their heads for about an hour.

The lights went back on, and he and Bimbo got to work

21

with the diagrams showing the attitudes of the bodies in death. The drawings would be photographed and filed, and later used if there was ever any trial. Working, he tried to keep his mind on the details, anything he might use. There was work ahead of him now, and none of it pleasant. He had no leads, and would have to ask a lot of questions. In Stearns County, people don't like questions. (A lot of the time, they don't even like answers.) He bent and, almost tenderly, drew a chalk line around the body of the little girl. The ambulance attendants came and went; one of them was sobbing, softly but steadily. The others coughed a lot and cleared their throats. *Jesus!* Nothing else, he thought, had happened in the county that night. No tie-in whatever, except maybe that hit-and-run cow death up at Sauk Centre, he thought grimly, which, he suspected, would later prove to have been the result of a combination of a teenage farm boy, a pickup truck, and an almost-empty case of Grain Belt "Strong."

There was a lot of work to do, and drawing the chalk line was just the beginning of it.

Finally, the ambulances were pulling out of the driveway, bound for the county morgue, to await the respective attentions of the coroner and the undertaker. Whippletree pulled a sweat-stained pad out of his breast pocket, and made a note to check on Koster's next of kin, should that be necessary. He leaned back on the ratty couch and rubbed his eyes. Outside, the eastern sky was beginning to show a faint ragged edge of pink, and the light framed by the cheap-curtained windows of the front room was no longer black. Bimbo came and went, getting the camera. Whippletree thought about what he knew. It was not much.

Bonnie, Mrs. Koster, had most likely been shot first, or the baby first and then Mrs. Koster. It made sense: the parents' room was first at the head of the stairs. Mrs. Koster had apparently been asleep, and whoever had done it would also have wanted to get her out of the way before trying to deal with the Reverend. Then, too, there was the fact that the other three children had all been awake, in attitudes of movement, of going somewhere, when their deaths had come. Koster must have been taken from the house and tied before the others were killed. That seemed to fit, because he'd been shot with a rifle, while the rest of the family had been shot with a shotgun, so there must have been at least two people involved. Whippletree had already contacted the state police laboratory, with whom county officials collaborated on fingerprints, forensics, etc., but he knew in his bones that, even with all the blood around, and even with the rain, footprints would be hard to find. Slick mud rubbers, probably.

He stood up, sat down again. It either had to be a hate murder, or a random act of death. It certainly could not have been robbery, unless the minister was secreting money from the Sunday collection, which, judging by the appearance of the Seventh Reformed Church and its parsonage, couldn't amount to much anyway.

He stood up again and walked around the room. Over in the corner, next to the door, was a battered old desk, with a chair behind it and a chair next to it. Here the Reverend probably talked to members of his church, counseled them, planned bake sales with them, listened to them tell him how to run the church better. On top of the desk, in a neat row, were some religious books: several copies of *The Life of Christ* in paperback; a book on Simon Peter: *Fisher of Men; Jesus in our Lives*, by a Percy Wimple; and a book on miracles, apparently, "Water into Wine," "Rising from the Dead," "Loaves and Fishes," etc. *That rising from the dead is a good idea*, Whippletree thought, *and it would make my job a lot easier.* He wrote down the names of all the books. Once, several years ago, he had cajoled Mel Betters into giving him travel expenses to a law enforcement conference in Chicago. At the conference, he had been told to take notes on everything at the scene of the crime because you never knew when it was going to come in handy. So now, in the green file cabinet back in his office, he had reams of notes, none of which had ever come in handy.

He surveyed the desk. A ring-clip folder was packed full of mimeographed church bulletins. At the top of each, right under the Seventh Reformed logo, was a "Quotation of the Week," the one for this week, August 15–21: "The Lord helps those who help themselves." *I'll say,* he thought, thinking again of Mel Betters and Bimbo Bonwit, *but that's pretty go-getter for a poverty-stricken clergyman, isn't it? Maybe he had trouble thinking them up.* He riffled through the folder and found them to be eclectic, running all the way from "The meek shall inherit the earth" to "A stitch in time saves nine." *Maybe there's something in this week's bulletin to give a clue,* he thought, but all it contained were announcements of usual weekly routine. The choir would meet for practice on such-and-such a date. Mrs. Withers and Mrs. Hockapuk were asking for volunteers to collect old clothes for Indian children on the reservation up north, and Mavis Kronenberg had visited her sister Lavinia at the latter's home in St. Cloud. The rest of the bulletins were just the same. Whippletree wondered again why anybody would want to be a minister and live a life filled with the meaningless chittering and scurrying of women who live for a mention of their names in the church bulletin. At that moment, he felt more strongly about it than he ordinarily would have because he knew that he would have to spend hours and days talking to people like Mrs. Withers and Mrs. Hockapuk, to try and find out if they had seen or heard or noticed or divined anything "suspicious" of late. *Maybe,* he thought, his eyes blurring with lack of sleep, *somebody didn't care for his sermons and this is revenge.*

"You're tired, old man," he told himself aloud.

Then there was the Bible, and in it two sheets of notepaper. The first sheet bore scribbled quotations, probably for use in a Sunday sermon. Beneath the quotations was a brief outline:

I. Announcements for week.

> Births to Eisners and (a name Whippletree could not decipher).
> Death: Lawrence Busby. Funeral at South Haven Cemetery.
> Marriage bans: Mary Prone to Dennis Bauch.

Mary Prone is getting married again! Whippletree thought, amazed. *To Bauch!* Well, maybe it figured. Mary, of the Club Valmar, had had just about every man in Stearns County, and Denny Bauch, an aging punk who drove a cattle truck when he did anything, had had a good share of the women, including many who would have nothing to do with him in daylight. *Nice they're finally getting together.*

II. Introduce topic: Love and Will

> Define Love—feeling akin to predetermination, knowing the mind of God.
> Define Will—knowing what must be done and doing it.
> Mention Damon and Pythias
> Mention story of Beth and (unintelligible)
> Tell how it feels to be overpoweringly in love—Bonnie and I when young—try to recapture.

Whippletree felt a little embarrassed, as though eavesdropping or opening somebody's mail. *Well, if the guy talked*

*about stuff like this in public, he must have believed it because . . .
. . . because a real man wouldn't,* he finished. *The poor weak
bastard. Why would anybody do this to a harmless guy like him?*

III. Resolution:

> Exhortation—be willing to love, do not be afraid.
> *describe* what it means to love, against all
> obstacles and the world's scorn.

The sheriff felt guilty now, after what he'd just been thinking. *That* had been scorn, and young Koster was right here
on paper saying he wasn't afraid of it. *Hell, don't know the kid
that well . . . meant him no harm . . .*

> Conclude: "Love is the greatest of all the mysteries, and to
> reach it we must be willing to suffer."

Underneath this he had written, then scratched out, "Bonnie
and the kids and our poor, poor life together." Then, "Ask
choir to sing Hymn 92. Benediction following."
   The quotations above the outline didn't move Whippletree
much.

> Isaiah. 50.7: For the Lord God helps me;
>   therefore I have not been confounded;
>   Therefore I have set my face like a
>   flint,
>   and I know I shall not be
>   put to shame.

*Face like a flint. Looked more like an usher in a movie house to
me.* Actually, the formal Bible language was making the
sheriff uneasy, reminding him of catechism classes long ago.

They were about all the education he had been able to get, because he had to take care of his mother and the younger kids in the family. *Forget about that,* he ordered himself. *You're sheriff of Stearns County, and that's all right. Turn your face like a flint,* he thought. He felt his face trying to smile.

Psalms 66. 18-19:   If I regard iniquity in my
                    heart
             the Lord will not hear me.
             But truly God has listened;
                he has given heed to the voice
                of my prayer.

2 Corinthians. 9.6:   The point is this: he who sows sparingly
             will also reap sparingly, and he who sows
             bountifully will also reap bountifully.

That was the only one that made any sense to Whippletree, and he figured Koster had his head at least partway on his shoulders. Even the farmers in his church could figure that one out. The other verses and the outline for the sermon were "church stuff," but then you can read just about anything into Bible quotations, and he was sure that anybody trained in the ministry could fit practically anything to the topic of a sermon, too.

The second sheet in the Bible was just a bunch of numbers, probably notes or codes for more verses and other sermons. He took the two papers from the Bible, as evidence, and made a brief inventory in his note pad of the books and material on the desk.

Bimbo came in with the camera.

"Here you are, sheriff." He was frowning like a big overgrown boy, unexpectedly told he can't go to the ball game after all.

Whippletree stuffed the note pad back into his breast pocket and reached for the camera, then had a wicked little thought, like a grin of the brain.

"No, Bimbo, you go ahead and take the pictures this time."

Bonwit's face lit up, then darkened. He sensed a trap. What if the sheriff hoped the pictures wouldn't turn out? *Then he could blame me.*

"Aw, Whip, now you said it yourself. The pictures turn out bad whenever I take them. An' this is a big case. We can't afford . . ."

"Oh, all right." Whippletree took the camera and headed for the stairs.

"You know, we could use a new camera and other new equipment, too," Bimbo said. "Come election time . . ."

"Drop it. Say, you heard that Mary Prone and Denny Bauch are set to tie the knot?"

"Oh, yeah," Bimbo said. He would have heard. He was pretty regular at Mary's Club Valmar. "You know, I think Bauch has got his eye on owning a chunk of that place. He was always a greedy one, if you ask me . . ."

"He who sows bountifully will also reap bountifully," Whippletree said, climbing the stairs again toward the blood and the chalk marks.

"What?" Bimbo wondered.

"Nothing. Forget it. Now, shut your mouth, set your face like flint, and see if you can stick one of those fingers of yours into the dial of a phone. Call my wife and tell her I won't be home for breakfast."

28

IV

Whippletree's schedule had always been irregular, and his wife, Sarah, had long since gotten used to it. She had had to. In the first place, he took his job seriously, and spent a lot of time at the office. Second, he was an old country boy, with a lifelong habit of long hours. Then, too, getting on toward sixty, he just didn't need the sleep he used to. But he was tired this morning, driving back to St. Cloud, although the feeling was as much sadness as it was fatigue. No matter what he thought about, the Koster house, the bodies, the bitter scent of mean, vicious destruction swept back over him. He tried to concentrate on the tall symmetrical rows of green corn, to get lost in the order of it. But that didn't work. He remembered the baby, torn apart in the crib. He tried to fol-·low the golden windrows of straw, fallen in perfect lines across the stubble of a wheat field, but his mind rebelled and followed itself back to the upstairs bedroom, and to the body of little Ruth Koster, trying to reach whatever refuge she must have believed the closet would provide. Something was happening in her house, and she awoke and did not know what it was. But knew that it was terrible, and knew that it was coming toward her in wild explosions that shook the house and flashed blue and white in the reverberating darkness. And then it had been her turn, and her life went out. At five, maybe six. Her life went out before she had even had a chance to understand it—if it could be understood. Halfway to a closet.

The feeling gripped Whippletree again. Of absolute rage, and vengeance. Maybe Koster wouldn't welcome it. Maybe he believed enough in that bromidal religious shit to take it and let it wash off in forgiveness—that is, *if* he lived. But the sheriff realized he was thinking as much of his own little girl, thirty-five years dead, as of Ruth Koster. Neither of them had had a chance. It was unfair and there was no way you could figure it out. Next to him, Axel Vogel slumped into a snorting, snoring doze, sweating like a hog. The sun was up, low in the east, and it stung the sheriff's eyes. Already the shimmering haze of August heat was building over the fields. It was going to be a "corker," as they said out here.

Jamie Lugosch had long since gone back to town, and Whippletree had left Bimbo and Farley on duty in Lake Eden to handle there whatever came up, which would be mostly inquiries from the local citizenry, and helping the state police lab boys when they showed up. He'd told— ordered—Bimbo not to go around asking questions just yet. The sheriff wanted to talk to Koster first, if he could, *before* he started an investigation of his own out in the lake town. And, besides, with Bimbo way out there, the gigantic deputy wouldn't get a chance to huddle with Mel Betters, and figure out a way to use this murderous night even before the investigation was properly begun. They would do it, too. He would put nothing past them, not in a regular year and certainly not in an election year.

Maybe I shouldn't have booked them last June, he thought, *but what could I do? There'd been a formal complaint.* And there *had* been. A righteous, dumpy Lake Eden matron, out for a round-the-block walk with her equally proper husband late one mild evening, had espied Denny Bauch's pink Grand Prix parked in an alley behind the Club Valmar. In the back seat was a woman—"naked as a jaybird, she was"—on her hands and knees, and Denny, similarly unattired, lying on his back directly beneath her. So busy had the two been that the older couple had had plenty of time for a good long look. As it was, they'd been incensed when the charge—later dismissed—was "creating a disturbance" rather than sodomy. Hell, how had Whippletree been expected to know the woman in the car was Lynn Betters, daughter of the chairman of the Stearns County Board of Commissioners. There were other things, of course, on which he and Mel Betters differed, but this one was a nettle under Betters's flesh.

Whippletree sped through the towns—St. Alazara, Cold Spring, Rockville—back to St. Cloud, where he dropped Vogel off at the office, and swung up about ten blocks to his roomy old gray stucco house on the north side. Sarah met him at the door. She was a full-bodied woman a few years younger than her husband, gentle, always trying for a cheery smile that never quite conquered a certain perpetual worry and concern.

"Bimbo called," she said. "He said something happened and that you'd be late."

At least he didn't go braying about the killings, Whippletree thought. "Yes, and I can't stay long. Just for a little coffee, if some's hot."

"There is. Of course there is."

Sarah was from the old school, and although it bothered Whippletree sometimes to see her always rushing after his needs—real or imagined—there was no way of changing her or getting her to calm down. *If we could have had other children, then maybe she . . .*

"What happened, dear? Or can you talk about it?"

The sheriff sat down wearily at the kitchen table with the too-bright yellow tablecloth and leaned forward, sipping the hot coffee.

"It's very bad," he said. "I don't know if you want to hear about it right now. Too early in the morning."

Her face whitened a little as the blood sank away. She had

31

a full, pretty face, with good color, but disaster or bad news showed fast. "I'll just worry 'til the *Tribune* comes out this afternoon," she said. "You'd best tell me now."

Right. Mel Betters would certainly write a little editorial on "crime wave," if not today, then tomorrow. Mel Betters owned the St. Cloud *Tribune.*

"There was a killing in Lake Eden," he said, putting his cup down. "Killings, actually. Five."

"Oh," she cried. "I knew it was something like that, the way Bimbo . . ."

"The way Bimbo what?"

"How he was so serious. You know. *Formal.* He's usually so happy and jolly on the phone. Do you know who did it?"

"No," he said. "I haven't the slightest idea." He told her about it, very sketchily. Circumstances. Name of the family. "I'm going up to the hospital in a minute. Got to try and talk to the guy."

Sarah had moved back against the sink, her kitchen position of retreat, like a fighter on the ropes. Small tears of horror and sympathy formed in the corners of her eyes. "I can't believe it. In Lake Eden? That's such a nice place. All those nice lake homes . . . so nice . . ."

"So I hear," Whippletree said. Mel Betters had a big house out there.

"And the Koster family sounded like such an ideal . . . wouldn't hurt anybody . . ."

"What do you mean, 'sounded'?"

"Why, there was an article in the *Trib* about them just a couple of weeks ago. About him, mostly. I put it on your desk."

She often did this, clipping news on county people so he could update his political files.

"Can I get it for you?"

"No, I'll . . ." he started to get up. But she was already halfway out of the room. He finished his coffee and slumped wearily in the straight-backed chair, bracing on his elbows over the table.

"Now here it is . . ." she said, putting it down in front of him.

Montana "Transplant" Takes Root In Lake Eden—Koster "Committed"

Lake Eden: On the second anniversary of his call to the Seventh Reformed Church, the Reverend Matthew Koster expressed "great happiness and satisfaction" with his church, his community, and his role in life. "I'm the luckiest man alive," he said at a meeting of the Ladies' Auxiliary, "I have God, I have love, I have a wonderful life, and a future that promises more of the same."

Yeah, it sure does, Whippletree thought.

Reverend Koster, who grew up on a wheat ranch in Montana and studied for the ministry at the Seventh Reformed Seminary near Missoula, did admit to finding life in Lake Eden different, at least at first. "Here you have so many things," he said. "Houses. Boats. New cars. Out there we had only the Big Sky. And maybe that was enough." The young minister was quick to point out, however, that he saw no evidence to indicate that possessions or "the good life" had turned Lake Edenians from a religious commitment. "I feel that commitment," he said. "I feel it every day. You only really live when you encounter and give in to a feeling that is more powerful than you are . . ."

Politician, the sheriff snorted, with a small feeling of satisfaction, having sensed in this exemplary young man a touch of everyday b.s. *Or maybe it isn't? Maybe he believes it.*

Mrs. Koster, or Bonnie, as she prefers to be called, married the minister eight years ago. "We were only eighteen," she said, "and Matt hadn't even decided on the ministry yet, but I'm glad he did. We don't have many things, God knows, but you make do."

The rest of the story went on to tell about the children, especially the baby, Matt Jr., born last fall. Whippletree set the paper aside, frowning. There was not a clue in it, no help at all. The short article was like a recapitulation of those sermon notes he had found in the Bible, with the same rhetoric—he thought of it as rhetoric, dispassionately but without contempt—and same stress on love.

"Are you thinking about something, dear?"

"Yes. I'm wondering why anybody would want to be a minister or a priest, and why they have to prate all the time about love. It gets a little too sticky, if you ask me."

Sarah came over and leaned down and put her arms around his big shoulders. She knew the public postures Stearns County "he-men" had to take, but she knew more, too. After Susan's death, those many years ago, he had never set foot inside a church again. She was a Catholic, and it bothered her, but he would not be moved. No God who would kill a child was worth a damn, and the prelates with their honeyed words were, at best, silly dreamers, and, at worst, con artists like the gypsies who came through town every spring and "tarred driveways" or "sealed roofs" with a compound containing dirty water and black coloring.

"I'm sure Reverend Koster was a fine young man," she said. "Just like it says in the *Trib*. But you have to remember that he was *young*, and that's the way he talked."

"I hope he *still* talks." Whippletree got up. He was thinking, *after this we'll see how much he talks about love and God!* It was not a bitter thought, but sad: he was not thinking of Koster, particularly. He was thinking of another young man in his mid-twenties who had been known by the name of Emil Whippletree, who had a wife named Sarah Whippletree, and in his arms the body of a dead little girl named Susan Whippletree. The wife was still here, and he knew what had happened to the little girl, but when he looked in the mirror sometimes or when his will failed him and he could not help but remember the girl, he often wondered whatever had become of that young man. But he was dead sure of one thing: love and God had had nothing to do with it.

He left his billed uniform hat on a hook behind the front door and put on instead a soft straw hat with the snap brim. It made him look not so tired, and with the day heating up the way it was, he could use it.

"When will you be home?" asked his wife, her worried look in full force.

He shrugged, positioning the hat. "I'll probably have to go on back out to Lake Eden. I don't know."

"Try to take it easy, will you? It's so hot . . ."

35

There had been times before, when he'd been working long hours on complicated cases, that he'd napped on a cot in one of the cells. If he had the time . . .

"We'll see. One thing's sure. I can't move as fast as I used to, so I'm bound to go a little slow. I'll call you or have one of the boys call if I have to go back out there today."

"All right," she said, standing up on her toes to kiss his stubbled cheek. "And shave, too. With the murders, I wouldn't be surprised if Mel Betters didn't stop by."

With his office in the courthouse right across the street, I wouldn't be surprised either. "I wouldn't shave a pig for Mel Betters," he growled.

She laughed, but still looked worried. Then he left. Getting into the car, he wondered what the difference was between the farmer, who had to worry about storms and hail, and the sheriff, who had to worry about elections. Then he forgot about it. The path of his life had been determined years ago, and it was too late to go back now. Besides, you can do something about winning an election. But when the hailstones come pounding down, you're screwed.

V

The St. Cloud hospital was farther up on the North Side, built high up on the banks of the Mississippi River. He pulled into a special parking area for emergency vehicles and climbed out. Morning visiting hours were beginning, and as he walked across the parking lot, people waved or nodded and a few of them said good morning, sheriff, or called him by name. Whippletree always liked that, the country friendliness, and it worried him a little sometimes that the younger people didn't seem to care as much, or to be as open. Except, of course, for Matthew Koster. It was funny when you thought about it. Koster, a young man, thought like most of the older people, a pattern of thought and belief that most young people casually rejected or scorned outright. The thought struck him, and he stopped in the lobby and wrote it down, in mental shorthand, in his note pad.

A goody two-shoes murder? Somebody couldn't stand all that love stuff?

Whippletree had never been able to shake a feeling of vague shame and guilt over his lack of formal education, but he figured he knew people. Even if he couldn't phrase it in the proper psychological terms employed in the courthouse by young county attorney Nicky Rollis, he could "read a person" pretty damn well. Now, stuffing the note pad and ball-point pen back into his pocket, he thought: *If it was sick hatred and envy of a person who claimed to be better or more pious, then the killer would have to have been somebody who knew Koster, and somebody who was a bully.*

Some local(s). In Lake Eden. A bully.

The guy was always a potential suspect for almost anything, and his name had been floating around in the back of the sheriff's mind for a while now, but usually for other stuff, penny-ante stuff: bar fights, accusations of rape, fencing stolen goods—you name it. But if you were looking for a bully, you were sure to find one in Denny Bauch.

Just to make it definite, he took out his note pad again and wrote Denny's name in big block letters next to "love stuff."

"How you doin', sheriff? Come to see Koster?"

He knew the thin, insinuating voice. Melvin Betters. He turned. "That's right, Mel."

Betters smirked. He stood half-a-head below the sheriff, a thin man with a thin agressive face and restless eyes and an unusually large mouth (*Fitting,* Whippletree thought) with the lower lip permanently outthrust. He looked like a pugnacious ferret. The sheriff did not like his looks, but he liked even less the fact that Betters did not play fair. The not playing fair made Whippletree somewhat afraid of Betters, in a way, because the sheriff himself could never find it in him *not* to play fair, even when his brain told him it would be the best thing to do.

"Well, I'm one up on you there." Betters was grinning. "I already been up to see him."

"How'd you find out? If you don't mind my asking. I thought it would be better to keep it quiet a little, and not get people stirred up, at least until we can . . ."

"Bimbo called," Betters snapped. "He figured I should know. Since, as you know, I *am* the chairman of the County Board."

"I heard about it, Mel. You tell me all the time. But I gave Bonwit strict instructions to keep his mouth shut."

"*You* may have, but I'm glad he had the brains to see it different. And as you'll recall, he *is* on my table of organization, *assigned* to you as deputy."

"Mel, you don't have to draw me a picture."

"Oh? No. No, I guess I don't, do I? You know I'll have to put the story in this afternoon's *Trib.* Don't want to cover anything like this up, right?"

The smaller man was enjoying himself now, having Whippletree doubly on the spot. *What a way to start the day.*

"Sure, Mel, of course we don't want anything covered up. Unless it's cocksucking in a pink Grand Prix . . ."

Betters, ever the animal of attack and response, thrust and parry, let his eyes change to *glare* in the middle of an instant. "It could of been Bauch did this, you know."

"It's occurred to me."

"Well, you run the son-of-a-bitch in."

"I can't. Not without proof."

Betters leaned forward and jabbed a finger into his chest, accentuating each syllable, *"Then . . . you . . . get . . . some."* He took his finger away and looked up. "I believe your name's gonna be in the papers."

Whippletree glared back. "Stop messing around with my office and personnel," he hissed.

"Oh? What's this?" Betters chortled. "What's this? Or— *what? What's* going to happen?"

The sheriff shrugged it off, disgusted. November would come soon enough. "You said you saw Koster. How is he?"

"He's sleeping. Out of intensive care, though. You're wasting a trip if you think you can talk to him now."

"I'll be the judge of that."

Betters laughed again. "Calm down, Emil. Calm down. We're all in this together."

"Then why don't you hold off on the story until we can get our feet on the ground with the investigation."

"Sorry. No can do. An election year, you know. Have to get it all out in the open."

The sheriff really saw red this time. That damn Betters. He knew Whippletree would never bring up the sodomy thing, being the kind of man he was. But, "You know, Mel, I always did wonder about that time Otto Ronsky shot Father Ripulski in that cornfield. How come *that* never got in the paper? The bishop paying you off, too?"

The commissioner just laughed again. "Won't do you no good. No good at all. Ripulski died of a heart attack . . ."

"He had a ten-gauge shotgun shell for a heart then, I guess . . ."

"And none of the Catholics would believe it anyway. You'd just lose votes bringing that up. Besides, everybody was in on it. The coroner. Nicky Rollis. *And you, too.*" He did his finger-in-the-chest thing again.

The hell with it, Whippletree thought. *Let it go. For now.*

"See you, Mel," he said, heading for the elevators.

"Call me when you bring Bauch in."

Whippletree didn't turn or reply.

"You call me, you hear," Betters said, a little too hard. People in the lobby, coming and going, turned and looked. Whippletree sensed it, but didn't do anything. He didn't have to. It was Mel Betters, standing there in the middle of the lobby, yelling to himself.

The sheriff restrained an urge to laugh, and pushed the elevator button. In the corner of his eye he could see Mel Betters hurry out of the hospital, scurrying, sliding, just like a ferret. He could almost hear the click of sharp claws on the marble floor.

VI

The Reverend Matthew Koster looked none too good.

Whippletree stopped at the door of the hospital room and saw the white bed with the oxygen tent, the tubes, and the bottle of plasma upside down on its metal stand. Two doctors were standing over the bed, talking softly. A young nurse hurried past him out of the room, averting her eyes when she saw the badge. One of the doctors turned, resident director Paul Petly. His picture was always in the paper, because of a good golf game and a wife in the Rosary Society.

"Morning, sheriff. I see you boys are keeping us busy."

"I'd just as soon skip it. He doesn't look too good, does he?"

Beneath the transparent plastic, Koster's eyelids fluttered and for a second his mouth worked in a chewing motion. He looked extraordinarily pale.

"He may not look too good," the second doctor said, "but he's one of the luckiest men I've come across in a while."

"How so?"

"Well, sheriff," Petly said, "he was shot at close range—there were powder burns—with a .22 caliber rifle. Shot in the chest."

From a chart on the bed, he picked up a clipboard and unsnapped an X ray of Koster's torso.

"See?" he said, pointing. "Right here, between the ribs, is the point of entry. The bullet came in just to the right of the upper portion of the stomach, just a little low left of the right lung, and *missed* the ribs while doing so. There was no damage. And, on exit, it also missed the spinal cord. The odds on that are . . ." He shook his head. "He's a minister, I understand."

"Seventh Reformed, in Lake Eden."

"Well, he must have been saying some prayers, because he certainly had them answered."

You haven't seen the other bodies, Doctor, Whippletree thought. "Then why does he look in such bad shape, if he was so lucky?"

"That's the anesthesia. We had to do a probe and cauterize. He'll be coming out of it anytime now."

Whippletree hesitated. "Has anyone told him about . . . about the rest of it? His family?"

"Excuse me," the second doctor said, "time for my rounds," and left the room. Petly's eyebrow went up a notch. "Ahh . . . not that I know of."

Right on time as usual, thought the sheriff. *Just my luck.* "Well, doc, if I'm going to have to do it, you better make sure

41

somebody is around here. I imagine he's not going to grin and bear it."

"Of course I'll stay," Petly said, reclipping the X ray to the board. "He's going to be very weak, and won't be able to say much now. I'll have to give him a sedative anyway."

Whippletree nodded and pulled up a chair, waiting. Underneath the tent, the patient began to stir again. His arms and legs were strapped down to prevent sudden movement, which would dislodge the tubes bringing liquid and blood into his body. The room was on the fourth floor, on the river side, and outside the sheriff could see the tops of trees falling away steeply as the riverbank fell away to the slow-moving Mississippi in the valley. Outside, the air was hazy with heat and pollen; inside it was cool with the air conditioning. The sheriff leaned back in the chair and felt the weight of his eyelids, fought against it.

Then Koster's head jerked, and he made a sound.

"Doc!" Whippletree said, leaning forward.

Petly went over and swung away a portion of the oxygen tent. Koster's eyes were open now. He was awake, but not yet totally conscious. They watched him swim upward towards them, and when the expression of fear and alarm came over his face, Whippletree knew he was back in action. *Too bad you have to come back to a memory like that,* he thought.

"You're going to be all right," Petly was saying, resolutely cheerful in the best of bedside manners. "Just relax. You're going to be fine."

Koster croaked something. Again. Whippletree leaned forward.

It was, "Bonnie? The kids?"

Petly looked at the sheriff and nodded. Whippletree leaned into the tent, and putting a hand on the man's shoulder, forced himself to meet the questioning eyes. "Son, I'm afraid they didn't make it," he said. "They . . . they were killed. Can you tell me what happened? I have to know."

Koster took that with wide-open eyes and no expression, and for a couple of seconds he might have been dead himself. Then, as if in a delayed reaction, his mouth flew open. He gave a long low moan of inconsolable loss, and tears formed in the corners of his eyes. He fought against them.

"Oh, my God," he was sobbing, his arms fighting the straps which tied him down. "Oh, my God!" Petly stepped to the door and asked a nurse for sedatives.

Whippletree waited, half inside the tent, his arm still gently restraining the young clergyman.

"Can you tell me what happened?" he repeated. "I promise I'll do everything in my power to find out who did it. Is there *any* help you can give me?"

Koster was sobbing openly now, his fine face grostesque and twisted as the tears flowed freely. The sheriff did not like to have to look at it, but he understood what the guy was going through.

"Anything at all?" he asked again.

"Just a minute more, sheriff. You can come back later. He'll have to stay here a week, anyway, maybe longer."

"Koster," the sheriff said a little roughly this time, to break through the wails of grief. "Koster, what happened?"

The minister made an effort and the crying stopped. "Two of them," he said. "They wore ski masks. One of them . . . big. The other not so big. They . . . they . . ." Here he broke off and began to sob again, then brought it under control. "We were sleeping . . . came into the house, made me go outside. Tied . . . tied me up. Then . . . back in the house . . . the big one . . . shots . . ."

43

This time he turned his head away and could not go on. Behind him, Whippletree sensed the doctor's impatience, and out of the corner of his eye he saw the nurse hold a syringe to the light.

"Did they *say* anything?" he asked. "Koster. Come on, remember. I want to help you. Did they *say* anything?"

The young man quieted, with effort, and seemed to be trying to remember. "No . . . no, nothing that made any . . . Wait, they kept saying 'Where is it?' The big one did. 'Where is it?' I didn't know what it was, but he kept asking, and then he came out of the house, after the shotgun blasts, and told the smaller one to . . . to shoot . . . and . . ." Here he broke off unable to continue, unable to do anything but ride along in the rush of his grief.

"Sheriff!" Petly was saying.

"All right," Whippletree said, stepping back. He had a few things, anyway. Two men, ski masks, looking for something. What? Was it some terrible mistake. The wrong house, wrong people? Or *was* there something of value in the house? Or had the search on the part of the killers been only a ruse, an excuse for some other motivation that was still concealed? The nurse stepped forward and gave Koster the injection, but it didn't seem to quiet him much.

"I'll be back later," he told Petly, walking with the doctor down the hospital corridor, fumbling for his note pad. "Is he in any danger?"

"Physically, no, not unless there are complications. But if he lets himself go—I mean, mentally. If he gives up . . ."

"Right." *If I were him I just might feel like it.* "Well, doc, I'd appreciate it if you'd give my office a call in case . . ."

"Certainly. You've got your row to hoe, sheriff. I'll help in any way I can."

Petly went off to his duties, and the sheriff stood waiting

for the elevator, scribbling notes about "motive" and "two masked men" and "shotgun blasts: not heard by neighbors because of storm."

Lucky neighbors.

VII

Deputy Alvin Ruehle monitored the radio and handled the phones during the day shift, aided by Alyce Pelser, a farm girl who was supposed to be a secretary but had trouble spelling her own name. She had done some undisclosed but apparently very important favors for Mel Betters once, and to show his gratitude he put her on his "table of organization." There were a hell of a lot people in Stearns County who were on it, and every single one of them—not to mention their families, friends, and distant cousins all the way out in Holdingford or Brooten—would show up at the ballot box in November.

"Hey, sheriff," Ruehle called, as Whippletree slouched in, "how's it goin'? Had a busy night, I heard."

Deputy Pollock, just coming off duty, sat with his feet up on a desk and his hands over his paunch. He tried to hide it that way, with little success. Now he yawned. "Sure as hell did. I guess I'll go on home and get some shuteye. Unless you want for me to go on out to Lake Eden? Sheriff?"

Whippletree sat down at his own battered desk. Alyce Pelser poured him a cup of coffee, her pock-marked face locked in concentration at the effort.

"No, you go on home. Bimbo and Farley are out there, and I'm driving out pretty soon. That's enough."

Pollock rose heavily and stumbled out, grunting his goodbyes.

"How's Koster?" Ruehle wanted to know.

"Not good."

"Talk to him?"

"Yeah. He did give me a few things. Apparently there were two men in on it. One used a shotgun on the family. The other used a .22 on him."

"Lucky he made it."

"That's what everybody seems to think."

"You want cream in this here coffee, sheriff? Jesus, I just don't know what to think," said Alyce Pelser. "What are you going to do?"

"No, black. I don't know. All I can do is start investigating."

"Oh, Bimbo already done that," Ruehle informed him.

"*What?*"

"Yeah. He called about fifteen minutes before you come in. He said Mel Betters give him a call and told him to get right on it."

"You want sugar, sheriff?" Alyce Pelser asked, occupied by the intricacies of her task.

"No, damnit, black. Where the hell can I reach Bimbo now?"

"He said he was going on over to the Club Valmar, try and find Denny Bauch."

Oh, Jesus Christ! Betters was determined to get Denny Bauch, so determined that any chance of a quiet, methodical investigation would be blown all to hell by noon, and certainly by the time the *Tribune* came out later in the day.

"See if you can raise him on the radio."

Ruehle loved to work the communications system, and he clicked on the power. "Bald Eagle," he said into the microphone. "Bald Eagle, this is Mountaintop. This is Mountaintop. Come in, Bald Eagle." *I should never have let Ruehle come*

46

up with those code names, Whippletree thought, the inside of his mouth curling from the effects of Alyce Pelser's coffee. *It makes us look like we're trying to be hotshots.* (The sheriff himself was "Lone Wolf.")

"Yeah, Alvin, what is it?" came Farley's voice.

"You're supposed to use the code name, dammit, Bill. Don't you learn anything? We might be overheard."

"Yeah? By who? I didn't get no fucking sleep and I . . ."

Whippletree stepped over and grabbed the mike. "Farley, where's Bimbo?"

"He's over in Mary Prone's trailer."

Mary Prone lived in a trailer, or "mobile home," parked just off to the side of the Club Valmar. The trailer got a lot of use.

"What's he doing in there?"

"He's looking for Denny Bauch. Mel Betters gives us a call an' . . ."

The sheriff spoke very slowly and distinctly. "Look, Bill, is there a pink Grand Prix parked anywhere around?"

Short pause. "Nope."

"Then, Bill, Bauch is *not there.* Because he never lets that damn car out of his sight. Now, you go get Bimbo before he gets his privates caught—sorry, Alyce—and tell him I want to talk . . ."

"Ah, hold it, sheriff, here he comes now. Hey, Bimbo," they could hear Farley yell, "Whip wants to talk to yah."

In a couple of seconds, Bimbo's booming growl came over the air. "Yeah, sheriff?"

"Wayne, what the hell are you doing out there in Lake Eden?"

A momentary offended silence. "Why, I'm starting in on the in-vest-ti-gash-un. Mel called and said . . ."

"I don't give a damn what Mel said. I don't want you out

47

there stomping around like an elephant in a field of daisies."

"Now, Whip, you got no call to go and get personal, I was just checking out Denny . . ."

"Leave him *alone.* I said leave him alone. Leave all of it alone, will you, until I get out there."

Bimbo's voice had a hurt, whining note to it now. "You just want all the glory for yourself, ain't that right?"

"It's hardly a matter of glory, Wayne, I . . ."

"Well, you'll be sorry. Mel tell you he was running me for sheriff this fall?"

So they *were* going to do it! Whippletree had been waiting for it, and now Betters had a big story and the time was ripe.

"No, he didn't, but you're not sheriff yet, so do as I say. Get back to the house and wait for the state boys."

"They're already there."

"Well, go back there and watch them. Maybe you can learn something. Or go to sleep under a tree. Only don't go around asking questions. I'm not ready yet."

"Seems you're *not ready* most of the . . ."

"Drop it. Now, since you've already started screwing this up, what did Mary Prone say?"

"Nothin'. She didn't say nothin'."

"You mean she didn't talk at all?" Which was next to impossible for Mary Prone, whose mouth was always working, one way or another.

"Naw. She wasn't in her trailer. She ain't anywheres around, far as I can see. Trixie said she ain't seen them, neither."

That would be Trixie Wade, Mary's friend, part-time barmaid and regular user of the trailer.

"Okay, Wayne," Whippletree said, with a sigh of exasperation. "Tell me exactly what happened, and exactly what you said, so I know the extent of the damage."

"Hell, sheriff, there ain't no damage. I just knock on the

trailer door and Trixie comes over and opens it. Clem Duck-worth is in there on the bed, looking a little sheepish, he-he-he, an' I say, Trixie, where's Denny Bauch? So she tries to lie to me, Whip. She says, 'I don't know,' an', 'What's it to you?' kind of huggin' herself with a little bittie nightie, he-he-he . . ."

Bimbo, you jerk, Whippletree was thinking.

"An' I said listen, Trixie, there's been a whole mess of murders over at the Koster house, an' we're lookin' for Denny . . ."

"Wayne, you *didn't* say that, did you?"

"Somethin' wrong?"

"Now do you know how fast, do you have *any idea* how fast word is going to spread. From Trixie Wade and Clem Duckworth? Do you have any idea *at all*?"

"But I thought . . ."

"No, you didn't. Anyway, where did she say Mary was?"

"Come to think of it, she never did say. She just said she wasn't there, an' she wasn't. Not in the trailer. Least as far as I could tell . . ."

"Oh, good going, Wayne. Real good going. Now get back to that house and wait until I show up. Then you and Farley can come on back here and get some sleep."

"But I don't want to miss the in-vest-ti-gashun. Don't you try and freeze me out of it."

"Wayne, rest easy. I'm sure you'll be involved all the way, you and Mel. So you just get on back to the Koster house, okay?"

Bimbo grumpily acquiesced. The sheriff handed the mike back to Ruehle.

"See you later," Bimbo was saying.

"No," Ruehle complained. "That's not the right way, dammit. You're supposed to say "Roger, 10-4. 10-4. You got that?"

VIII

Whippletree took care of some routine paperwork, checked the morning mail—nothing much—and quickly scanned the advertisements for bumper stickers, posters, and brochures. All those companies knew when you were running again, and they couldn't wait to get your money. They didn't care if you won or lost. He put them aside. He was tired. "Alyce," he said, "go on over to the bar-and-grill and get me a roast beef sandwich, will you?" He put his feet up on the desk and pulled out his note pad again, not seeing it, really, for a little while. Here he was, one term away from a pension, and things were ganging up on him. It was a lot of things. Mel Betters and Bimbo. Age, fatigue, some depression. The memories and doubts about your life that come unbidden as you get older. Old disappointment, all of it. And now these murders, with so few clues to go on. It could easily be made out by his enemies that the sheriff just couldn't cut the mustard anymore. And it *would* be made out that way. Mel Betters loved that kind of an opportunity to put pressure on people.

Idly, he picked up one of the advertisements for campaign posters. What slogan should he use this year? When he'd first run for sheriff, he'd used "Win with Whip," a catchy one, Sarah had said at the time, but lately, after a long time in the job—too long, some people seemed to think—it had been simply "Re-elect Emil." He could use that one again, and if he did, well, there were several thousand posters and bumper stickers left from the last campaign. But this time he was really in a horse race. It was just one of those years. The common feeling was that he'd been around too long. He'd heard it himself. Out in the dance halls, where he was sometimes called to quell bar fights. There he would be, out at, say, Cedar Point Pavilion in St. Alazara, having to face down whiskey-crazed Paul Meyer, maybe, the idiot of that particular village, who'd gotten into a bottle-flinging battle across the dance floor with Virgil Konig over whether a John Deere tractor was really better than an Oliver. He would get it all settled down, and people would come over and say, "Yeah, Whip, you can sure do the job, but ain't you gettin' a little tired of it?" Time for a change.

He wondered what kind of slogan Mel Betters would think up for Bimbo. Did Bimbo have a chance? In Stearns County, he sure as hell did. Where else would it be a claim to fame to have a name like that?

The thing about little Wayne Bonwit was that he was never, ever, little. He started out in life as a physical giant and kept on growing. Whelped at thirteen pounds, ten ounces, starting off heavier than a lot of calves and most sheep, young Wayne Bonwit just kept right on growing. He was a slow-moving kid with a small head and a big appetite, ready to chortle at almost anything, and ready to bask in the glow of rustic admiration. He smiled and he ate and he accepted accolades due him—"That there kid is sure gonna be a help come hayin' season"—and he kept on growing and growing and *growing*!

Wayne Bonwit had the further good fortune of being born in Stearns County, where being six-four at sixteen was something of an oddity, (he eventually made six-seven and a half), and certainly a help, first, on the basketball team of the local high school in the town of Kimball, and later for purposes of image and identity when, too lazy to farm, he followed a hunch into "public life." In fact, it was in high school that he first developed a taste for public recognition, which accrued to him because of his success in dunking a basketball. None of the other teams had a chance against Wayne Bonwit, then known as "Bonnie," and the wallopings sustained by the powerhouses of Sauk Rapids, Sartell, Melrose, Alexandria, and Meier Grove were of truly historic dimensions. In Stearns County, that was good for instant recognition, and after church on Sunday in Bonwit's home town of St. Augusta, the awed, ass-scratching farmers would gather around and say, "Yo, Bonnie, that there was a heck of a game against Brooten," and, "How's the weather up there?" "How's it around my ass?" Wayne would respond, a remark invariably met by appreciative guffaws. *That Bonwit, an athlete and sharp in the head besides!* He would go far.

It was in his last year as a dunker for Kimball High School, when he took the team to a respectable third-place finish at the fabled tournaments in Minneapolis, that he acquired his trademark nickname. By this time he didn't see any sense in keeping the training rules laid down by the dog trainer who doubled as the high school's basketball coach, and he was a nighttime regular at Freddie's, the local tavern. He could easily put away five, six pitchers a night, all the while downing steak sandwiches, potato chips, and strips of fried fatback, a local delicacy. There was a song on the jukebox that year, an idiotic piece of popular drivel that assaulted the brain and stuck there, that Freddie and all the regulars—Butch Ronsky, Cyril "Hubcap" Zipp, Alf Bascomb, and "Dinky" Starkopf—played constantly. It went:

Bimbo Bimbo where you gonna go-ee-ooo?
Bimbo Bimbo what you gonna do-ee-ooo?
Bimbo Bimbo when you gonna
Gr-o-o-o-w?

52

The Fields of Eden

* * *

Big joke: "grow." Hence, "Bimbo." It stuck. Within the space of less than a year, Wayne Bonwit had become "Bimbo" throughout Stearns County, aided by the headlines on the sports page in the St. Cloud *Tribune*:

KIMBALL HIGH SCHOOL "KILLERS" WIN TOURNAMENT BID:
CRUSH BROOTEN BULLS, "BIMBO" BONWIT SCORES 69.

Sheriff Whippletree vaguely recalled those days. It was just about the time he was getting over losing the farm, changing his life, getting established as sheriff. He couldn't remember if he'd ever seen Bimbo play a game of basketball but never, not even in his darkest hours, had he ever suspected that it would be this pea-headed, blond giant of an ex-farm boy who would rise up almost twenty years later and threaten to put the old kibosh on his retirement plans.

Had Bimbo thought of any such thing at the time—which was highly unlikely—it would have seemed most unrealistic to him as well. He graduated from high school, having confronted the elemental and unavoidable criterion that no one could play a fifth year, regardless of academic standing, and now he had nothing to do. College was out. He would never get in, and, besides, he didn't want to work hard. Farming, likewise, was lonely and unglamorous, hence ruled out summarily. About the only things left were show business and politics, and, at nineteen, he had no idea how to get into show business nor any understanding of politics, except you had to go around and visit the bars and drink with the boys.

Bimbo never worried about anything, never thought about much, and never, ever, doubted that good things were going to happen to him. All he had to do was keep on grinning and wait for the right time. In this, Whippletree knew, they were

53

exact opposites. The sheriff's daddy had died early, when he was only fifteen, leaving a mortgaged farm down along the flood basin of the Mississippi, a distraught wife, and five other kids, from thirteen down to six months, all dependent on Emil. Stearns County was also one of those places where it is considered a kind of challenge to the law of evolution to engage in charity or to help somebody out, and the locals sat around waiting to see what Emil would be able to do. He pulled it out of the fire that time—got his brothers and sisters educated and paid off the mortgage *that time.* He had not gone to high school. He had never been a basketball star. Sometimes when he pondered the mystery of clumsy, irresponsible—many would say lovable—Bimbo Bonwit, the sheriff tried to gauge how much of his attitude toward the big guy resulted from envy, or a long-buried resentment at the inequities of life. He knew there was a part of that in him—he tried to be a honest man—and yet the image of Bonwit taking over his job as sheriff seemed preposterous, insulting. Natural forces had taken away three things in his life: his father, his daughter, and his farm. Were they now circling to take away his livelihood and peace of mind at this late date?

No, he told himself. *No natural forces. Things happen. Mel Betters is circling, and that's all.*

Yet it was hard to state it cleanly, or to believe it. Because during all those years of readjusting, moving off the farm, running for sheriff, getting established, Bimbo was running around the county, driving a truck here, working on construction there, serving as a good-natured and virtually impregnable bouncer at county dance halls. Getting known by all, like an easygoing, ubiquitous *natural force.* Church picnics weren't the same, weren't complete, if Bimbo didn't show up, and every year he was invited back to Kimball High School to "talk to the boys" and he would always go, ducking his head and aw-shucksing it, and then dribble up and down the court, beer belly bouncing, and shoot a few. Now and then, going through his twenties, he tried a couple of things. Auditioned in far-off Minneapolis for a role in a TV cowboy series. That didn't work out. Some other guy got it. Favoritism, the neighbors claimed. Then he started running for office. First he tried local things, stuff in his own township, like constable, regional supervisor, assistant commissioner. He always lost, but by very close margins. People were having a little trouble shifting their minds from "lovable old Bimbo" to "candidate Bimbo" not to mention "commissioner Bimbo," or whatever. But, election after election, he branched out, and pretty soon he was running for county jobs like agricultural agent or county planner, and still almost winning. He did very, very well out in the rural areas, where he was better known and where his basketball prowess had not been forgotten. He ran all right, but not all that well, in St. Cloud, where at least some of the voters regarded themselves as too sophisticated for Bimbo's "style."

But at last Bimbo won. Not untypically, he won while losing, during his last time out in the contest for county planner. On election night, when they were putting the vote tallies together over at the courthouse, it soon became clear that Bimbo, who had formed an alliance with Mel Betters and his slate of candidates, was actually carrying the rural townships on his coattails for the wily St. Cloud factotum. In spite of Betters's vacation home out at Lake Eden, or maybe because of it, he was resented and mistrusted in the outlying regions. In appreciation, Bimbo went on Betters's "table of organization," and after the election Whippletree came to the office one morning to find that he had a new deputy who was already dreaming dreams of being the Matt Dillon of Stearns County.

"Goddam it, Mel," Whippletree had raged, sitting over bourbon on ice in the publisher's office at the *Tribune*, "this is the limit! How can I run an outfit efficiently if it gets to be a patronage dumping ground for all your boys?"

Betters just let his mouth widen in a smile. "Whip, I got to put them somewheres, now don't I. And did you check your vote figures? You were down considerable from last election. Barely squeaked by with the St. Cloud vote, and dropped near twelve percent overall out in the county. And I am commissioner, you know. I got the right to put these guys where they'll do the most good."

"Most good for what? Your politics?"

"Come on, now. Come on, Whip. Welfare of the county, is all. Welfare of the county. That's what I'm thinkin' of."

The sheriff had left Betters that time with an uneasy feeling that their relationship, usually respectful but distant, had taken a sudden turn. His vote tallies had gone down. He was losing ground. And Bimbo Bonwit, now Betters's big new buddy, would be hanging around the office every day, every week, every month, watching and going back to report on what he saw. You go along for years and build up a reputation and think of yourself in a pretty good way, and then, through no fault of your own, through nothing you can put your finger on, the ground slowly shifts beneath you, like a foreboding, like a premonition, like the still, utterly motionless *unmoving* just before a landslide. Or like the last moment before the current of the Mississippi comes washing up over the bank, spreading over your fields like the tide, to take away your rich black hard-bought earth. To take away your life.

IX

Alyce Pelser came back from the bar-and-grill on Court-house Square and set the wax-paper wrapped sandwich down on the sheriff's desk.

"Thanks, Alyce," he said, "I love a good roast beef sandwich."

"Uh-oh," she said.

"What's wrong?"

"I forgot what it was you said you wanted. That there is liverwurst. They make a real good liverwurst sandwich over at the . . ."

Whippletree hated liverwurst, but if he made a fuss Alyce would take all afternoon getting over her humiliation. He'd rather be quick about it, and leave her in shape to answer the phones while he was out in Lake Eden.

"Thanks, Alyce," he said, "you did a good thing. Alvin, go get yourself some lunch. When you get back I'll be leaving for Lake Eden."

Ruehle went out, and the sheriff pulled a piece of yellow paper off a pad, wrote "Koster Case" on top of it, pulled the note pad out of his breast pocket, and the two pages he'd taken from Koster's Bible. First, he made up a small receipt for the two pages and told Alyce to mail it to the minister, care of the hospital. Then he took another look at the notes for the sermon. It was hard to know how to interpret them, and what he really had to do was have a long talk with Koster when he recovered a little. Barring a psychological accident, a thrill killing, Whippletree figured there must have been a *personal* reason for what had happened. Life was a personal thing, after all. He looked at the words on the paper, *love, poverty, Bonnie and the kids,* and they didn't tell him much. *Scorn, set your face like flint, sow and reap bountifully.* What did all that mean, really? The sheriff was not a man who dealt with words. He was often uncomfortable with them. They were fleeting and indefinite, stinging, even maddening, like the slimy insinuations of a tricky editorial by Betters in the *Tribune.* But if you could get out in the country and stand in a man's backyard and look him in the eye and feel the grip of his hand and judge the timbre of his voice, *then,* then you had something. That was why he had to start slowly, talking easily and casually to people out around Lake Eden. He had to do it his own way, because only in that way would he begin to understand why anyone might think of attacking the family of a harmless man.

He pulled a Manila folder out of a lower drawer, marked it "Koster," tore out the pages of his note pad and put them inside. Also the sermon notes and the other page with those numbers on it. What could they mean? Bible chapter and verse?

QM 23 B46   QM 23.2 E48   QM 23 F713

"Hey, sheriff, I'm back," Ruehle yelled, coming up the steps and into the office.

"Alvin, you scared me!" wailed Alyce, spilling a cup of coffee.

"Sorry. Sheriff, you goin' now?"

"Yeah." Whippletree stood up. He felt stiff and old and tired. "This time of day, takes me nearly an hour to get out to Lake Eden. You take care of things this afternoon, okay? Radio me if anything big comes up. Anything *big.*"

"Like what's big?" Ruehle wondered.

Whippletree grabbed his straw hat from his desk. "Murder or rape," he said. And of course if there's a complaint about skinnydipping I would certainly want to know."

Ruehle took that in and ran it around in his head.

"Skinnydipping?" he asked.

"That's a sin," Alyce declared.

"Use your damn head, Alvin. I got to go. I got an hour's drive."

"You better get that helicopter, sheriff. That's what you should do."

Whippletree gave his deputy a look. "Where'd you hear that again?"

"Over at the bar-and-grill. At lunch. Everybody's talkin' about the Koster killings . . ."

Everybody? Already? "And so?"

"They said you might have saved some of 'em if you had the chopper. But that if you couldn't work your way through the politics of it, looks like . . ."

Ruehle was a dull, but decent sort. He stopped and hung his head.

"Go on, Alvin. I'm a big boy. I can take it."

"Looks like you can't do the job you're paid to do," the deputy concluded reluctantly, averting his eyes. "I didn't say nothin', sheriff. I didn't know what . . ."

"That's all right, don't worry about it. You just do your job and everything'll be okay. Now, listen. This afternoon, when the *Tribune* comes out, there'll probably be a story or something in it about the murders, and there'll probably be some phone calls too. Some people will scream . . ."

Alyce put her hand to her mouth, her eyes wide.

". . . and some will want to know about the murders and what I'm doing about them. Now, listen carefully. *Don't* get into conversations with the callers. *Don't!* Just listen, and take their names, if they give them. A lot of people won't. A lot of people just want to blow off steam. But when they're finished talking, tell them this: 'The sheriff is in the field investigating the case and will have a statement by tomorrow.' You got that?"

Ruehle nodded and so did Alyce.

Then Whippletree walked out of the office and into the heat.

"Checking out the Case"

I

Bimbo called on the radio and told Whippletree that the state lab boys were finding all kinds of prints and were still working, but would need prints of the Koster corpses and of Koster himself, since none of them—ha ha—had records. The sheriff, taking the call en route, relayed it to Alvin and told him to get the coroner and the St. Cloud police specialist right on it. Then, to check how the news was spreading, he stopped in Rockville and then St. Alazara, under the pretext of buying a soda (on account of the heat). He was not encouraged.

"On your way out to the murder, sheriff? Ain't you a little late?" asked an old lady at the Rockville Market. An old-fashioned general store that still had home-dilled pickles in a barrel of brine and something that looked like a baby scale to weigh fat lengths of wurst.

"J–J–Jeez, sheriff," stammered Hercules Rasmussen, storekeeper at the "Wagonwheel" in St. Alazara, "we heard all about it. My God, what're . . . what're you goin' to d–d–*do?*"

A small crowd of oldsters, just killing the time at the store, gathered around.

"Well, I guess we're going to try and catch them," Whippletree said, trying for a calm approach.

"Them?" somebody asked, alarmed. "There was more than one?"

Whippletree nodded. "We think so."

"Jeeeezzz!" Hercules Rasmussen said. He shuddered. "I hope . . ."

"You got Bimbo helping you on this one?" an old man quavered. Whippletree recalled that Bimbo was from out this way. "Sure," he said, as graciously as he could, "he's out there now."

"Well, you might just as well stay home then, Whip," the old timer cackled fiercely. "I reckon Bimbo'll have it covered and taken care of by the time you show up."

The only way he'll have it covered is if he sets his ass down on it. Whippletree thought, feeling himself smile.

"Yonder comes the Reverend Mauslocher," called one of the old men, pointing to the rectory across the way.

"See you," Whippletree said, getting out of the Wagonwheel store and into his car. He waved at Mauslocher, who struck him as one of those judgmental types who knew it all. *So they shoot a guy like Koster and leave Mauslocher running around. It figures.* All he needed was a session with an overbearing second-guesser.

"How you doin', Reverend?" he managed to wave, before pulling out of St. Alazara. By the time he got to Lake Eden it was almost mid-afternoon, and Bimbo was dozing in the shade of a box elder next to the Seventh Reformed.

"Where's Farley?"

"Oh?" Bimbo rubbed his eyes. "He went on over to the Valmar for a beer. He said he had to have something wet. You know, it's hotter than hell, sheriff, an' . . . "

"I don't care, as long as he doesn't start asking a lot of damnfool questions."

"Aw, he *can't*." Bimbo stood up and stretched, his arms reaching up into the lower branches.

"What?"

"I said he can't ask no questions. Mary Prone ain't back yet."

"Not back yet? How do you know?"

Bonwit looked a little sheepish. "Well, we spelled each other. I was over there havin' a quick one, an' Trixie's behind the bar today. Mary's not there."

"Where'd she go?"

"I didn't ask. You told me, sheriff, remember, you didn't want me to ask no questions . . ."

"Right. Right. What about Denny Bauch?"

"Ain't seen him neither. I didn't ask and Trixie didn't say."

"Good work, Bimbo," Whippletree said, with just the touch of an edge on it, and swung his glance around the churchyard. The grass on the lawn was burning, and even in the shade it was dry, in spite of the rain the night before. Out of the shade, the air was hazy and almost visible, somnolent. There was no breeze and nothing moved, and then he caught a flicker of movement—or he thought he did—up in the belltower of the church. He straightened and stared at it, but whatever it was, if anything, was gone now.

"Something up?" Bimbo hissed, looking around, looking all over.

"I just thought I—" the sheriff began, when a man in white shirtsleeves and loosened tie, carrying a black case, came out of the house. He looked pale, expressionless, and very tired.

"You the Stearns County sheriff?"

"I am," Whippletree said, offering his hand.

They shook. "Russ Arledge, state laboratories." He looked at Bimbo. "You got yourself some real deputies here, sheriff."

"Well, there's no lying about that. What'd you find in the house?"

"Prints all over. Of course we don't know yet if they belong to anyone besides members of the family. And there was plenty of buckshot. I'm heading back now for the Twin Cities as soon as my partner finishes the photos he's making in there. Man, is it *hot*." He pulled out an already-soggy handkerchief and mopped his forehead. "They sure didn't have any air conditioning in that house. Nor much of anything else, either," he added, easing into the shade.

The sheriff saw it again, and this time it was no mere thought, or the visual prevarication of fatigue: movement in the belltower. Keeping the church in peripheral vision, he turned again to Bimbo.

"When Mr. Arledge's partner finishes up in there, I want you to secure the house and lock it. We're going to have to hunt the lawn and the gardens in the nearby houses. See if we can't find that .22 bullet the Reverend was hit with."

"How we goin' to do that?" the big deputy complained.

"How's the Reverend?" Mr. Arledge said.

There it was again, a quick dark shape rising up over the wooden slats of the tower, then dropping down again. It was a human head.

"With a metal detector and our eyes, dammit," Whippletree said. "He's expected to recover if grief doesn't get him," he told Arledge, all the time wondering what to do. Wait until Arledge and his partner got out of there? Or call it right now and go on up.

"Bimbo, anybody been around here today? In the church? Come up to the house, or anything?"

"Naw, naw. You give the orders on that, remember, sheriff? Bill an' me ain't let anybody in, and there weren't many who even came close."

Yes, and you've been asleep under the tree. the sheriff thought, unless, just by chance, Jamie Lugosch had come by last night early enough to scare somebody up there, who, since then, hadn't had a chance to get down.

They stood around about ten more minutes, until Jiggsy Potoff, the lab photographer, came out, packing up his gear. "We'll let you know if these prints turn up anything in the computer files," Arledge promised again, and they left in their state motor pool Plymouth. Meantime, Bill Farley drove back in the patrol car. Getting out, he belched. "Drop over at the Valmar and have a cold one, whydontcha, sheriff? Me and Bimbo'll handle whatever comes up here . . ."

"Bimbo, last night when you checked the church, did you go in it?"

"Eh-yup. We sure did, we . . ."

The movement again, quick and unmistakable against the white clapboard of the belltower, against the August blue of the sky.

"Check the tower?"

Confoundment. "W–w–well, no, that is . . ."

"Okay. Don't . . . *don't* look now. Don't move. You got that?"

Farley managed a sleepy look of alertness; Bimbo almost tensed. "We in trouble, Whip?" he hissed. "I'll . . ."

"Now listen carefully and *don't* look " Whippletree repeated once again, having learned long ago that, where his staff was concerned, there could never be one admonishment too many. "I think there's somebody up in the belltower."

65

He held his breath and watched while Bimbo's brain fought against the impulse in his neck muscles. The brain won out and Whippletree almost sighed. Farley, standing with his back to the tower, didn't have as much temptation.

"Good. Here's what we'll do. Farley, you stay right here. Sit down by the tree or something. Make it look like you're going to be here for awhile, but don't look at the goodam belltower, got it?"

Farley nodded.

"I'll stroll on back to the house. But I'll duck in the back door of the church and head up to the stairway in front, the one that goes up to the tower. Bimbo, while I'm doing that, you kind of amble over to your patrol car, and *make it look natural*. Where's your riot gun?"

The deputy's eyes were wide. "In the trunk."

"Okay, you get it out, real slow and careful. Got that?"

Nod nod nod.

"Now give me time. At least five minutes. In exactly five minutes, Bimbo, I want you to say something like 'Okay, up in the belltower, stand up with your hands above your head,' or something like that. Got it?"

Bimbo's lips moved as he rehearsed the words, the whites of his eyes still prominent with surprise.

"Okay, let's go."

Whippletree headed in front of the church, where the little white-lettered sign for this Sunday's sermon said:

"The Lord Shall Give Acceptance

And Grant Us Rest."

He stopped at the back entrance and slowly eased open the door. It creaked faintly. *Now,* he thought, *if "The Lord" is with me and Ruthie Koster, this door won't squeak anymore.* He moved it a little further. It squeaked again. Whippletree almost smiled. The door protested because its hinges were rusty and its wood was rain-swollen, and he would find Ruthie Koster's murderer if he was smart enough and tough enough and that was all there was to it. You "accepted" what you could, and if you got any "rest" it was because you made yourself forget.

He pushed the door open all the way—the noise wasn't bad—and stood inside the church. One minute had elapsed so far. The church was bare, just the necessities. A spare lectern instead of a pulpit. An altar so unadorned it might simply have been a table. A couple of flower stands, empty. The United States flag on one side, and on the other the flag of the state of Minnesota, with the figure of the plowman bent against the sunset. Many of the people who summered out here in Lake Eden attended Seventh Reformed on Sundays. *They must like to look at that plowman working away,* Whippletree thought, *before they go on back to the lake for water skiing and a barbecue.*

Quickly, he walked down the length of the church, past the rows of wooden pews, keeping to the side of the building. The floor was old, wooden, and would be very noisy in the center where it sagged. Then he was at the steps in the rear that led up to the choir loft and the belltower above it. The stairs, also of wood, were all but guaranteed to play a little number as he climbed.

Outside, he heard Bimbo slam the trunk shut. He had a little under three minutes. Great. Whoever was up there would see Bimbo with the riot gun in his hand, just casually standing down there on the lawn. Or maybe Bimbo was just fiddling around, waiting for the right time. Maybe. He started climbing, and made it quickly and pretty quietly up into the choir loft. The stairway to the belltower was an old, rickety spiral up a shaft that was no wider than a closet. It was hardly ever used, because the bell was chimed by pulling on a rope that hung down into the choir loft. Carefully, he placed one foot on the bottom stair.

"Hey, you lousy bastard," he heard Bimbo roar outside. "Up there in the tower. Yeah, *you*! You get your ass out of there with your hands up."

Oh, Christ, Whippletree thought, and for an instant debated inside his skull whether to rush up into the tower or to stay where he was and keep his mouth shut, ambushing whoever it was if he came down the stairs.

He didn't have to decide.

"Don't shoot! Please don't shoot!" somebody up there shrieked in a high-pitched voice. It sounded practically insane with fear.

"That's it, that's the boy," Bimbo was yowling. "Sheriff! Hey, sheriff!"

"Yeah?"

"Go on up. I got him covered."

"Does he have a weapon?" Whippletree called.

"Nope. Just a punk kid with his hands high as they'll go, and probably shittin' a brick."

The sheriff took it easy up the stairs, which were none too steady, and eased into the small square balcony around the old bell, his .45 extended with the safety off. Standing there in front of him was a boy about sixteen, seventeen maybe, thin, with longish brown hair. He had a thin face and looked almost ready to cry. The sheriff could see his legs shaking inside his bluejeans. Down on the floor next to him was a packet of sheet music in a plastic bag. Next to that was a smaller plastic bag with small red cylinders in it. And next to that was an old shotgun, twelve-gauge by the look of it.

"Easy does it, son," Whippletree said soothingly. "Easy

does it. Nobody wants to hurt you. Now, you just turn easy and go on down the stairs. All we want to do is talk to you."

"I swear I didn't do it," quavered the kid. "I swear I didn't have a thing to do with it."

"You do what the sheriff says or I'll blow your fuckin' head off," yelled Bimbo Bonwit, down there on the grass.

"Come on now, son."

The kid turned, still with his hands up, and eased toward the top of the stairway. Whippletree, keeping the bell between them, moved around, gathered up the weapon, and the spent shotgun shells. He didn't look, but he could tell by the feel that there were five of them. One for Ruthie, one for Bonnie, one each for Ben and Paul, and one for baby Matt. *Neat boy,* he thought.

The young man turned slightly and Whippletree tensed. Harmless as the kid appeared, it didn't pay to take chances. He jerked the .45 authoritatively.

"Please . . ." the boy pleaded.

"What?"

"My music. Right there in the bag. Please bring my music."

II

The music was his story, and he clung to it for dear life.

"I . . . I heard about what happened," he begged them to believe, hunched fearfully on the hood of the squad car, with the sheriff and Farley listening and Bimbo pacing back and forth, flexing his muscles. ("I'll make him talk, Whip. Don't you worry. I'll make him sing a few songs.") "I heard there were killings and the church was gonna be locked up for a while, and I wanted to make sure and get my music out."

69

"This stuff?" The sheriff inspected the contents of the plastic bag. About a dozen pieces of sheet music, from "Rock of Ages" to "A Mighty Fortress is our God."

The boy nodded. "I'm the . . . I *was* the organist. I came back to get my music before . . . somebody took it . . . or it . . . got lost . . ."

"He's lying," Farley put in. "He's lying, sheriff. Look at the way he don't look you in the eye."

The kid looked Farley in the eye, not for long, but he did it, and repeated, "I came back for my sheet music," with as much definitiveness as he could muster under the circumstances. Across the lawn separating the parsonage and the church from other houses, people were coming out onto their porches now, looking over.

"You say you *were* the organist?" Whippletree prodded. "What happened?"

The boy looked away and bit his lip. Oddly, he seemed more emotionally threatened by this question than by Bimbo and the circumstances of his apprehension.

"Why aren't you now?"

It took a while before he spit it out. "Because the . . . because . . . *because Koster kicked me out!*" he finally gritted.

"There you got it, Whip," Bimbo yelped. "There you got the whole thing. Look how mad the kid is. He couldn't play the organ anymore, and so he . . . "

"Quiet, Wayne . . . " the sheriff said, and from across the lawn a couple of little kids started chirping. He couldn't make it out clearly, something about "*Fingers, fingers . . .*"

"Son, what's your name?"

"Abner Fensterwald."

Whippletree ran that through the mini-computer in his head. There were a bunch of Fensterwalds out near St. Rosa, but here in Lake Eden there was . . .

"Your dad Elwood Fensterwald?"

The boy nodded.

Whippletree considered it. Fensterwald Dairies. The man was tight-assed and, for Stearns County, well off, a somber, even dour man, but straight as they come and honest as the day is long. Even Bimbo recognized the name and looked a little abashed. There would be no political headway in raking Elwood Fensterwald's kid over the coals, no matter what he had done.

Across the broad, hot lawn, more kids were chanting "*Fingers, fingers,*" and a little girl shouted, "Play us a five finger exercise, hey, Abs?"

The boy was ducking his head and swinging it from side to side, as if to shake off the sound, which seemed to disturb him.

"Hey, over there, keep it quiet," Whippletree commanded, and then, as if reluctantly, mothers started getting their shouting kids in line.

"Son, I'm taking you out to your pa's house," Whippletree said, and the boy made no response. "But first tell me . . . "

"Don't you have to read him his rights, sheriff? " Bimbo asked, with a dull gleam in his eye.

Whippletree gave him a look. "Son, tell me, how did you get that shotgun? And the empty shells?"

Abner Fensterwald didn't hesitate. In fact, he even looked glad of the question. "They were in the music seat," he said. "Right in the music seat. When the men were in the house and that other deputy . . . " he pointed at Farley " . . . fell asleep under the tree, I went in the back way and just figured I'd get in quick and get out. I knew my music was in the seat in the choir loft. That's where I always kept it, but Koster wouldn't . . . wouldn't let me in . . . ." Here he broke down for a little while. ". . . and I wanted to get it. So I went up to the loft and opened the music seat and there the gun was."

The sheriff held up the shotgun. A very old, well-cared-for

71

twelve-gauge, single-barrel, single-shot. "This one right here?"

Abner Fensterwald nodded.

"And what are you doing with it?"

"I . . . well, it wasn't supposed to be there . . ." Abner faltered.

"That the murder weapon, sheriff?" asked Bimbo eagerly.

"Might be. Twelve gauge. Maybe whoever did it hid it in there. But you can't tell for sure with a shotgun like you can with a rifle, when you have the bullet. And we don't have any such bullet."

No further ahead than before, actually. Or maybe they were.

"And this bag of spent shells was in that music seat with the gun?"

Abner nodded again.

"So what'd you do?"

"I . . . I made a big mistake, sheriff." The kid looked up at Whippletree, asking for understanding. "I was so surprised, I reached in and picked it up. Picked up the gun."

"And then?"

"And then my mind started working lickety-split and I remembered about fingerprints and everything and I . . ."

"You wiped it off, didn't you?"

"Right, and when I heard the patrol car come back I ran up in the tower. I was waiting until you left and . . ."

"I think he's the one did it," Bimbo barked. "You were going to dump the gun, hey, kid?"

"Yes, but I didn't . . ."

"Easy does it, Wayne. I want you and Farley to do a real thorough search of this place. *Real* thorough. You get Ruehle on the radio and get whatever help you need, and a metal detector, too."

"Aww, sheriff," Farley complained, "we ain't had no sleep in . . ."

"You been sleeping most of the day, and drinking beer besides. Now, get on it. I want this place scoured top to bottom, and I want that lawn and the trees and houses over there checked for that alleged .22 slug. But it couldn't have gone far. If they shot him over by the laundry poles and it went through his body, well, it couldn't have had much speed left."

"You're working us more than the alloted hours," Bimbo pointed out, putting his big ham hands on his hips.

"Yeah? Well, this is just the start. You're still working for me, remember? If you don't do what I tell you to do, I'll put you on report and bring it up come election time."

The big deputy was stunned by that, and it dawned slowly in his gelid-blue eyes that Whip had a few aces he could play, too.

"That ain't fair," he said, kicking at the grass.

"Yeah," Whippletree said. "Now you get started. Son," he said to Abner, "get in my car, will you? We'll go on out to your pa's place. First I want to have a look at something."

Cradling the shotgun under his arm, and stuffing the shells in a hip pocket, he walked over to the side of the house where the laundry lines were. It was a simple arrangement. Four shaky metal poles set into the grass, two poles on one end, two at the other, forming a rectangle. The poles were about five feet apart, joined by a thin wooden crossbar to which clotheslines were attached. The lines ran about twenty feet from one set of poles to the other. Last night, Koster had been tied to one set of poles, almost as if in a parody of crucifixion. Whippletree checked the knots. Amateur job. Slipknots tossed over the tops of the poles, and then tightened by the sagging weight of Koster's body, bound wrists

73

tied to the other end of the ropes. Well, when you are already shot through the chest, a couple of slipknots and a couple of shaky washpoles are enough to do the job and keep you where you are.

He led the boy back to his patrol car.

"Do you have to tell my pa?" the kid said. It would have been pleading had he not already been resigned to it.

"Sorry. But this looks like a simple thing to me, although it's too bad you panicked when you saw that gun. 'Course, anybody might've."

"Do you think it was really the gun that . . . " Abner looked over into the backseat, where the sheriff had put the weapon.

"I think so," Whippletree said, figuring, *Now, if Lugosch showed up last night right after the shootings, whoever did it must have been right in the church, stashed the gun there, and gotten out. But what about the rifle?*

He turned onto the main street that ran through the town of Lake Eden, past a Deep Rock gas station — Harvey Ahlers owned that one — past the Catholic church with its high steeple — out here the religious split was about fifty per cent Roman Catholic and fifty per cent Protestant, represented by Seventh Reformed. There was little hostility between the two groups because nobody took religion that seriously around here, or at least that's what Whippletree had always thought up till now, except that the Catholic girls said the Protestant girls were "loose" and the feeling was reciprocal. Across from the church was the Club Valmar, a collection of pickup trucks and cars clustered around it now in late afternoon, with the trailer off to one side, sort of in the back, and no pink Grand Prix anywhere around. Or? On impulse, Whippletree swung around into the alley in back, but it wasn't there. A suspicion was beginning to take shape in his mind:

perhaps Mel Betters wasn't all that wrong about Denny Bauch's involvement. It was unlike Bauch not to hang around the Valmar this time of day, and if Mary Prone was missing, too . . .

But that had to wait. He went past Fern Rehnquist's Market, the Great Northern Elevator Company and feed store, and past Bob Bucholtz's squat veteranarian's office, set right next to his new ranch-style house. That was downtown Lake Eden, not counting the hundred-odd houses set behind the business establishments on Main Street, nor the North Star Dance Hall outside of town, just a couple hundred yards from the lake itself. He had been at the North Star many a hot summer night, breaking up fights. Fights over women or young girls. Fights because of too much booze or simply too much energy. Or fights between the young men of various towns: "My town (Elrosa) is better than your town (Luxemburg) and I'm going to prove it by breaking your head open with this tire iron!" That sort of thing.

He braked at the stop sign by the fork. Here the road separated, one fork turning into a gravel trail down into the trees that sheltered the lake homes, and the other leading out into farm country. Just then a silver Mercedes 450 SL coupe came roaring up the rise out of the lake area, raising a billowing cloud of dust. The car would obviously have shot right on through the stop sign, had it not been for the sheriff's car right there, but now it braked and skidded right up to the sign and a little bit beyond. He had no trouble recognizing the car or the woman in it. The straight dark hair, deep tan, big dark glasses, and full red promissory mouth of Lynn Betters, which, when she saw him, curled into something like a snarl. Her shoulders, brown and bare, lifted slightly in an impenitent shrug, and her breasts rose and fell inside an inadequate halter top.

"Better take it easy, ma'am," Whippletree said out the window.

"What's it to you? " she spat. Spoiled little rich kid, good licking would do her no harm. "Haven't you got enough to do in St. Cloud? Have to be out here bothering decent . . ."

The sheriff knew she was angry about that Bauch incident, but it had been her own fault, dammit. There were plenty of places out in the country to do whatever she wanted, with Denny Bauch or anybody else.

"I said slow down," he told her in his official voice, not kidding now and not willing to take any guff. He gave her a look to back it up, and the words so obviously forming on that luscious mouth were recalled at the last moment. She snapped her head straight forward, salvaging in petulance whatever dignity she could, and drove off slowly.

Abner, who'd been watching the woman closely, let out something like a sigh.

"She's a looker, isn't she, son? What, about twenty-three, twenty-four?"

"Twenty-two," the kid said, too quickly. He realized it and said "Twenty-two," again, slower this time, as if to appear disinterested. Whippletree smiled. "You know her?"

"Aw, I seen her around. She comes to church sometimes."

"Church? In town? Seventh Reformed?"

"Yeah."

"I didn't know the Betters were Seventh Reformed." *In fact*, he thought, *I can't recall Mel Betters being much of anything*. Betters had been a nominal churchgoer while his wife was alive, but when she died he kind of chucked it.

"Well, from what I hear," Abner began, "you know, talk around Lake Eden . . ." He hesitated.

"Go on." Whippletree stepped on the gas and headed down the fork for the farm country.

"There was this thing happened between Miss Betters and

some guy, some hood, in a . . . in a car back of the Valmar . . ."

The kid was going on haltingly, with a furious adolescent
blush.

"I know about that, son."

"And . . . anyway, from what I heard, her father made
her go pretty regular to see the Reverend Koster. It was supposed to get her straightened out, or something."

The sheriff would have laughed, had the young man not
been with him. Koster, that idealistic love-and-respect
preacher, barely out of the seminary, was going to straighten
out Lynn Betters? Who had already been thrice corrupted by
too much money, too much freedom, and too much appetite
for the pleasures of the flesh? Of course, Koster did have all
those kids, so he'd had a little experience, but ministers and
priests always put another kind of tag on that sort of sex. It
was the old game, the rhetorical double-shuffle—the same
thing is different, depending upon your purposes and intent.
Well, Mel Betters must have figured his daughter was pretty
far gone to turn her over to a preacher.

"He made her go every week for a talk or something,"
Abner was saying.

The Fensterwald farm was a couple miles off yet. Conversation lapsed. The sheriff was thinking, wasn't it about time
for the *Tribune* to be out on the streets and on the front
porches back in St. Cloud? And, he guessed, the kid was
wondering what his old man was going to say when he saw
the sheriff's car driving up. Or maybe he was just thinking of
the pubic charms of Lynn Betters. Better that. Do himself
some good. Then, on impulse, he asked:

"What did you think of the Reverend Koster?"

The kid sat up straight, jerked up straight, really, next to
Whippletree.

"What do you mean?" he said evasively.

77

Evasiveness? Why that reaction? "Nothing special. Just what did you think of him? "

Abner hemmed and hawed a little and then said he didn't want to say anything.

"Why not?"

"Because Pa is on the board of trustees of the Seventh Reformed, chairman, I guess, and I don't want to be talking about . . ."

"Well, come on now, son. You must have an opinion. The man . . . how did you put it? *Kicked* you out as organist?"

Abner clenched his fists, bit his lip, and looked out the window at the broad rolling fields of wheat that started here in Western Stearns and swept on through the Dakotas and all the way into Montana. Koster had come from Montana.

"I hate his guts," the kid said then, still looking out the window. The fury was unexpected, but real.

"Because of the organist thing?" Whippletree prodded.

Abner nodded curtly, saying no more, although the sheriff guessed that wasn't all of it or even the end of it.

The radio snarled electronically and Whippletree grabbed the mike and flicked a switch on the dashboard.

"Lone Wolf, this is Mountaintop; Lone Wolf? Come in Lone Wolf?"

That damn Ruehle. Here he was with an impressionable kid in the car and the deputy was coming on with that *Mission Impossible* stuff.

"Can it," he said, mostly for Abner's benefit. "I'm here. What's up?"

"Hey, sheriff," Ruehle said. "It's up for grabs here. The *Trib* came out and the murders are all over page one. Somehow they got a photographer into the minister's room at the hospital, and the guy must have talked and talked. It's all in there. The two guys in ski masks and everything. And the phone's been ringing off the hook."

"Look, Alvin. Just tell them what I told you. I'll have a statement to make tomorrow. Now, what else is in the paper?"

"You're not going to like it."

"I don't care if I like it or not, dammit, tell me."

"Well, I better read you the part then." There was a short pause while Alvin breathed heavily into the mike. "Oh, yeah, here it is. Ready?"

"Shoot."

"Mr. Melvin Betters, chairman of the Stearns County Board of Commissioners, met and spoke with Reverend Koster at the St. Cloud Hospital at noon today. Emerging from the session, which he described as 'heart-rending,' Mr. Betters said that, based on the Reverend's description of his assailants, and on the supportive reports of Deputy Wayne Bonwit, a highly probable suspect has been determined. This suspect, whose name cannot yet be revealed for legal reasons, is also known to be missing."

"And here's the bad part," Alvin said.

"Could it be any worse?"

"Oh, yes it could, and it's already a big topic at the Courthouse Bar-and-Grill. It says, "Mr. Betters also stated that, based on his knowledge of the situation at the time the paper went to press, Sheriff Whippletree had ordered his deputies not to make inquiries into the absence of the chief suspect."

Whippletree blew up, scaring the hell out of young Fensterwald.

"Goddam it, Alvin," he yelled into the mike, "anybody else calls and asks questions, you tell them Mel Betters is a goddam liar, and on top of that, he's full of shit, now . . ."

"But Whip . . ."

"An' you tell 'em, too, by God, that . . ."

"But Whip . . ."

" . . . that I'm still the sheriff and I'll . . ."

"But Whip . . ."

"What the hell is it *now*?"

"I can't tell them *that*. You know what you told us about talking good."

Poor old literal Alvin. "Yeah, I know. You just tell them what I told you, and leave it at that."

"Jeez, sheriff . . ."

"Yeah?"

"You know, sheriff, I really like working here at the office, and all, but, Jeez, it's hard bein' in the middle. I mean, here I am on Mel's TO, an' Bimbo is running for sheriff this time around, and, hell, you've been real good to me . . ."

"Later. We'll take care of it later. The important thing right now is to stay cool and find those killers. Now, I'll be out at Fensterwald's place, something came up. You call my wife and tell her I'll probably be home around nightfall. Okay?"

"Right, Sheriff."

"Did you get that stuff out to Bimbo? The metal detector and the help."

"Sure thing. I sent out Pollock and Lugosch, to give him a hand."

"Good grief," said the sheriff. "Okay, Alvin, we'll have to make it as we can."

He put the mike back.

"Then you don't think I killed 'em," Abner blurted.

Whippletree looked over. Skinny teenage kid. Gangly, with his face taking on the big nose of a man, the joints of his body overgrown. A boy midway from one thing to another, neither one or the other, and not sure of anything either. He had been that boy one time. He hadn't been caught in a church with a possible murder weapon, but he'd had his own burdens, and he remembered.

"Hell, no," he said. "You look more a bank robber or a gigolo to me."

For the first time since the tower, Abner Fensterwald smiled, almost in pleasure, as if he was actually an all-right guy.

Too bad his old man wasn't so sure.

III

A huge double gate, open, led onto the properties of Fensterwald Dairy Farms, heralded by a sign next to the roadside. The drive curved easily through a meadow and a rich field of flowering clover. Then you came over a small rise, and great white barns, six of them, stood in a row, with smaller farm buildings around them, and, across a wide yard, surrounded by a wide green lawn, an old, large, lovingly-cared-for farmhouse. Elwood Fensterwald had an office in a room on the side of the house, with a separate entrance, and when he saw the sheriff's car in the yard, he came out. He had small, shrewd eyes, and one of the tightest mouths Whippletree had ever seen. "I don't make money smiling," he was known to have said, the only humorous remark ever attributed to him. "I'm like that Hefner fellow. I make money off tits." That he even knew about Hefner was astounding in itself. Most of his life, if not all of it, was surrounded, encompassed, and summed up in production figures and milk prices , and records of butterfat yield.

"Abner, you little bastard, you get into some kind of trouble?" he snarled good-humoredly, walking up to the patrol car. Whippletree got out, taking the shotgun with him.

"Pa . . ." Abner started.

"Elwood, there's a little bit of a problem, I think," the sheriff said, "an' maybe if the two of us was just to talk it over . . ."

"He ain't done nothin', has he? If so I'll kick his ass around a while."

The boy, flustered, humiliated, said nothing and stared at his hands. *Fingers.*

"Nope, not that I can see. Can we . . . ?"

"Sure. Come on into the office. Abs, you get changed and get on the chores, hear? Now you got that silly organ-grinding out of your system, might as well do some real man's work."

The kid went off into the house, and Fensterwald, scratching the back of his neck, led Whippletree up the steps into his small office. It was as dry and grim as he was, with an old roll-top desk, its compartments crammed with old papers, a table with a calculator on it, boxes and crates with files in them all over the floor, and pictures of at least a hundred different cows on the wall. Under each was a small plaque bearing the cow's date of birth, names of sire and dam, and production figures. Lined against a wall, neglected, were trophies won at state and county fairs. Trophies didn't mean a damn thing to old man Fensterwald. They represented the past. The past wasn't worth a piece of shit. It was the future that was important, and what you could make out of it. One of his problems had always been that he thought of his son as a piece of the past, not of the future, a trick of the mind accomplished by having convinced himself that he would never die. Whippletree, sitting down, holding the shotgun and the bag of shells, wondered why so many people put such store in having children and then treat them so badly all their lives. *You probably think that way because you never had the chance. Susan!*

"Nice gun you got there," Elwood admitted. "Looks just like my old Winchester twelve-gauge."

Whippletree's breath caught somewhere around his heart like a ball of fire.

"What?" he heard himself asking.

"A Winchester twelve. Got mine in nineteen hundred and twenty-two. Hunted with it for years, when I was young. Retired it years ago, one of the finest pieces I ever owned, too."

"Where is it now?" It came out like a croak.

Old Elwood Fensterwald was not a successful man for nothing. He cocked his eye sharply, and put two and two together. "Goddam," he said, as if in wonder, "that little shit-ass didn't really go on and do it, did he?"

"Do what?"

"C'mon, sheriff. I warn't born yesterday. He told me he was goin' to kill Koster, 'cause of what happened. Well, I guess he didn't even do a good job at that. Koster's still alive, I hear?"

"He was as of this noon. Now, what's this about something that 'happened'? Your boy threatened the Kosters? Reverend Koster?"

"Hell, I don't think he actually went up to the Reverend and threatened *him*. He just told me he was goin' to kill him. I just took it like he was spoutin' off, talking big, know what I mean, 'cause of what happened."

"*What* happened?"

"You mean you ain't heard about that? You must be the only man, woman, and child in the whole county who hasn't. You see, it's this way. Koster caught my kid up in the choir loft last week, just before choir practice. He was the organist, you know. An' he was jerkin' off. Kicked him right off the choir, told him to go home." Fensterwald snickered. "Guess he didn't want anybody double-timing on another organ."

So that was it! *Fingers. Play me a five-finger exercise, Abs.*

"Just like the dipshit, too. Here I am on the board of trustees for that church, an' my own kid has to go and make a scene like that. I told him, you want to beat your meat, go out

83

behind the barn like a decent all-American boy, or get yourself some girl and stick it in her, but . . . so he actually went
ahead and done it . . ."

"I don't think so," Whippletree said, repeating the story
Abner had told him about finding the gun and the shells in
the music seat.

Fensterwald listened, unimpressed. "Well, there's one way
we can find out. Let's go down to the game room in the basement."

Elwood said nothing on the way down the stairs. He
seemed to be thinking the whole thing over, and the situation
wasn't at all as amusing as it had first been.

"Haven't been down here for a long time," he said. "Too
busy. Now, let's see . . ."

He turned on a light and slid open a chest-high length of
panel. Behind it were hunting and sports weapons of every
conceivable kind. Archery sets, traps for mink, muskrat,
wolf, even a big bear trap, from the old days. Rifles of various
caliber and age, and shotguns. He ran his hand on down the
racks.

"Now, wait a minute. Was an old .22 supposed to be here,
as I recall. And hey, wait a minute, my old Smith and Wesson
double-barrel is gone an' . . ."

Double barrel? Whippletree thought.

Elwood Fensterwald looked up angrily. "Six of my best
guns are missing," he snarled. "The oldest ones, too, *an'* my
1922 Winchester twelve."

"Is this it?" The sheriff offered him the gun.

"Easy enough to find out. All's we have to do is . . ." He
took the weapon, turned it upside down and held it to the
light, checking up inside the trigger housing. He cursed.

"What is it?"

"I always mark my guns," he said. "Put my initials in tiny

letters up under the housing, where hardly anybody can see it, or even find it, if they're looking."

"Is it there? Your mark."

"No, but here. You take a look."

The sheriff did, and saw a small patch, rubbed or filed, where such initials might have been.

"You have the numbers on the gun?"

"Nope. No registration necessary back then."

That's right, Whippletree thought suddenly. "You have any break-in around here, lately? Theft? Anything like that?"

"I doubt it, but I'll check." Fensterwald scratched his head, then his chin. "So you think Abner actually . . ."

"Hell, Elwood, I don't see how he could."

"Yeah, I doubt it. But it don't look too good, now, does it? Here I am a trustee, and everybody knows about my boy pounding his pud in the choir loft, and . . ."

"How did *you* feel when Koster kicked your son out as organist?" the sheriff asked, and followed it up with, "What do you know about Koster, anyway? He's a young man hard to figure for an old farmboy like me."

Fensterwald gave him a look and nodded shrewdly. "I'm not one likes to talk about my fellow man," he lied brazenly, "but then these are special circumstances, wouldn't you say?"

"I would."

"Then let's go up an' get us both a bottle of Grain Belt an' go sit out on the porch. It's a hot day."

"Well, he's been here for about two years now, that's the start of it," Fensterwald began, out on the shaded porch. Cold moist droplets collected on the dark brown beer bottles, and the sheriff held the bottle against his forehead for a moment.

"Old Reverend Runde went on to his reward, an' we were needin' a new man. Pretty hard to get somebody out here in the country these days. A lot of 'em don't mind it in the summer, when the lake people are all over, but in the winter, when it gets around to blowin', you can get locked up in your house for more'n a week at a time. Well, you know about that. Anyway, I guess, even so, Koster never had it so good. First time he come down here, I recall, he was just about to graduate from that there seminary up in Montana. He was lookin' for work. Well, I'll tell you frankly, Emil, I may be on the trustee board, an' the missus will come as quick over a church picnic as she does with me pumping away for an hour, but this churchgoin' stuff, an' decent young men becoming ministers, practically *women* if you ask me, is just too damn much. 'Course I got my business to think of. Well, he comes down here, for us to talk to him and see what kind of goods he got, an' about all he says is 'Why, you've got *so much* down here. You've got *fortunes* down here,' as though every manjack with a TV set is right away landed gentry with an extra asshole for hire, like some of those executives down in Edina that couldn't pour piss out of a boot if the instructions were written on the heel. Well, you know the other two trustees? Morris Weiderman and Caleb Clowers?"

Whippletree nodded.

"Yeah, I thought so. You know pret' near everybody, ain't that so?"

"You milk cows, Elwood. I got to know people."

"When you goin' to give Bimbo Bonwit a crack at somethin' important? He's pretty well thought of out here."

"I've got him handling the investigation back at the parsonage right now," Whippletree said, suppressing a sigh. "Anyway, about Koster?"

"Well, like I said, he come down here and told us he was finishing up at the seminary, and had a family and all, so that meant he was settled. Of course, the women thought he was the greatest thing next to a feathered cock, an' he seemed all right at first. I liked his wife a whole lot, an' the kids were well taken care of. It's just . . ."

"Just what?"

"It's just he was so *hard.*"

"Koster was hard?"

"Oh, I don't mean it the way it sounds. Not hard, so's he could drive a fence line in a day, but, you know . . . " The dairyman sought a word that would best describe what he meant, found he didn't have many to choose from, but tried anyway, "Koster was a horse's ass, if you ask me."

If Whippletree knew nothing else, he knew the vernacular of Stearns County.

"One of those, huh?"

"Yeah," said Fensterwald, warming to his subject, "he's one of these guys don't give a man the benefit of the doubt. Don't give a man nothing. Like with my kid. What the hell did he do, now, that we ain't all done? Except now I'm beginning to wonder, but anyway . . . 'Course he was dumb enough to try it right behind the organ in the choir loft. But Koster goes an' makes an example of him. Hauls him up, big surprise, when the rest of the choir gets there, and *tells everybody about it.* Nobody would've known otherwise. Sure, the guy considers the thing sinful and unnatural and all that, and always rails away in sermons, denouncin' sex, denouncin' fornication, especially about Denny Bauch and Mary Prone . . ."

"Hold on a minute, Elwood. You mean from the pulpit?" Whippletree thought of the slender Koster waving an outraged fist over the spindly lectern at the Seventh Reformed. "You mean he actually named *names* and . . . practices committed? From the pulpit?"

"That Koster was a demon against sex if I ever saw one. I

87

often wondered how he'd gotten around to having himself four kids. Maybe he was like a nun, and it was on his mind all the time. Maybe he just couldn't stand anybody to have it free, like Bauch."

The sheriff pictured Denny Bauch. The body that was not particularly big, but well-shaped, graceful like an animal, indolent. The perpetual smirk, halfway between a sneer and a smile, that you always wanted to smash, even if you were a nice guy. And the big, greasy 'Fifties pompadour, a kind of tipoff to where Bauch was, where he was at. Well, it was true: the Bauches and the Kosters of the world hated the sight of one another like dogs and cats. It was a matter of physiognomy, to start with.

"Koster sure laid old Denny low a couple of times," Fensterwald was saying.

"Such as?" asked the sheriff.

"Whip, you'll find me regular in attendance on Sunday, but that don't mean I got to listen to what's goin' on. Close as I can recall, it was around June he started denouncin' sex in particularly strong terms. And the Valmar. He got to be death on the Club Valmar. You would of thought it was Sodom and Gomorrah all rolled into one."

"That's what I thought it was."

Fensterwald snorted in amusement. "He kept on ranting about the 'higher love' and the 'higher life' until old Miz Hockapuk like to creamed her drawers."

"She liked it?"

"Hell, she loved it. Lot of people loved it, having a nice-lookin' young guy like that tell them all about sin. Don't get me wrong. *I'm* the one couldn't put a handle on the guy, but then I'm just an old country boy. I call a spade a spade, and to me a screw is just a screw, except it feels good. But to hear young Matt Koster talk about it was like listenin' to someone who was so good at describin' the flavor of chocolate ice cream that you could actually *taste* it just listenin' to him."

"I thought you told me he was *against* having fun?"

"Well, now, drinkin' was out, so that pretty well cut out the Valmar, although I think it was more because of Bauch that he hated the Valmar. But he was real concerned about sex being that 'higher love' I was talking about."

"Why did he hate Bauch so much?"

"Because why do any of us? No, I don't hate the guy. He's just a shiftless, lyin', stealing son-of-a-bitch. He sure gets his share of ass, though. I'll give the bastard that much."

"You heard that Mary Prone and Denny are getting ready to get hitched?"

"Yeah. That's a good one. I don't see why he bothers. He's been hosin' her brains out for a couple years already. It seems to me he just wants to get a chunk of the Valmar. The place does real good enough in summer to support a long trip to Florida come January, when the blizzards start up."

"Bauch is not one to pass up an angle, and I'm sure Mary can make a man happy, if she puts her mind to it."

"It ain't her mind she puts to it, Whip. Now what are we gonna do about my kid?"

Whippletree thought it over. The shotgun would have to be test fired on new shells, to determine whether or not the firing pin left a mark similar to the mark on the five shells Abner said he'd found in the music seat. It seemed the gun *was* Fensterwald's, or might be, and with the other weapons missing, somebody could have been in the house at one time or another and that somebody could have taken the weapons. Of course, it was a little unusual, but the missing guns were valuable as collector's items. Somebody would have to know what they were doing.

"Bauch ever come out here?"

Elwood Fensterwald glanced up quickly, and once again anticipated what the angle was.

"Quite a few times, but he never got down in the basement, if that's what you mean. 'Course it could of been when we were gone down to Sioux Falls in July, to look for breedin' bulls. But what would Bauch know about guns? I thought stolen tires or TV sets was more his speed."

Whippletree nodded. "I just have to run down every possibility. That gun got in that church some way."

"Well, I figure it's my gun and I damn sure want to know *why*."

"Technically, Elwood, looking at it from a certain angle, I should book your boy on suspicion, especially since we don't have any other suspect, and in his case, with his threat and all, it seems he sure had cause. But I just don't think he did it. Now . . ."

"Whip, anything you do is all right with me. A little stay in the old jailhouse might make a man of him."

"I doubt it, but here's the thing—if people find out about him being in there with the gun, they're goin' to start yowlin' and howlin'. They're scared and I don't blame them. So let's you and me keep this under our hats, and I'll get the gun down to St. Paul for ballistics. Okay?"

"I'm with you on that, all right. But you do what you have to do. I would."

Whippletree and the dairyman walked back out into the big yard. The white paint on the big barns gleamed in the late-afternoon sun. The sheriff wondered what it would have been like to have a place this big, something he had wanted and was on his way to getting just when the big flood came, back in forty-one. He'd been all paid up on the place, then had taken out a second mortgage to put his younger brother, Herb, through law school, and his sister, Vera, into nursing.

Bought a new combine, too, and put up a big new dairy barn for himself. Got way overextended. Then the flood came; and that was the end of it. Now, standing in the yard, with Abner and the gun on his mind, he had a slight, niggling feeling that he was overextending himself again. Too much trust, maybe? Or was it only because he was suddenly thinking of the lost years?

Fensterwald looked around proudly. "Yeah, I sure got a nice place here. Koster could never get over it. He even brought his old man out here to see it."

"Koster's father?"

"Yeah. An old guy from Montana. Wheat rancher, I think he said. Didn't say much, just looked around. Didn't seem to have much in common with the boy."

Probably not, Whippletree was thinking.

"I think the kid was tryin' to mend fences with the old man, or somethin'. The guy came down from Missoula on a visit in June, took one look and went back. Then, in July, Koster took off a week and headed back there all by himself. Left the wife and kids here."

The connection was vague, but anything helped. "You say his sermons started getting a . . . a little more colorful around June?"

Elwood, caught off-guard by what he regarded as a change in the subject matter, said, "What? Oh—oh, yeah. All summer he ain't been quite the same as before . . ."

Then they saw young Abner, kind of poking his head out around a corner of one of the barns. Whippletree waved him over, and after what appeared to be a moment of debate, the kid reluctantly slouched toward them.

"We got you set up for the ee-lectric chair, Abs," chortled his father.

The kid blushed, and appeared ready to start crying.

91

The sheriff tried a laugh. Big joke, ha-ha. "I'm taking the gun in for tests, son," he said. "Most likely nothing will come of it. You just stick around home now, hear? And stay out of church towers."

There was something indefinable in the boy's expression that Whippletree couldn't quite put his finger on, as if he weren't all that appreciative of what was being done for him. Or was it something else? The sheriff couldn't read it. Hard to tell about these youngsters, and with teenagers, next to impossible. They could be slippery and obsequious as a four-bit nigger with towels and a whisk broom, like at that Chicago Hotel, time of the crime conference.

Abner was busy studying the texture of the gravel down at the toe of his shoe. He nodded.

"Okay, I guess that's it." He shook Elwood's hand.

"Remember what I said, Emil. Get Bimbo on this. Bimbo'll help you out on this one, all right."

IV

The Club Valmar, for the time being, was really just the Club *Mar,* if you could even call it a "club." It was a small-town tavern, and that was all, with a long bar on one side, gouged and burned with cigarettes, and a mirror behind it, foggy with the grease of a thousand cheap hamburgers and "steak" sandwiches that Mary cooked in the back. There was a pool table in the middle of the floor, the green felt thin and torn in places, and booths along the wall. There was a juke-box, a pinball game, and a cigarette machine. The johns were in back. That was all.

Mary's first husband had been Val Hennesey, who, unfor-

tunately, developed an excessive liking for the chief commodity in their jointly-run establishment, and who, when
sampling said product, developed an overwhelming desire to
apply his belt to Mary's behind, this to exorcise in his own
mind what he believed to be her infidelity, and to discourage,
with the long black marks he engraved upon her soft flesh,
her desire to expose that flesh to any Tom, Dick, or Harry, or
Denny Bauch or even Bimbo who might happen to walk into
the Valmar and ask for a beer and a shot of Guggenheimer's.
When, eventually, Mary got around to kicking Val out, people figured it was only fitting that she reassume her maiden
name. She left the red neon sign—VALMAR—on the front
of the place "as a remembrance," and besides, it was paid for.
Lately people in Lake Eden, running out of things to talk
about or think about, wondered if it might soon become the
DENMAR or the MARDEN. It was a den of some kind, all
right, they were sure of that.

Whippletree slowed down, as he drove through town, and
once again checked the cars outside the Valmar. No pink
Grand Prix. It was becoming a problem for sure now, because Bauch *was* a suspect, and if he didn't show up pretty
damn soon, there was going to have to be an all-points out
for him, and that would make him very mean. He was a suspect to everybody, or almost everybody, and he was one of
the suspects in the sheriff's mind, too, but Whippletree just
didn't peg the guy for a killer, no matter what. So Koster *had*
denounced him from the pulpit. So what? The Denny Bauch
Whippletree knew—*if* he really knew the guy—would take
this as a mark of distinction, good publicity, you might say.
And so Koster had gone into moralistic rages against the Valmar and Mary Prone? Again, unless Bauch's approaching
nuptials had dramatically altered his personality, these were
things that had been said in the village for a long time. Hell,

Mary Prone didn't even care. She did what she wanted to do, and laughed, and so did Bauch.

Something was wrong about the whole damn thing, but Mel Betters and the *Trib* wouldn't wait until he figured it out.

He stopped his patrol car next to Mary's trailer, got out, and walked up the wide concrete steps and into the bar. Outside, it was not yet twilight, but it could have been close to midnight in the bar. Dull lights glowed at either end of the mirror, dully reflecting Trixie Wade's tangled, ash-blond hair. Cutesy little electric candles glowed on the tables of the booths, and the light in the jukebox flickered with the throbbing bass of some song, the only lyrics of which seemed to be "Rock-a-me-hon-eee" repeated over and over, interspersed at odd intervals with the howl of man or dog. It was enough to give orgasm a bad name.

Whippletree slid onto a stool, let his eyes adjust to the gloom, and motioned Trixie to cut the decibel level. She reached beneath the bar and did something and "rock-a-me-hon-eee" faded with a final desperate howl.

"Hey, Trix, what the fuck ya doin'?" called a runty-looking guy in work clothes, who was making out with some heavily-mascaraed teenybopper in the back booth. She was obviously too young even to be *in* there. The sheriff turned around and let him see the badge, and that sure as hell took care of that. The drinkers at the bar, half a dozen of them, most of whom Whippletree knew vaguely, stared into their shot glasses and listened as hard as they could. *The killings! He's here about the killings!*

"How's Trix?"

"Couldn't be better. You wanna beer?" Her mouth went up and down on the chewing gum. Her eyes were afraid, but bold.

"Give me a Hamm's. Where's Mary?"

She reached into the cooler, grabbed a bottle, and with one long deft motion, twisted off the top, swung the bottle over the bar, and poured it into a glass.

She didn't look at him. "Bimbo asked me that this morning. You mean you still don't know?"

He didn't like the tone of her voice. She was trying too hard to be tough and nonchalant, and so she crossed over into something more like insolence. She realized it, but trapped inside her lower-class idea of courage, couldn't back off gracefully. Her mouth went around and around. "Been trying to find her all day, haven't ya?" she said, making it worse.

Down along the bar, Whippletree was sure he heard somebody snicker. He was just too damn tired for that kind of crap.

"All right," he told her, raising his voice just a notch, "how much did you charge Clem Duckworth for last night?"

Her mouth stopped, and he had the feeling she would like nothing better than to give him a good female slap across the chops.

"What're you talkin' about?" she blurted, with fading defiance.

"Look, Trixie, you know as well as I do. There's hardly a woman in Stearns County would give Clem Duckworth a ride unless he paid for it, and you know we have laws against that kind of thing. Now, do I have to go find Clem and get him to tell a long, involved story for the St. Cloud *Tribune,* or are you and I going to have a nice little talk right here?"

She gave him a look that was hatred, fear, and defeat wrapped in one. "Can we go back inna kitchen, then, at least?"

He nodded and went around the bar. "Hold your water, boys," Trixie called. "Be out inna minute."

Nobody said much, but when they were back in the kitchen, Whippletree could hear the excited hiss of whispered speculation from the bar.

"So whattaya want to know?" Her mouth was working again.

The kitchen was filthy. A refrigerator yellow with neglect. Tiled floor with stains and sticky spills all over. On a table, a bag of hamburger buns had been left open. Some buns had fallen on the floor. Trixie bent over, giving him the benefit of her cleavage, which was impressive, if fleshy. "Lucky we keep the floors clean around here," she said, putting the buns back into the plastic bag.

"When did you see Mary last?" Whippletree asked.

"Let's see now," she started, thinking up a lie, "I . . ."

"Save it. I'm not kidding. I haven't had much sleep for practically two days and a bunch of people are dead. I've been running all over the county, and there's not one more game I want to play today. Where's Mary Prone and Denny?"

Trapped, and aware of his anger, Trixie wavered, then: "They're over in Brooten."

That was a town twenty miles away.

"Since when?"

"Since an hour ago. Mary called me. They're over drinking at the Brooten Rod and Gun."

"What did she call about?"

"To tell me where she was."

"Why would she have to do that?"

"I don't know."

"When did you see her last?"

Trixie looked away. "Last night," she said, after a moment.

"When last night?"

"About a little after suppertime. Then she told me to take over and she and Denny . . . left."

"Left from here? Where were they headed?"

"I don't know. They didn't tell me."

"Does this happen too often? That Mary leaves the club and takes off?"

It didn't, and they both knew it.

"When she called, did she say where she'd . . . she and Denny . . . had been?"

"No."

"Did you tell her about the Koster murders?"

"I didn't have to. She knew about it."

"How did she find out?"

"I don't know. But she knew about it."

If it was in the Tribune, *then it's probably on the radio by now,* he thought, *or word-of-mouth up to Brooten. It could easily go that fast. But if she—they—had prior knowledge . . .*

"Why would she be so interested in the Koster case?" he asked her.

Trixie, suddenly and surprisingly, went through a strange little catharsis.

"Because Denny was *scared,*" she said, then stopped, as though she'd told too much.

"Scared?" That hardly sounded like Bauch. "Of what?"

"Because of that fight with Koster."

The sheriff felt himself take a step backward. There was Trixie Wade, all right, hangdog, dirty-blonde, cheap, and scared.

"*What?*" he heard himself saying, very slowly.

"I don't know about it," she added quickly. "I just heard about it. I wasn't here that night. That was a long time ago."

"How long ago?"

She thought a minute. "Sometime before the Fourth of July. I went up to see my parents in Bemidji. I go once each year an' . . ."

97

"What started the fight?" He remembered Elwood Fensterwald's stories about Koster's attacks, the sermons.

"I don't know. But they had one. Out back, in the alley."

It was getting high time to have a face-to-face with Denny Bauch. "Are they still at the Rod and Gun?"

"They didn't say where they was goin'," she said sullenly. "Look, I got to get back to the customers . . ."

"Okay, you go ahead. And thanks."

She didn't tell him he was welcome. A few men called "S'long, sheriff," as he went out. Back in the car, he debated what to do. Could drive up to Brooten and see what he could do about Bauch. But the guy might not even be there. So he drove over to Fern Rehnquist's Market and used the phone on the wall outside.

"Denny Bauch there?"

"Who wants 'im?" came the voice on the wire.

"Emil Whippletree."

Short pause, auditory double take. "Hey, sheriff! Why didn't you say so? Naw, he just left. Mary Prone was with 'im."

"You know where they went?"

"Haven't the slightest. Hey, you want me to tell him to give you a call when I see him again?"

Sure, he thought. "Are they coming back there tonight?"

"Can't say."

"Okay, if you see him."

"You get up here, sheriff, drop in. Buy you a beer."

"Thanks."

He said good evening to old Fern and "how's business." Fern and a few customers gathered around looking worried, just as they had in Rockville and St. Alazara earlier this afternoon, and wondered who could've done such an awful thing and did he find out yet who had done it?

"Got a few leads, but I can't talk about them yet," he explained, and was it just insecurity, or did he see a look of doubt, disbelief, on the faces of some of the people? *Whippletree's losing his touch,* they probably thought.

Well, they ought to see just how far this thing would've come if Bimbo had been in charge.

Now, Emil, it hasn't come too far. You'd better put out an APB on Bauch and bring him in. No, wait a little while longer. You already know he's scared, and now Trixie will get in touch and tell him you're interested in talking to him. That's enough. Bauch is no killer. Is he?

Back at the church, Bimbo was stretched out next to a patrol car, asleep. Farley and Pollock were dozing inside, and Jamie Lugosch paced up and down the parsonage lawn.

His face lit up when he saw the sheriff.

"We found the bullet!" he cried.

One little bit of good news, and it was a tight market for that kind of thing. "Where?"

"Just a couple yards past the laundry lines, in the grass. It's pretty wasted though."

Farley took him over to the car, and from a little metal box, using a pair of tweezers, he extracted a small, irregular-shaped lump. Whippletree had seen them before. It was a slug, and from the rising stink of it, there was no doubt that it had been in the body of man or animal. It was a quality of bullets: the first characteristic necessary for a good ballistics man is a strong stomach. But this bullet was not going to be of much use to anybody. The formalities would be adhered to, nonetheless.

"Pollock, how'd you like a ride down to St. Paul?"

"Aw, Whip!"

"Yeah, you're goin' to have to be the one. You're the only one got any regular sleep today or last night. I want you to take this .22 slug down to the state laboratories, and also this shotgun and shells. Tell them I want the gun test-fired, to see if it's the same gun that was used with these empties. That an' the .22 is all we got to go on. I assume you boys didn't come across a .22 rifle here this afternoon?"

"Nope, Whip, we sure didn't." Bimbo sat up, yawning. "What about that Fensterwald kid?" The big deputy had that dull glint in his eye again, a bush-league reflection of the perpetual gleam that Melvin Betters always walked around with.

"I left him with his pa. He didn't do anything."

"Yeah, we only caught him in the church with a shotgun, and he supposedly swore to get the Reverend first chance he got, 'cause of that J-O thing."

"Where'd you hear about that?"

"Some church women come over here this afternoon while we was working, brought us lemonade. Told us about a lot of local goings-on. A Miz Mildred Hockapuk an' a Miz Withers, I think it was. Ain't that right, Bill?"

Farley grunted in affirmation.

"I hope you didn't feel you had to discuss the case with them in great detail," Whippletree said.

"Naw, but when they told us about young Fensterwald and the murder threat, I knew that was our man."

"Boy. Anyway, he's back on his old man's place, if we need him."

"I don't think it's right to leave a prime suspect running around," Bimbo grouched, while Farley, Lugosch, and Pollock studiously avoided any look or gesture that might put them on one side or the other. Bimbo was standing out more and more now, Whippletree observed, and the situation would not get any better between now and November.

"Wayne, I've known Elwood Fensterwald for forty years. Don't worry about it. I'll take the responsibility."

100

"Well, all right, if you . . ."

"You come up with Denny Bauch yet?" Farley wanted to know. "Don't you think we better try and bring him in."

"I know where he is, and my hunch is that he'll be back to-morrow. Then I'll talk to him. Meantime, there's nothing to tie him to the . . ."

"Lot you know," Bimbo interrupted, sure of his shot this time and ready to take it. "Miz Hockapuk said there was a terrible hassle between Denny and the Reverend sometime early in the summer. I'd say that's enough to look into Denny, wouldn't you?"

So, Whippletree thought. He felt pressured. "We'll do it my way," he said. "We don't know what that was about. Could be totally unrelated. That was over two months ago, and there's nothing to connect Denny Bauch with this place at the time of the killings." *Not that I know of yet,* he qualified. Or was he just resisting a confrontation with Bauch because Mel Betters had practically ordered him to put the bum away?

"And just what else did the good ladies know?"

"This Koster must have been some kind of a saint," Pollock said. "They couldn't say enough good things about the guy. How he gave a share of his tiny salary to charity every month. How he always had time to solve everybody's marriage prob-lems, or talk to their kids, if they needed it . . ."

He sure did a great job on Abner Fensterwald, Whippletree reflected.

" . . . an' how he was probably the reason Lynn Betters stopped whoring around the way she used to do."

"You're speaking of the daughter of Stearns County's finest," said the sheriff, not bothering to keep the sarcasm out. Still, it might be a good move, just to hassle old Mel—*and* Lynn—if he were to go out and have a talk with her. After all, she might know something, have some clue. Although he doubted she went much further than water skiing, rock music, clothes, cars, and serving the demands of her body. He could just about imagine juicy little stuck-up Miss Betters putting on her innocent, reformed act with the parson in order to get credit-card privileges back from her father. (Mel Betters: "Well, what say, Reverend? How's my kid coming along? Gettin' those hellin'-around ideas out of her head, hey?" "Oh, yessir, yessir. She certainly is. I'm sure she's *never* going to stray again . . .") What was it now? Reverend Koster was death on sex? Well, unless Lynn had worn granny dresses made out of burlap bags to her counseling sessions, she was a walking advertisement for the commodity.

"Okay, let's move. Pollock, get goin'. You can probably make it before dark. You know the way? Cut around by the airport and then over to St. Paul. It's right next to the Capitol."

"I been there."

"The rest of us'll hit back for St. Cloud. Bimbo, you can move out now. Farley, go with him. Jamie, get the car started, I got something to do yet in the house."

He went inside and stood for a moment in the front room, just listening. There was no sound or, rather, there was a total absence of motion, breathing, life, a hollowness heavy and saddening. He strained to hear, to feel, but the alien visitor had come and gone, taking its bloody nourishment, sated for a time. The sound of his footsteps as he walked over to the Reverend's desk echoed in the room, but in his mind was the upstairs bedroom and the body of Ruthie Koster crumpled up on the floor.

Don't worry, his mind said to her. *Don't worry, it's still yesterday and I'll be with you all night. Nothing is going to happen.*

"You're a damn silly old fool," he said aloud. "Blubbering about it isn't going to solve anything either."

He picked up the folder with Koster's sermon outlines in it and left the house, carefully locking the door.

V

Sarah had her worried smile on when he came in at a little after eleven, and she reheated the pot roast she'd prepared for dinner.

"I hoped you'd make it back. Better try and get some sleep tonight. You can't run this way day in, day out and stay on top of . . ." She didn't finish. "You got raked over the coals pretty good in the *Trib*. You want to see it?"

"No. Alvin called on the radio and read me the meat of it."

"Emil . . . I've . . . I've got this feeling . . ."

He cut the meat, dashed a little salt on it, poured on some of her rich gravy, and took a big forkful. "Uh-huh?" he asked chewing.

"Don't talk with your mouth full. This feeling . . . that, I mean, do you think it's going to be all right?"

He nodded and went on eating. "What?" he managed to say.

She thought about it a little more before going on. "Well, I don't want to worry you. Lord knows you've got enough problems already. But I've had this feeling again, like I had that time before, back in the year we had that second mortgage on the home place . . ."

She always called it the "home place," as though now they were living somewhere else, someplace comfortable enough, but a little strange, transitory . . .

We are, he admitted, and probably because of the fatigue, or because he knew Sarah was worrying again and that there was nothing he could do to stop it, a glimmer of memory

103

came back, a memory of the night it was all wiped away, the "home place" and everything else, too. Mid-March, it was, with one of those quick deadly thaws that occur maybe once every ten–fifteen years in the upper Midwest. People who own and work the land on the rich bottom of the Mississippi valley hate and fear these thaws. They shrink back in apprehension and picture the head-high drifts of snow melting quickly and inexorably up there to the north, up there in the hundreds of thousands of acres of wilderness, and they can see in their mind's eye the meltwater running down the slopes, among the pine forest, becoming pools that rise and pour out of hollows and become rivulets that gather into the melting streams, the ice gone too, by now, and spill crashing into the tributaries of the Mississippi, then into it, and then crash down along the length of it, roaring like a tunnel of thunder, moving like the night, and rising, rising. And that year the rain had come, too. For days men worked along the banks, sandbagging until they dropped, listening to the sound of the river, like the dull rumble of fate, until the sound of it echoed in the caverns of their brains, even in sleep. But still the river rose, and still it rained. It rained for four days and into the fifth night, and that was enough. He had gone back to the house late that night, convinced the river had crested, and gone to sleep. "It's over," he remembered telling Sarah, busy putting Susan to bed, "I think it's crested, and the storm appears to be breaking up," and then they had all gone to sleep, and while they slept, *while they slept . . . If I just don't think about that now,* he told himself, sitting here in this cheerful kitchen thirty-five years later, *if I just concentrate on chewing this meat and getting this piece of lettuce on my fork, then it will be all right . . .*

"I mean, well," Sarah worried, getting around to it, "do you think you'll win this one last time? It's all we need, but that story in the paper . . ."

"I wouldn't worry about that yet," he said, as soothingly as he could. "Remember, I've been around a long time. I've got a lot of friends out in the county."

He remembered the looks on the faces of some of the people "out in the county" today. The questioning, doubting looks. And the fear. "You think old Whip can still handle the job?" "Well I don't know. He used to be able to, but, hell, he's been around, now, how long's it been . . . ?"

"I don't think you have to worry about that," he said again.

"What's that folder?" she asked, noticing the big ring-clip folder of sermon notes and church bulletins.

He told her.

"What've you got this for?"

"I thought I might find something in it."

"You're not doing so well on the case, are you? You haven't figured out how it happened?"

There was no point in trying to lie out of it. She was a worrier by nature—not to mention experience—and she knew him too well. "No." he said. "There are only a couple of possibilities. But I know the people involved, and for all their drawbacks . . ." he was thinking of Bauch " . . . I'd need more to bring them in. A man with a stronger stomach might have done it already, but . . ." he was thinking of Abner Fensterwald " . . . you get to know people in twenty years. Say, did you ever hear of a minister fighting?"

"Fighting? Like how?"

"Like a knock-down drag-out behind-the-bar brawl, is how I understand it."

He told her what Trixie Wade had revealed about Bauch and Koster. "As near as I can figure, Bauch somehow came across Koster in that alley and beat the stuffing out of him. For what he'd been saying about Bauch and Mary and the Valmar. But Koster never said anything about it, far as I know. Certainly he never filed assault charges. Anyway, that happened in June, and a couple of people say he changed in June, and . . ."

"Changed?"

"Got more tough, strident. Started denouncing things a lot, like the Valmar."

"Wait a minute," she said. "You just told me he started condemning things more *after* the fight. Then what was the fight about?"

Whippletree thought that over. "Well, maybe he thought to change things in town, quietly, you know, have a talk with Denny . . ." He had to laugh at that. Have a talk with Denny Bauch to persuade him to be a good little boy? It was a joke even to think of, but Koster, idealistic and—what had the paper said?—"committed," might have figured he could do it.

"I'm going over to the hospital in the morning, anyway. I'll ask him then."

Sarah opened the folder and read the notes for the sermon of the previous Sunday.

"Oh, that poor man," Sarah cried, reading the sheet of paper. "See how much he loved his family, and how poor they were. And how brave he was."

"How can you tell?" He always felt a little twinge of jealousy when she found, or thought she found, good qualities in other men.

"Don't go into a huff, now. You know, right here, where he says you have to be willing to love, now . . ."

"Well, he's a minister, for God sakes, an' he's supposed to . . ."

"There, you know what I mean. The poor man didn't even get a chance to get a talk ready for next Sunday. Now he won't have to give one."

"Yeah. All he had a chance to do was put up the marquee sign in front of the church." What had it been, now? "The Lord Shall Grant Us Rest?" He better.

"Don't call it a marquee."

"It's the same damn thing," he said, grouchily affectionate. "Now, let me take a look at this. Maybe he said something to offend somebody out there. It might be something so slight he didn't even know about it. You know how those things go."

This kind of thing was not exactly his main line of work, and Whippletree knew it. All those words or little phrases stood for a whole series of interconnected ideas to a man who had book learning, but to the sheriff they were not much more than words. Take that talk the Reverend might have given this Sunday, if his family had not been taken away from him. *The Lord shall grant us rest.* Now, what did that mean? Could mean a lot of different things, but to Emil Whippletree it meant that some people thought there was a Lord who, after they died, would tell them they didn't have to struggle anymore, and there was absolutely nothing wrong with believing in that kind of hogwash if it made you happy. He went back to the one for last Sunday, the "Love and Will" one. That was the one the women seemed to go for, right? Well, they liked the gushy stuff and he reckoned it was a part of their natures, but he just couldn't see it much himself. Then another thing struck him, and in spite of his situation and the fact that he was making no headway on the Koster case, he thought, *all the Miz Hockapuks get themselves hot and bothered listening to a young man who is unavailable to them anyway by reason of marriage and ministry telling them not to do the things they have all done or very much wanted to do.*

He shook his head, took out his note pad, and jotted a memo, "See Mrs. Hockapuk and friends." Then, with no great measure of optimism, he returned to the ring-clip folder.

Let's see, they said he changed or something along about June . . . riffling through the pages . . . *it must be in one of*

107

these sermons somewhere and somebody must've heard it and got pissed off . . . He went back a ways.

Sunday, March 28. Theme: "Patience and Forbearance."

Psalm 37, Verse 34:   Wait on the Lord, and keep his way,
and he shall exalt thee
to inherit the land:
You will look upon the destruction
of the wicked.

Far back along the borders of cognition, too far to be wholly conscious, the sheriff had a sense of something almost formless and insubstantial, like the smoke from a campfire drifting over the hills. He turned back all the way to the beginning of the year, to Sunday, January 11. There, below the usual announcements of the living to be solaced and the dead to be remembered, was another rather untroubled theme:

"Promise of the Earth."

Isaiah, 41. 1–19:   I will open the rivers in high places,
And fountains in the midst of the valleys . . .
I will put in the wilderness the cedar,
the acacia, the myrtle and the olive . . .

Whippletree checked several more, all of them from early in the year, and found them to be pretty much of a type. They were tuned to the people of Lake Eden, at least to the year-'rounders. Maybe that's it! he thought suddenly. Koster gives the regular parishioners what they want to hear during the main part of the year, and then in the summer when the lake people show up, he gives them hell. For their own benefit and the good of their souls, and also for the amusement of the less prosperous, mostly rural year-'rounders. Just to put that thesis to a little test, he flipped ahead to June 20. The "lakers" would be pretty much out there by then, and showing up for Sunday services. Sure enough:

Theme: "Tyranny of the Flesh."

Psalm 38, Verses 7–8: For my loins are filled with burning, and there is no soundness in my flesh. I am utterly spent and crushed; I groan because of the tumult of my heart.

"What do you make of this?" he asked Sarah, who'd finished cleaning up the plates. She came over from the sink, drying her hands on a dish towel. "Look at this part about the 'flesh' and the 'loins.' They all get around to talking about it sooner or later . . ."

"Hush," she replied, bending to look it over. She read it, then: "Well, if he meant it, for himself, that is, maybe he was feeling a little down. Maybe he just got into a rut like the rest of us."

"But it doesn't fit with the sermons from the rest of the year."

"You can't give the people the same thing all the time. Why don't you ask him? It could be somebody in his church was having a problem, and this was his way of talking about it."

Whippletree nodded. *Could also be*, he thought, *job plateau.* He knew about that from personal experience. At first, after he'd just become sheriff, he was a ball of fire, and loved every minute of it. But after a while, it had started to dull a little, to become a chore. That was the job plateau—the point you reach sooner or later when you say *what the hell am I doing this for?*

Anyway, Koster could sure find things in the Bible. Pretty

words, and powerful, too. The sheriff would never forget the old priest who'd taught him his catechism when he was a boy. He could say "pleasures of the flesh" in a way that drew *fel-leesssch* out into syllables. It had sounded loathsome and horrible at eight or nine, but around thirteen or fourteen, when Whippletree stopped going, it had gotten to sound more like an advertisement.

" 'Bout eleven-thirty," Sarah was saying. "You have a big day for tomorrow?"

"Got to go to the hospital. And maybe I'll have to go out to Lake Eden again . . ."

He said "maybe" because he knew he'd have to, especially if that lab report from St. Paul came back as he thought it would. But if he said "maybe" it gave her all night to get used to the idea of his being out of town the next day.

"I hope it's settled soon," she said, worrying again. "If it drags on and on and gets in the paper every day, well . . ."

She didn't have to finish.

"You go on up," he said. "I'll be there in a minute."

He heard her climbing the stairs and took out his note pad again. There were a few more possibilities now. He listed them:

1. A goody two-shoes murder.

2. Koster said something in a sermon that bugged somebody.

3. "Where is it?" Something in the Koster house?

4. Koster in some unknown conflict with somebody: Bauch.

Then, just to complete the picture, he wrote:

110

5.   Abner Fensterwald (?)

He sat back and looked them over, and was dissatisfied. Particularly with item # 2. It didn't say what it might. He thought again of the sermons. Being a minister could be tricky, especially in Stearns County. *What if*, he mused, *what if* one or more of Koster's parishioners had come to him with some problem, and then he used it for a sermon? *What if* the nature of that problem was already pretty well known around town? *If* that was the way it had happened, there would be some faces red with both anger and embarrassment, hearing their situation described from the pulpit. Denny Bauch and Mary Prone, obviously. And there had been that fight. Or something else he didn't know about yet?

Well, Koster was on the recovery list now, and he might be able to help. Time for that in the morning. He almost staggered, getting up from the chair. *Sarah, you're not the only one who wants this thing wrapped up quick.*

VI

The young Reverend might have been on the recovery list, but he looked pretty damn sick. They had moved him to a private room that looked out over the parking lot side of the hospital, and all you could see were cars and trees above the roofs of houses and the sprawl of a shopping center in the distance. The land here, west of the river, was very flat. The Reverend was flat on his back, with a white face, a white hospital gown, and a white sheet. A thin black hose came out from under the sheet and ran into a small bottle next to the bed. "His wound is draining," Dr. Petly had told Whippletree

111

before they went in. "It looks satisfactory to me, but I'm worried more about his mental state. Try not to . . ."

"I've got to know some things. The only way I can do that is to ask him . . ."

"Well, go easy, will you, sheriff? The man's been through . . ."

"I've got an idea what he's been through. I saw what was in that house."

Whippletree had not spoken angrily, but there was a tone in it unfamiliar to Petly, who drew back. "I'm just trying . . ."

"Aw, forget it, Paul. Too much on my mind."

"Saw the paper yesterday, huh?"

"I heard about it. Say, can Koster have visitors? I mean people from Lake Eden? Think that would cheer him up?"

"There've been a few calls down at the desk, and some women from his church were here yesterday afternoon. I told them to hold off until today. Then it should be all right. Short visits, though. If he feels up to it."

"How will you know?"

"I'll ask him."

"Does he know I'm here?"

"I told him you were coming. He's anxious to see you. But, remember, not long, and don't get him worked up. He's a nervous, high-strung young man, as it is, and after what . . ."

"Okay, okay. Show me in."

Koster turned his head slightly as they entered, and blinked. There was no expression whatever on his pale face, as if the after-grief numbness had set in, protecting him from feeling.

"You want me, Emil?" Petly asked.

"What? No, no, that's okay." The doctor left and Whippletree approached the bed. "Well, son, this may sound stupid, but how are you feelin'?"

Koster turned his head back to the ceiling and mumbled something.

"What?"

"I said I'm not sure," he said a little more strongly. "I never thought I'd have a new life, and I'm not quite sure I want it." He managed a wan smile, that was almost, but not quite, replaced by a quick flood of welling tears.

"I got to ask you some questions."

Koster nodded once, his fine-boned but square chin upthrust. Whippletree could see the blood pulsing in a vein in his throat.

"Now, take it easy and take your time. I've been working out in Lake Eden, come up with a few things, too, but I need your story."

The Reverend turned his head slightly, curious. "You've caught . . ."

The sheriff shook his head. "No, but some leads. I'll tell you in a minute. First, what do you remember that night? About that night?"

The Reverend took a deep breath. "I wish I remembered nothing," he said. But then he told it.

"It was getting pretty late, maybe almost eleven. The kids were . . ." He paused and choked a little at the mention of his children. " . . . asleep. I heard the baby fussing, and Bonnie went up and said she'd give him his bottle and then go to bed herself. I was down at my desk working on my sermon. Then you could feel it getting cooler, and I went outside and looked at the sky. The wind was coming, and I was pretty sure there'd be a thunderstorm. So I closed the windows and then the electricity went out . . ."

"Lock the doors?"

"No, we never did. There didn't seem to . . . to be any reason. So I went up to bed in the dark. It was starting to rain then. The thunder and everything."

"Did the children wake up?"

"No. They never did, anyway. They weren't afraid of storms."

"So you went to sleep."

"Yes, and the next thing I knew somebody was bending over me and there was a hand on my throat. It was dark and at first I couldn't see, but then a stroke of lightning showed me the mask."

"What kind of a mask?"

"One of those winter masks, ski masks, I guess, over the head, but with a place for the eyes."

"What did you do? "

"I froze. I'm not . . . not what you'd call a . . . hero type, I'm sorry to say, and the surprise . . .'"

"I understand. In a situation like that, there aren't going to be many heroes anyway."

Koster looked relieved at the sheriff's remark. "He told me to get up and . . .'"

"He? You could tell by his voice?"

"Well, he whispered, but yes. And his size."

"Big man?"

"Bigger than I. Not that big, but well-built. I said, whispered, '*Don't hurt my family.*' He just yanked me out of bed, pushed me over to the wall, and asked 'Where is it?' 'What?' I asked. 'You know damn well,' he said. 'Now where is it, or do we have to tear this place apart?'"

That might be necessary now, the sheriff was thinking. Item # 3. "Something in the Koster House."

"Reverend," he asked. "Is there anything in that house

114

that anybody might want? Anything that might be hidden in there?"

"Have you been inside? Yes? I hardly think so. It's been the parsonage of Seventh Reformed for fifty years. Nobody's ever lived in it except the ministers and their wives and families, and none of them have been blessed with . . . with what are called worldly goods."

His voice was weak, but he managed to put a little spirit into it. Whippletree smiled. "Then what?"

"It made him mad that I didn't know what he was talking about, and he shoved me out of the bedroom and down the stairs. The other one was waiting down there. With a gun."

"A rifle?"

"I don't know about guns. It was a long gun. Not a pistol. The one downstairs was smaller than the other one."

"Where was the shotgun then? I mean, did the one upstairs have the . . . a gun when he woke you up?"

"Yes, yes he did, and downstairs both of them pointed their guns at me and asked '*Where is it? You tell us where it is, you bastard, or you'll . . . you'll be sorry.*'" And here he did break off, turning his head away and weeping quietly. Whippletree twisted in the chair beside the bed, wishing he had the knack for this kind of thing. Well, Bimbo Bonwit sure as hell didn't have it either. Hoping to make it easier for the young man, he asked, "Did they take you outside before the shootings in the house?"

Koster pulled himself together and nodded. "Yes. It was storming terribly now, and they pushed me out into it . . ."

"Why did they do that? What purpose would it serve to get all wet?"

"The little one suggested it. She said, '*Get him out of here and we'll work on the family.*'"

115

"How do you know it was a woman?"

"Just an impression. Size. Tone of her whisper. It was more like hissing."

"What were the two of them wearing?"

"Well, it was dark and everything was happening so fast, I . . . I think, well, dark clothing, gloves . . ."

"Gloves?"

"Yes, and . . ."

"What about their shoes?"

"They had on those . . . those rubbers."

Whippletree nodded, pleased with himself. He had guessed as much.

"And then they took me out and tied me to the laundry poles."

"Who did?"

"The big one did it, and the other one stood watching with the rifle. It was raining like mad, and I remember worrying about the lightning hitting those metal laundry poles." He paused. "That's funny, isn't it? Worrying about lightning. Anyway, the big one went back inside. I screamed at him, *'Don't hurt my family,'* and a little while later I heard the shots."

"The neighbors didn't hear you yelling for help? Or the shooting?"

"I could hardly hear the shooting myself, because of the thunder. All I could see were the flashes of light from the windows upstairs."

Blasts of the gun. The sheriff thought of Ruthie. "How long was the man inside?"

"I don't know. Ten minutes, maybe. No, more than that."

"What did you think he was doing?"

"I thought he was asking my wife the same stupid question

116

the woman kept asking me, out there in the rain. Where is it? Where is *what?* was all I could say."

"Did she . . . or, the one out with you, believe you?"

"I don't think so."

"What did you think when you heard the shots and saw the flashes?"

Koster bit his lip and fought off an attack of tears. "I didn't think . . . I hoped, no, I thought it was . . . it wasn't happening. And then the big one came out and said something like, 'That's it, there's nothing there anymore,' and sort of laughed . . . and . . . and . . .'"

"Then they shot you? The smaller one?"

"Yes. She said, 'Then I'll pay the bastard back good,' and raised her gun and shot me, just like that."

"Too bad she was such a poor shot, huh?" Whippletree said, trying for a joke. Koster did not react. "And then they left me there," he said. "To die!" He said it bitterly, with real vehemence.

And he has a right, too, Whippletree thought. "Son, now I'm going to ask you a question. It's very important, and it involves the lives of other people just as much as what happened the other night. Son, do you think Denny Bauch was one of those two?"

Koster weighed it for a long time. "There was that laugh," he said. "There was that laugh . . .'"

Whippletree knew. Denny Bauch had a sneering, mocking laugh that sometimes made you want to punch his balls in. Whippletree had wanted to do it himself, a time or two.

"But are you sure? Are you sure enough for me to go over to see county attorney Rollis right now and have the papers drawn up?"

"Yes," Koster decided.

"Good. All right, good. But now let's say you're in a court-room, and Bauch gets himself a smartass lawyer from down in Minneapolis, and he gets you up there on the stand . . ."

Koster was getting even paler now.

" . . . and he waves his finger in your face and says, 'Reverend, all you have to identify my client as the killer is his laugh!' Now, that's the way it's going to go, unless . . ."

"But . . ."

"And so far I haven't even checked out whatever alibis Bauch has. If any. So . . ."

"But it was Denny Bauch!"

"You know that, and I might think that, however . . ."

The minister gave Whippletree a sudden, hard stare, as if suddenly revealing another side of his personality, a side the sheriff had sensed in the sermon outlines. "You haven't even checked on Bauch yet?" he asked coldly.

Whippletree met his eyes. "I've ruined more than one thing in my life by jumping in too fast," he said. "There are going to be people, and Mr. Smartass Lawyer will be first among 'em, who are going to want to know about your fight with Denny Bauch, and why it happened, and maybe if you aren't just getting even . . ."

Koster looked abashed and a little afraid. He looked away. "I'm not proud of that," he said. "I'm not a strong man, he . . . he just . . . just beat me and beat me, and . . . and *laughed*. Believe me, I know that laugh."

"How did the fight start?"

"I was out for a walk and . . ."

"A walk past the Valmar? I heard you didn't care much for the Valmar."

"I don't," Koster said emphatically. That other personality again, the moral, minister side of him, that ran along with

118

but was so different from the "young kid" side. "That place is a degradation, a scum, and destroys the church, the town . . ."

"What happened?"

"I was just walking along down Main Street, as I often do, and he came out of . . . that place. He said 'I hear you've been shooting off your mouth about me, choirboy, and now I'm going to whip you good.' And he came down the steps at me."

"What did you do?"

Koster turned his head away, this time in shame.

"I ran," he said quietly. "I ran around in back. I thought I could get back through the alley, into somebody's house, or something. But he . . . he caught me back there . . . and . . ."

"Well, hell, Reverend, why didn't you call my office? Why didn't you report it?"

The minister, his eyes still averted, said, "That would have hurt me more than the beating."

Whippletree could understand that. Gently, he said, "Isn't it a little dangerous to go saying things like I've heard? About Bauch and the Valmar? From the pulpit?"

"It was my duty," Koster said.

Whippletree nodded to himself. "And you think the other one, the little one with him, the one who shot you, was Mary Prone? If you do, you better hurry with your charges, because when they get married neither one of them will have to testify against the other."

"Oh, I might be mistaken on that, but I thought it was a woman. Because of the slight build and the voice. But it could have been somebody else."

"Any idea who?"

Koster waited a moment. "Either Mary Prone or Abner Fensterwald," he said quietly. "That's the same thing I told county attorney Rollis."

Whippletree sat up straight in his chair, trying not to show his surprise and irritation.

"Nicky Rollis was here? Why didn't you say so?"

"You didn't ask. And he told me . . ." Koster broke off.

"He told you what?"

The Reverend looked at him, that straight hard glance again. "He told me you'd ask a lot of questions and that would be about the end of it." He lifted his head from the pillow, an effort of obvious difficulty. "And I guess he was right. Wasn't he? Well, now I've answered your questions and given you your chance to do something. And if you don't . . ."

"And if I don't?" Whippletree's only conscious reaction now was one of surprise, mingled with mild shock.

"Attorney Rollis said the matter would be taken out of your hands."

Oh he did, did he? So they were really going to move in on him now. "Son, it's not that easy," he heard himself saying. "I've got my responsibilities, and I'm going to carry them out."

"Well, you just go and . . . do . . . that . . ." Koster said, and then, this time, he was in a real throe of tears. *Poor kid, the pressure.*

The sheriff pressed a button that said "Nurse" and one showed up in less than a minute. She took in the situation at a glance. "You'd better leave now."

"Right. I think I will. But I might have to come back . . ."

"Get out," Koster said, between sobs.

The nurse nodded. Whippletree backed toward the door. "But if you want me to help you, I may need to talk to you again."

Koster said nothing and went on crying.

"He's having some visitors this afternoon," the nurse said. "Really. He's tired. You'd better go."

Before he left the hospital, he sought out Dr. Petly. "You didn't tell me Rollis was in here this morning."

The doctor looked sheepish. "Well, he said it was a courtesy call. Unofficial, you might say."

It sure was. "Well, I'll have to come back another time."

"How did it go?"

"Not too well. I left the patient a little bit upset."

"That's not good. I approved visitors for him this afternoon. I thought it would do him good. He *said* he wanted visitors."

"Not me, I guess. But I'll have to come back. Who's he got coming in later?"

"Some women in his church, from out at Lake Eden. A Mrs. Hockapuk called. She told me the Reverend has been meeting with a number of them for what she called "personal conferences." You know, people with special problems. They feel it would be good if they could show their solidarity now that he's got a problem."

"I'll say."

Petly looked around, as if afraid of being overheard. "And, Emil . . ."

"Yeah."

"Just between you and me, understand, one of the women in that group this afternoon'll be Lynn Betters. So if the Reverend's upset about whatever you did up there, I don't have to draw you pictures as to who gets the news."

Whippletree nodded and said nothing.

Petly seemed unable to decide what to say. Finally, "Emil, I just want you to know it's a damn shame. I see how they're boxing you in."

He looked genuinely sympathetic. "It's not November yet," the sheriff said lamely.

"Ever think of early retirement," Petly was asking.

"I can't. You don't stop in the middle of an operation, and I don't stop in the middle of a job."

"That's the spirit," Petly said, with very little.

VII

In Sheriff Emil Whippletree's vernacular, Nicky Rollis had been born a prick and kept on growing. He was a thin, sharp-nosed, fast-talking spouter of big words and acidulous opinions. To see him in the courtroom was one of the wonders of all the counties north of Minehaha Falls. There he was, a thin, sharp beanpole type, arms going like a semaphore run amuck, probing into everything, *everything*, and out of his mouth flowed, unabated and unbroken and as grating to the sheriff as chalk on blackboard, the most amazing words Whippletree had ever heard. Everything from the "technical contemporary applications of the Code of Hammurabai" to the "debilitating neurotic implications of excessive maternal affection." Hell, what was all that? In the first case, Whippletree hadn't the slightest idea. In the second case, he was talking about a mama's boy. Why didn't he just go and use words the way ordinary people did?

Because he's a lawyer, that's why. And he likes to snow the juries. And, Emil, what the hell is he trying to pull now?

The sheriff thought it over as he headed down Seventh Avenue, a tree-lined street with big old houses built after the First World War. In the distance, the dome of the courthouse glittered in the early-morning sun. Rollis and Betters had offices in the courthouse, the better to set up whatever it was they were doing. And, whatever it was, it wasn't likely that it would do the sheriff a whole lot of good. An "unofficial" visit to Koster would not only serve the purpose of reducing or removing any confidence he might have had in the sheriff, but would also serve to give Rollis information about the killings in advance. According to a procedure that had been followed for years, the sheriff and the Stearns County attorney worked according to a fairly informal plan. If something happened out in the county that required the sheriff to file legal papers on somebody, he would go to the county attorney and do it. Rollis had a slightly similar arrangement with the cops in the St. Cloud municipality, but, in general, Whippletree had first authority in the outlying areas. Once arraignment was held and indictment sought, matters went into the usual routine, and all the sheriff did after that — if he was involved at all — was to testify at the trial. But it *was* quite possible, and now it even seemed quite probable, for Rollis to go ahead on his own. *If* he had enough evidence to support a charge. So that must be why they — Rollis and Betters — had tried to get to Koster first.

What was the point of all the rush, though? According to the Reverend, he had told them Denny Bauch was one of the killers. So much for that, but where was the proof? The sheriff thought a lot of things about Nicky Rollis, but he had never considered him a fool. And the matter of the accomplice was likewise perplexing. Mary Prone *or* Abner Fensterwald? You didn't bring up charges on one person *or* another. It was too bad the Reverend was in such a disturbed state. *Well*, he thought, wheeling into the parking lot behind the jail, *Abner had motive, Denny had motive, and Mary Prone had motive. To hassle Koster, maybe — but to kill him?*

And on the other hand, Betters wanted to fix it up even-

123

Steven with Denny Bauch for that morals thing with Lynn. He wouldn't hesitate to bring in somebody else, like Mary Prone, if he had to. But would he be bold enough to take on Elwood Fensterwald, who was a big man in the county? It hardly seemed smart, and Whippletree had never said that Mel Betters was a stupid man.

Or are they just setting me up? he asked himself again. *Fixing it so my job's harder, and making me look the fool?*

So. He had to talk to the Reverend again. Maybe the guy really didn't know who'd come into his house, done what they'd done. Maybe he was using the incident to get even with a few people. Whippletree remembered that stern, moralistic side of Koster's personality, which had come to the surface when their conversation had turned to Bauch and the Valmar. Bars, drinking, sex. It seemed to Whippletree a little extreme to kick an organist out of the church for what Fensterwald had done, but the sheriff knew one thing—these moralistic types are hard to live with. They don't often give the benefit of the doubt. He would have to get back to Koster.

And he was going to have to have a good long talk with Denny Bauch.

He climbed out of his car, went around the office side of the building, and climbed the steps. Was that kink in his back due to sleeping wrong, or was it rheumatism again? No, too hot for rheumatism. This was August, after all.

"Good morning," he called, as cheerfully as he could.

It was Pollock's day on the radio, but he wasn't there. Still not back from the Twin Cities. *Dammit, should have remembered.* And Axel Vogel, on duty last night, had already gone home. That left poor old Alyce Pelser with both the phones and the radio, and she was already distraught at a quarter-past-ten.

"Sheriff!" she cried, both in relief and desperation. "You

got to get over to the courthouse. Attorney Rollis's already called twice."

"Screw him," Whippletree said, with enough anger to astound poor old Alyce. "If he wants to see me, let him walk across the street. Now, calm down. Anything happen so far?"

"No. Nothing much." Alyce ran her hand through her black, chop-cut hair. It could have stood a shampoo. "There was this call from Lake Eden. From a Mr. Fensterwald. He said to get in touch with him right away. Then somebody else called from out there. You know of a Dennis Bauch?"

Jesus! They must have mentioned Bauch here in the office five dozen times in the last few days, and Alyce . . .

"What about him?"

"Somebody called to say that he was in town last night."

"In town? Lake Eden?"

"That's what they said. He was seen at the Club Valmar late last night."

"Who was it called? "

"They didn't leave no name. They said you'd be interested in the news. Oh, and this come in yesterday afternoon's mail. I was gonna give you a call, but I figured why bother you."

She handed him a small white envelope, opened. The postmark read "Brooten, Minn." He took out a lined index card, on which cutout letters had been pasted. He read it.

You ARE Wrong on this No You AR easking TR ouble Look Out Iam Not Scared of YOU!

Look out was heavily underlined.

"What is it that you're wrong about?" Alyce wanted to know.

"Just exactly what *I* was thinking. Well, whoever isn't scared of me certainly goes through a lot of trouble not to tell me who he is. Now, call Elwood Fensterwald for me, will you?"

Alyce went over to the phone and began riffling through the directory. Whippletree checked the night report. Not much. Bar fight in Melrose. Missing cattle report in St. Anna. Had been a small rustling band around lately. Assault and battery charges as a result of a contested ball game between the Waite Park "Moose" and the St. Augusta "Gussies." And a fistic altercation between a game warden and a sportsman out at Clearwater Lake, involving the number of fish found in said sportsman's boat. A hundred and ten.

"I can't find no Elwoods in this here book," Alyce called.

The sheriff was just about to tell her Fensterwald started with an "F" when Pollock chugged his bulk up the steps and into the office.

"I busted a gut tryin' to get back here," he wheezed, his paunch going in and out along with his thick chest. "Did Alyce tell you?"

"Uh-," Alyce said, "I forgot he called and told me . . ."

"Quiet. What is it?" Whippletree asked.

"Here's the lab results," the chunky deputy said, sitting down next to the sheriff's desk. Whippletree took a look. He glanced hurriedly through the rambling details of who had conducted the gunshot test and where and how, and got to the meat of it.

Conclusion: Five expended twelve-gauge shotgun shells provided by Office of the Stearns County

Sheriff were definitely fired within the past
48 hours by a twelve-gauge weapon, of the
kind manufactured by the Winchester Company, Chicago, Illinois, circa 1922. Registration lacking as to ownership. Study of the
weapon negative as to fingerprints. Minis-
cule dried specks of human blood were
found on the area near the barrel of the gun,
type "A" Negative.

"Alyce, did that coroner's report get over here yet?"

"Ummmm . . ." There followed much pushing and shov-
ing of papers and files. "Uh, yeah, here it is."

He did a fast check. A couple of the Kosters had had "A"
Negative, and Ruthie, the little girl, was one of them. If he
was right, she'd been the last one shot, so . . .

"I guess we've got the murder weapon then," he muttered
grimly. *That meant young Fensterwald was in it up to his over-
worked* . . . He checked the second report.

Conclusion: The .22 caliber rifle slug provided to this laboratory by Office of the Stearns County
Sheriff was found to be in such a state of
deterioration, it will be impossible to determine the exact weapon from which it was
fired, even if such weapon were forthcom-
ing.

And, last, the fingerprint report:

Conclusion: Fingerprints taken from the Koster domicile
under the supervision of Mr. Russ Arledge
were numerous and, members of the Koster
family excepted, indeterminate, with a single
qualification. A set of fingerprints taken
from the Reverend Koster's working desk in
the living room of the residence, from the

doorjamb at the main entrance to the house, and from the stair railing leading to the second story of the residence, were matched to files of the State Police of the State of Minnesota, and to the files of the Federal Bureau of Investigation. The match was found to be positive, and the record of the individual is attached.

Whippletree turned the page hastily, while Alyce Pelser opened her mouth wide and deputy Pollock glowed in the glory of a message delivered and a job well done.

BAUCH, Dennis LeRoy
D.O.B.   8 April 1946   St. Cloud, Minn.
Last known residence: 22 Elm St. Lake Eden, Minn.
Occupation: Truck Driver, Fishing Guide, Hunting Guide
Married: No

RECORD OF ARRESTS:

3 Oct 1957, vandalism, breaking and entering, Lake Eden Elementary School. Remanded to custody of parents.

11 January 1959. Throwing brick through front plate glass window of Rehnquist Market. Remanded to custody of parents.

5 June 1960. Shot and killed prize breeding bull, property of Mr. Elwood Fensterwald, RR # 3, Lake Eden. Served two years at Minnesota State Boys Correctional Facility, Red Wing, Minn.

6 June 1962. Vandalism. Drove car through gate of Fensterwald Dairies, RR # 3, Lake Eden. Restitution made and charges dismissed.

22 May 1963. Attempted rape. Charges brought by parents of MarySue Hull, St. Cloud, Minn. Case dismissed for lack of evidence that coercion was applied.

The Fields of Eden

Probably one of the few times he didn't get it all handed to him,
Whippletree thought, reading.

16 October 1965. Assault and battery. Charges dismissed.

And so it went, on and on, sometimes one or two a year,
sometimes skipping a year, until the last entry:

8 June 1976. Disturbing the peace. Lake Eden, Minnesota.
Charges dismissed for lack of evidence.

Just disturbed an old lady's peace of mind, Whippletree
thought. *And the peace of mind of the Chairman of the Board of
Commissioners.* He went down the list of offenses again. It ran
the gamut. Possession of stolen goods, dismissed. More
fights, charges dropped. Accusation of sodomy under a boat
on the south shore of Lake Eden, denied by companion, witness failed to testify. Fencing stolen goods, dismissed for lack
of evidence. On it went. This was the Denny Bauch they all
knew. An aging punk who had stayed — mostly — just this
side of the law, except for that once in Red Wing. Well, that's
the way the law is written. If you can stay out of jail, you may
not be a good man, but the world will consider you a pretty
smart one.

But there was the evidence. Several sets of prints, including one leading to the upstairs of the Koster house. This time
old Denny might just have strayed over the line. Combination: past record, temper, violent nature, familiarity with
firearms, and *motive.* "Ain't nobody gonna hassle ol' Denny.
Ain't gonna stand for that from some wimpy-dicked *minister!*
Gonna teach that cocksucker a lesson, you better believe it. *I
am not scared of you!*"

Probably couldn't find a newspaper or magazine with
"ain't" in it.

129

Well, Denny, get set. You and I are going to have to have a little talk.

"I guess we got 'im, hey sheriff," Pollock said.

"Who? Bauch or Fensterwald?"

"Fensterwald?" Pollock looked confused.

"Reverend Koster says Fensterwald might have been the second one. I just got back from talking to him at the hospital."

"But everybody's saying it was Mary Prone."

"Who's everybody?"

"Well, all the boys at the bar-and-grill. And around."

"And *around*, huh. I can just about imagine. But Elwood Fensterwald is missing a shotgun, and funny a shotgun should show up in church with his kid, who had a little motive of his own."

Pollock scratched his head. The phone rang. "It's for you," Alyce said.

"Nicky Rollis here, sheriff. How you doin'?"

"I could be better."

"Say, would you be able to come over here for a short time. I think we might be able to have a most productive conversation."

"Yeah. About what?"

"Well, the Koster case, obviously. I've just had an opportunity to peruse the state reports, and I think it's clear that some kind of decision is at hand on this trying matter . . ."

"Hold it a minute, Nick." Whippletree put his hand over the receiver. "Pollock, you know anything about Rollis getting copies of these reports?"

The deputy started sputtering. "Well, sheriff, they told me down in St. Paul that the C.A.'d called, an' if I wouldn't just drop off a set of copies . . ."

"You could've let me handle that." He lifted his hand off

the receiver. "You know, Nick, why don't you just drop on over here."

"Now, Emil, I'd like that a lot. I'd like that. I surely would. But the problem is more than protocol, you understand. I'm afraid you've made some rather serious errors in the implementation of the Koster investigation so far, and I'll have to cover those with you."

Serious errors. Like what? But the hell with this young pup. If they wanted a grave dug for Emil Whippletree, they had better plan on doing the work.

"I'll be here for about an hour, Nicky, before I head on out toward Lake Eden. If you want to see me, I'll be here. Come on over anytime."

There was a breathing silence at the other end of the line, and then the phone clicked.

"Hey, where's Bimbo?" the sheriff remembered, putting down the phone with just the slightest feeling of satisfaction. "I thought he was on the duty roster for a.m. today."

"Oh, he was here," Alyce said. "He was here before. Then he had to go on over to see county attorney Rollis."

It wasn't more than a minute or two before Bimbo came lumbering in, ducking his head and hunching his shoulders to avoid the top of the doorframe. He was carrying an official, sealed "County Attorney's Office" envelope.

"Sorry I got to do this, sheriff," he said, handing it over. "It's just I got worried about the way things are goin'."

"I bet you did." Whippletree tried to be casual as he tore it open, and kept his face blank as he read it.

"Nothin' personal, sheriff," Bimbo was saying, kicking at the floor with his colossal shoe. "It's just . . ."

"Shut up," Whippletree said, immediately regretting it. But he couldn't help adding, "If you want to let Mel Betters

use you, that's your business. But don't go around with your
phony apologies for it."

And they were using Bimbo, all right. And well. Whippletree read the brief letter and realized he was in trouble.

Sheriff Emil Whippletree
Stearns County Sheriff's Office
St. Cloud, Minnesota

Dear Sheriff Whippletree:

I regret that I must inform you that it
has come to my attention through reli-
able sources that in a legal sense you
may have seriously compromised any
meaningful prosecution re: the Koster
case. A young man, whose name I will
not mention here, or at this time, was
discovered in the Seventh Reformed
Church in Lake Eden with a shotgun
and expended shotgun shells. The
weapon is probably that which killed
Mrs. Koster and the four Koster children. Upon the apprehension of the
suspect, you neither read him his rights,
as is required by law, nor did you take
the suspect into custody. Instead, you
chose to deal personally and privately
with suspect's parent. I realize that for
many years you may have become habi-
tuated to a person-to-person relationship with members of the community,
but you must realize that in a case as serious as that which presently confronts
us, we cannot afford the short cuts and
the end-runs that jeopardize prosecution. Moreover, it has been reliably re-

132

ported as well that, on the night of the
incident, you ordered both police cars
and ambulances to proceed without
flashing lights or sirens. Such equipment is provided county vehicles for the
safety of other citizens who might be on
the roadways . . .

In Stearns County in the middle of the night! Whippletree
snarled to himself.

. . . and it should be so used. Your failure to procure a helicopter for use of
the sheriff's office might also have re-
tarded matters considerably on that
fateful eve.

Finally, although I shrink from such
an admonition, I must urge you,
throughout the course of this investigation, to "go by the book," as it were, or
measures may have to be undertaken by
me to insure the proper conduct of this
most serious matter.

Sincerely,

NICHOLAS ROLLIS J.D.
County Attorney

Whippletree sat there at his desk for a moment. He felt the
anger rise in him, but it was tired anger, tinged with discour-
agement. Sure, on the surface of it, Rollis was right. Sure, le-
gally, strictly speaking, that was the way it should have been
done. But, goddam it, Fensterwald could not have had the
balls to do or even to help in doing what had been done in
the Koster house. *Could he?* And he'd known Elwood Fen-

sterwald since the two of them were young bucks, for Christ sakes, since before Nicky Rollis had even been *born*. Since before he'd been a quiver in his old man's cock.

"He asked you want to send a message back, I should take it," Bimbo offered, hunching around the office and not meeting the sheriff's eyes. "You got a message?"

Whippletree thought it over. "I sure have," he decided. "You run over there right now, Bimbo, and tell Nicky Rollis I'll reply to his letter when I have the time. And you tell him, too, that it's not worth the paper it's printed on, and when the time comes I'll show it around to prove what a jerk he is."

Having said it, Whippletree felt better. Bimbo looked surprised.

"Go on, I told you. Get the hell over there and tell him. Or do I have to put you on report for failure to perform instructions?"

And there, in big old Bimbo's eyes, way back so far, way down so deep that it was only a tiny spark of light that faded quickly, was a flash of heavy Bonwit anger. *What the hell*, Whippletree thought. *I finally got down that far.* Bimbo lurched out.

"I think he was a little pissed," Pollock opined.

"Maybe. Too bad. Alyce, when any calls come in for Bimbo this afternoon, send him to the ones that are the farthest away. You got that?"

She nodded, looking fearful.

"Don't worry. He's got to do it as long as I'm sheriff. And he's going to do it, too, by God, as long as he's working for Rollis and Betters as well as me." He slammed his hand down on his desk for emphasis, but he knew he was still in a bind. They did have a couple of things on him that were important, and that could be used. Sure, he could explain them, but if he didn't solve the Koster case, his explanations wouldn't be worth a pitcher of warm spit.

Before he got off to Lake Eden, three things happened.

First, Elwood Fensterwald called again. He didn't sound too happy. "Emil," he said, "I got a little news for you. I got to thinking what a dildo my kid is, with that church business and the gun and all, so I took a horsewhip to him. Tied him to a tree and went to work. You know what he said? He said that gun was *my* gun and that *he* took it to the church. He still denies the shootings, though, the little bastard. What should I do?"

"Nothing. I'll be out in an hour."

Second, a messenger arrived from the *Tribune* with the galleys of an article for the afternoon's paper. There was a little note attached. "I owe you the chance to check this for accuracy." It was signed "Mel Betters." It said, in part:

> The investigation into the Lake Eden slayings is proceeding slowly. According to official sources, several possible suspects have been placed at the scene of the crime, as a result of direct evidence. Sheriff Emil Whippletree, however, who is conducting the investigation, has at this time not acted upon such information, and the suspects remain at large . . .

It went on to say that sober citizens throughout the county were becoming "increasingly alarmed" over the contretemps and demanding that something be done. It quoted a few, like Mrs. Bertha Ravitch, of Pearl Lake: "I just think it's terrible when you have to lock your doors nights. It's like there's a monster running around loose." And, of course, the "objective" reporters of the *Tribune* did not pass up a chance to plug the favorite son:

> Deputy Sheriff Wayne "Bimbo" Bonwit, bleary-eyed from lack of sleep sustained during the course of the investigation, said, "Well, yes, the orders are for us to go slow on this, and I always follow orders, but I do appreciate the concern of the folks of the county to get this thing settled as soon as possible . . .

Bleary-eyed, Whippletree thought. "Alyce, when Bimbo gets back from his tough assignment, here's what you tell him. From me. And he better do it just as fast as he wants. I want that Koster house, and the church, rechecked. Inside and out. Every nook and cranny. Every hollow should be checked, every flowerbed turned up. You name it. Tell him to go over and get Koster's permission at the hospital. If he can't get it, tell him to go over and get a warrant from Judge Reisinger. If he has any problems, get me on the radio."

"Who's goin' out there with him?" Pollock asked.

"Farley and Ruehle. This may be the day I have to deal with Denny Bauch, and I can count on them backing me up if I need it."

The chunky deputy looked crestfallen. "But I need you here at 'Mountaintop,'" the sheriff added, making him feel better. "A steady hand on the tiller, and all that stuff."

The deputy cheered slightly. "You know, it's not easy being a deputy this time of year. Lots of things are going on that make it pretty hard."

"Hang with it," Whippletree said, as cheerfully as he could. "One way or another, it'll be over in a couple of months."

The third and last thing to delay his departure occurred as he was putting on his straw hat. Phone call. "For you," Alyce said, holding out the receiver. He took it, expecting Rollis or maybe Betters, feeling aggressive. But it was the voice of a woman, husky, sultry.

"Sheriff Whippletree?"

"Yes."

"I've got to talk to you."

"About what?"

"About the Koster case."

"Who is this?"

"I don't want to say over the phone. But you'd know me if you saw me."

Whippletree snorted. "Give me a hint," he said drily.

"You think I drive a little too fast," she said. "Or is it just that you have a thing against sports cars?"

Lynn Betters. "I see," he said.

"I'll be at home," she purred.

"Rumors and Bad News"

I

If I spot the pink Grand Prix, I'll hit the Valmar first, Whippletree figured. So he cruised through the town of Lake Eden, feeling the heads turn on the few people who were out in the August heat. He cut behind the back alley, but saw only Mary's trailer. It could wait until later. *Can only do one damn thing at a time.*

Elwood Fensterwald met him in the yard and took him, without a word, into his office on the side of the farmhouse. Inside, shivering in a straight-backed chair, was young Abner. The back of his T-shirt was ripped in places, and blood showed through in long stripes. He had cried himself out and now was feeling the increasing pain of the untreated cuts of the whip.

"Tell the sheriff how you lied, you little son-of-a-bitch," Elwood snarled.

139

The kid coughed and tried to look at the sheriff, but failed.
"Take it easy, son," Whippletree said, "Elwood, you know
there's laws against what you did, too."

"Oh, yeah? Well, wait until you hear this. Cough it up,
Abs."

The kid shivered some more and hugged himself. "Take it
easy, son. Just go ahead. All I want to know is what really
happened."

The story that came out was broken several times with
spates of trembling and choking, but it was not going to
make the Koster situation any easier.

"Well, you already know what the . . . the Reverend did
to me, an' I . . . I wanted to . . . to *scare* him a little. But
only just to scare him. That's all, I swear that's all . . ."

"Just go on."

" . . . so I took the shotgun out of Pa's rack downstairs
and I took the pickup and drove into town . . ."

"This was on the day of the killings?"

"Yes, that afternoon. An' I went up to the house, you
know . . . an' asked Miz Koster where he was. She didn't
know. She said maybe he had to go away on a call, or maybe
he just went out for a walk downtown, which he sometimes
did. But I hadn't seen him on the street when I was driving
over to the church. 'Course, he could of been in Rehnquist's.
Anyway, she asked me if I wanted to come in and wait, but I
said no, and went back to the pickup. That's where I'd left
the gun. I sat there for a little while wondering what to do,
then I took the gun into the church. That way, if he came
into the church, I could scare him there, and if he went past
the church on his way back to the house, I could jump out
behind . . . behind . . . him . . ."

"But he didn't come back?"

"No. Or I couldn't wait to find out. Because some women

of the Auxiliary came into the church then, for a meeting, or something. I ran up to the choir loft . . ." He stopped here for a moment, remembering this was where all the trouble had started in the first place " . . . and waited there for awhile. I'd broken the gun barrel and stock to take it into the church, but with those women downstairs, they could of recognized what it was at that short distance, even with the gun broken down . . ."

"Why didn't you tell me this before?"

"I . . . I didn't think it was important . . ." Then, knowing this was ridiculous, "I was scared."

"Son, you're in serious trouble. You took a weapon to the church on the day of the murder. A weapon that fired the shells found next to it. Where were you on the night of the murder?"

Abner hesitated, looked around wildly. Old Elwood reached into a desk drawer and produced a thick braided coil of whip.

"I was . . . was out by the lake that night," Abner quavered.

"By yourself?"

"Yes."

"Why? It was a stormy night."

"I had the pickup, and anyway, the storm came up sudden. It was a nice night until then."

"Why weren't you home?"

"I . . . I don't . . ." He risked it. " . . . I don't like it, home."

Whippletree could see that. And understand why. "Now, about the shells. Those were your father's shells, too?"

Abner shook his head.

"Look," Elwood interrupted. "Emil, just between you, me, an' the shithouse, if it comes to that, I'm gonna say the kid

141

was here at the house all night. Because this is the thing. I ain't fired that gun in over thirty years, nor even hunted for practically twenty, an' I ain't had a shell in the house for any of them guns in near as long. I ain't even been down there in the basement to *look* at 'em."

"You bought the shells?" Whippletree prodded.

Abner shook his head dismally and shivered.

"I don't think he's lyin' about that one, Emil. I hit him many a good stroke on that there question, an' he didn't change his story."

"I've got just two more questions, son. First, when you went downstairs to get the shotgun, were any of the others missing?"

"I don't . . . don't . . . know. I don't know how many there are, anyway. Or were."

"Were there any empty places in the rack?" Elwood asked.

"Sure there were. Yeah, at least a couple."

"Well, there shouldn'ta been!"

"And you just took that one gun? The shotgun?"

Abner nodded glumly. He seemed to be passing into some kind of a chill.

"The other question is this: How did you get out of the church?"

"I waited until their meeting was over. Those women. Then I went down and got out the back door quick, while they were milling around out in front."

"And left the shotgun in the music seat?"

Nod. "I figured I'd go back for it later, an' my music. I didn't want to chance taking it out right then."

"So the next day, after the killings, you went back, and that's when me and my deputies spotted you in the belltower?"

Another nod. "And . . ."

"And what?"

"And I went back there that night."

"What? The night of the murders? What time?"

"It must of been around ten-thirty, eleven. Before the storm started. Before I went out to the lake."

Oh, God, Whippletree thought, *he might easily have been there when the killers were already inside the house.* "Was the electricity still on then?" he asked. "Can you remember?"

"Yes. That's why I didn't try going in the church. I was afraid he'd see me."

"Who? Reverend Koster?"

"Yes. Him and his wife were downstairs. I could see him through the window. Then she went up the stairs. He was still walking around down there, walking around. It made me nervous. The storm was starting up then, and I headed out to the lake . . ."

Abner raised his hand to his head, swayed in the chair.

"An' . . . and that's the . . . truth . . ."

Whippletree moved forward. Abner swayed. Whippletree caught him, as he slumped in the chair and fell forward in a dead faint. The blood was crusting on his whiptorn back.

"Hey, we got the story now, all right," Elwood chuckled. "Looks like I better get a bucket of water an' . . ."

"No. Call an ambulance. I want this boy in the hospital."

"What?" Elwood was incredulous. "Hell, if you think he needs lookin' after, there's always old Doc Bates over to St. Alazara . . ."

"Elwood, you shouldn't've done what you did here, an' you know it. Now, you get an ambulance out here or I will."

"All right, all right." Reluctantly, the old farmer reached for the phone. "But at least we got it settled, right?"

"Not quite. I'm going to hold the boy on suspicion."

This time even Elwood was speechless in disbelief.

"I got to. I just got to. I don't believe he did it, not really, but he was too close to the place with a gun, at the worst possible time, and he's admitted it. Besides, although it's only circumstantial, you're missing some other guns, and the twelve-gauge is going down in the books as the murder weapon. Unless we can find the rest of your guns, and the thief or thieves who took them, there's nobody else connected. At least not to the twelve-gauge. Except Abner. Did he say anything about those initials in the trigger housing?"

The elder Fensterwald nodded, as if considering for the first time the gravity of the whole affair. So far, he might have figured, I'm free an' clear. Other people got killed. Other people are involved. Not me. But now it was a little different. "Yeah, he told me he filed it off. When I was whuppin' 'im."

The two men looked at each other.

"What are you waitin' for?" Elwood asked.

"I'm waiting for you to call that ambulance. Then I have to get in touch with my office. There's going to have to be a guard on the hospital room. Your son is now in custody."

He hated to do it, but it had to be done. *And now,* he thought, feeling a little uncomfortable with the defensiveness of the thought, *now you can have something positive for a statement to the damn* Tribune.

II

It was about two-thirty, heading back toward Lake Eden, and he stopped at the fork in the road. Down through the thick green trees he saw the dark still waters of the lake, a sheet of cool glass. Ahead of him, across the green-brown fields, heat rose in shimmering waves. It danced on the blacktop highway, sheen, mirror, mirage. He was thirsty, goddam, was he thirsty. Lynn Betters would have to wait a little. He tromped down on the accelerator and headed for the Valmar. That was business, too, after all. Trixie Wade must have seen and talked to Denny and Mary.

But when he came in out of the sun, it was Mary Prone herself behind the bar, in front of the grease-streaked mirror and bottles of cheap booze. The place was cool, deserted. She looked up, frightened and surprised.

Mary Prone was not a good-looking woman, at least not the kind you get used to seeing on the covers of magazines or in the Sunday newspaper ads for underwear and negligees. Her hair was a nondescript brown and always a little tangled. How it got a little tangled was one of the ongoing topics of conversation around the lake, at Rehnquist's, in the councils of the Seventh Reformed. Her face was a little too strong for a "pretty" woman, her nose too large, her mouth too wide and full. A man's hands might tangle in that hair when she used that mouth. Her breasts were also full, too heavy, and she was a little on the short side. But, like many of the strangest things, it all added up to something greater than the sum of its parts, the mystery of a woman's flesh, and what it could do to a man. Most of which, in Mary's case, it had already done. She exuded the ancient scent, unlocked the primeval memory in a man's brain of the musty promise of rut and ecstasy, with no holds barred, no quarter given, and no strings attached. In the spread of her strong thighs and in the rocking curve of her lush hips, a man turned elemental as wind or fire. She knew how to put a man's brain in his groin, and then destroy it. Not one of the many who had lost their minds in the pulsing tug and pull of her had ever been known to complain.

There she was. Behind the bar. What Denny Bauch was getting.

The sheriff took off his hat, sat down at the bar. "Where's Denny?" he asked.

Unlike Trixie Wade, Mary was a strong woman. She had had to be. Losing her parents very young, then enduring a long girlhood and part of adolescence at the pious, restrictive County Seat Orphans' Home—at that time under the direction of Father Ripulski, later shot in the head by farmer Ronsky—and then shipped out to a crude farm couple way up in Moorhead, practically at the edge of nowhere, she had had to adapt. She adapted. At eighteen, she ran away from Moorhead, even though the nuns at the orphans' home had given the "foster parents" the idea that Mary would stay and work for them until she was at least twenty-one. Returning to St. Cloud, the only place she knew, and one of the few she had ever heard about—Stearns County looked upon itself much in the manner of ancient China, as center of the world—Mary got herself a job cleaning rooms at Schwagum's Motel, later serving part-time as a cocktail waitress in the lounge. It was here she met Val Hennessey. When he got tired of drinking at his own place, The Tap, out in Lake Eden, he went into the "big town" and tied on a good one, staying at Schwagum's overnight and hoping to pick up some women to get his rocks off. Pretty soon it was Mary. She learned fast (she had had to adapt) and very soon it was Mr. and Mrs. Val Hennessey, and The Tap achieved the distinction of Club Valmar, new center of the summer social set in Lake Eden. Very soon she learned about Hennessey's Irish drinking habits—the part he'd kept from her during their "courtship" at Schwagum's—and bruises, black eyes, and twisted arms marked the course of her married life. She'd had enough of that at the orphanage and at the farm up in Moorhead. On her own, in secret, she went to St. Cloud, got herself a lawyer—young Nicky Rollis, before he graduated into county politics—and took Hennessey for everything he was worth. Which amounted to the club, a three-year-old Cadillac Coupe de Ville with an automatic transmission, a stock of liquor and several half-kegs of Grain Belt beer, three hundred dollars in change money, and a mobile home parked next to the club. More than she'd ever had in her life, and more than she'd ever dreamed of having. She sat back—or laid back—and began to enjoy life.

But she wasn't enjoying herself right now, there behind the bar. Whippletree could see it. Still, she stayed cool.

"I said where's Denny?" he asked again.

"So how about a beer, sheriff? You look pretty hot to me." She got a glass and held it under the foaming tap.

"Thanks," he said, grateful. In a very personal way, he admired Mary Prone, in spite of the stories about her. She'd had it harder than he, in a lot of ways, and she'd survived. So far. All you can ever say about any human condition is "so far."

She brought over the beer and looked him straight in the eye. "Good luck," she said. "I don't know where Denny is right now."

He picked up a slight inflection in her voice which betrayed something, something important and indefinite.

"Right now?" He took a good long swallow of the cold beer, felt the coldness of the glass against his hand. "Then, let's say, just between us, where was he the night before last?"

Mary was pretty well tanned from the summer, but the question cut down her color a shade or two.

147

"He was with me," she said, a little too quickly.

"And where were you?"

"We . . . we both were . . . up by Brainerd. We had some things to talk over, so we took off for a day. We went camping. Then, when we heard the news . . ."

"How did that happen?"

"We stopped off at the Rod and Gun Club in Brooten. On our way back. We heard about it there."

"When was this?"

"Afternoon. About three. Four. The day after . . . it happened."

"You know, I got a so-called letter in the mail, came with a Brooten postmark. You know anything about that?"

She seemed to hesitate. Then, "I told him not to. But he was . . . worried about the situation."

"Why? You say you were out camping over a hundred miles from here. Why worry? That is, unless nobody saw the two of you."

She looked away. "That's . . . that's right. No one did. But you and Denny have had a few run-ins before, and he thinks you have it in for him. So after the problems here this summer . . ."

"You mean the stories and Koster's sermons?"

"Yes. Here, let me freshen that beer. Like a shot of something? Rye? Bourbon?"

"No. Thanks, anyway. What about the fight?"

"Oh, that was nothing." She waved it away, or tried. "Denny just lost his cool. After that, it was like trying to live in a glass house. Being the talk of the town from the pulpit of your own church is not a pleasant feeling."

Nor being subject number one in the Tribune, Whippletree thought.

"That was what the fight was about? The sermons? Why

did Koster keep on giving them then? After he'd already been beaten up."

"I don't . . . I don't know . . . anyway, it's been . . ."

For a moment she lost her composure, and Whippletree thought she was going to break down, but anger saved her.

"Nobody knows Denny, really," she snapped. "He's had a hard time, just like most of us, but he's going to do better. That's why we had to get away from here and talk things over. It's the end of the summer, and I'm tired. We just had to." She paused. "At the worst possible time," she added, in a quieter voice.

Whippletree nodded. *Denny was going to get better.* There probably was never a bride, born, made, or manufactured, who didn't have that same thought.

"Still, you had your banns published with Seventh Reformed. Why was that?"

"It's . . . it's been my church. Ever since I got out here. Which was before the Reverend Koster!" She pronounced the name sarcastically.

"You don't care for him much, is that it?"

She gave him a straight, honest look. "That stuck-up little candy-ass," she said, with a working girl's contempt. "Old Reverend Runde would come in and have a beer, just like a normal human being. But not that diddley Koster."

Well, another precinct heard from, he thought.

"With his talk groups and his 'counseling' sessions, and all that. The dipshit! Letting Lynn Betters pull the wool over his eyes . . ."

"Hold on a minute. What do you mean?"

The thought of it brought all the color back to her face. "Come on, Emil. You remember the time that old biddy got you out here? Because of in back? Denny and . . . her? In his car . . . ?"

149

Clearly she did not like the idea of her fiancé sixty-nining the competition right out behind her place of business. He nodded.

"And her hotshot old man got her to go in for some of Matthew Koster's *moral guidance!* The dirty little hussy! Just so she could get her credit cards back. Pretty soon she's running around town with her nose as high as Mrs. Hockapuk, for Christ sake. As though she's some kind of holier-than-thou buddy of . . . God, or something. Hell, she's . . ." Mary paused, thinking of a way to phrase it " . . . she's not even as good as me."

"You're all right, Mary," he said. "But the situation's no good. In the first place, where were you camping?"

"On Dutchman's Bluff. Up by Gull Lake, north of Brainerd."

"And you can't prove it?"

She looked down, but didn't even bother to shake her head.

"Nobody else there? Even a gas charge. Anything?"

She shook her head this time. "We fueled up here. It takes less than a tank, both ways. And the place we camped isn't . . . isn't really campground. We just found a place in the woods."

"Denny's cute letter isn't going to help things any, either."

"Well, how can that affect anything? There's nothing to put him here in Lake Eden on the night of . . ."

"Mary, if you know where Denny is, tell him to get in touch with me. He can call the office anytime, and they'll call me on the radio. The longer this drags on, the worse it's going to get for everybody."

"But . . ."

"There're no buts this time out. Denny has a . . . a not-so-good reputation, and, hard as it is, he's got to be checked

150

on this. By the way, what's he doing over at the Rod and Gun all the time?"

"He's not there all the time."

"He seems pretty much a regular. The bartender I talked to on the phone sure seemed to know him well enough."

"Well, that's where he picks up clients. You know, he's a hunting and fishing guide sometimes."

"That where he might be today? Out fishing?"

"No. Too hot."

That was true. Leaving the cool, dark Valmar and going back into the sun was brutal. All down Main Street, the tiny elms planted in the spring dropped and suffered in the heat, leaves curling at the edges, and the grass on lawns was sick and sere and brittle. This was the country. People watered their lawns when it rained. Sliding into the car seat, Whippletree winced, wishing he'd had the sense to park facing away from the sun, or at least on the shady side of the Valmar.

Before heading out to Betters's place, he stopped by the parsonage. Bimbo was out there, sweating away, digging up the heat-riven flowerbeds, and cursing as he worked.

"Hey, there, deputy," Whippletree said, goading him a little, "you finding anything?"

Bimbo gave him a slow, dull glower. More and more, he was expressing his feelings directly, and his primary feeling was hostility.

"What am I lookin' for?" he growled.

"A murder weapon. Or the .22 they used on Koster. Anything."

He heard a faint knocking from inside the house. It ceased for several moments, then began again.

"That Alvin and Bill?"

"Alvin. Ruehle's doing the walls. Bill is down in the cellar."

He tossed a spadeful of earth to one side and leaned on the

shovel. "Sheriff, there's *nothin'* of any value in this whole damn place. *What is it? What is it?* Who could believe there'd be anything in here?"

"I don't," Whippletree said. "I told you you're supposed to be looking for a weapon."

"Aw, Whip, now there ain't . . ."

"I'm not so sure. First place, the shotgun didn't move too far. Now, it hardly seems to me that the perpetrators"—Bimbo brightened, hearing the technical word—"would leave one weapon and take the other one, the .22, now does it?"

Slowly, very slowly, Bimbo turned that around once or twice in his head, and seemed to like the idea.

"So you think . . ."

"Exactly. So when you finish on the house, get on the church again. Look in the piping. Anyplace where there's metal. The detector might have missed the rifle before, because of that. But finish the flowerbeds first."

"But, jeez, Whip, it's so hot."

"Sure is, isn't it?" Whippletree said. "And I've got to go out to Lake Eden. Talk to Lynn Betters."

Bimbo almost groaned.

The sheriff checked Farley and Ruehle, giving them a little encouragement, some symbolic patting-on-the-head, then headed out toward the lake. But, going by Ahler's Deep Rock gas station, he saw something. He was thinking about what to ask Lynn Betters and how to approach her, and he saw something that, at first, his brain did not fully receive. It took a moment of recapitulation before the wordless impulse passed up and into his conscious being: color *color* COLOR. A glimpse of pink metal, a corner of it, glinting in the sun behind Ahlers's station.

He braked, swung around on the deserted street, and pulled up beside the garage. Gasoline fumes rode the air, and the heavy smell of grease hung around the front of the place. Ahlers, working on some guy's muffler, wiped his forehead with a dirty rag, leaving a streak of grease on it, and came over.

"Howdy, sheriff."

"That Bauch's Grand Prix out there behind your place?"

"Sure is," Ahlers cackled lewdly. He lowered his voice and leaned toward the patrol car. "Brought it in here to get the come stains off." He cackled again, louder than before. "What can I do fer yuh?"

"When did he bring the car in?"

"This morning. Just drove in, parked it hisself, and said to give it a lube and oil change when I got around to it. No hurry, he said."

Whippletree thanked the old guy and drove off. That probably meant Bauch was in town, probably had been in the back room at the Valmar all along. He tried to remember the way he'd put it to Mary Prone: *Tell him to get in touch with me . . . the longer this drags on, the worse it's going to get for everybody . . .* That didn't sound too bad. Shouldn't scare the guy away, anyway. Thank God I didn't mention Bauch's fingerprints in the house. If he's scared already, that would make him run for sure. But then, you never did know just how to figure Denny Bauch, bridegroom-to-be.

III

Mel Betters lived well all year around. Whippletree drove down the long, twisting road—trail, really—that led along the lake, and way up to the north end, where the big houses were. Other places along the lake had everything from two-

room cottages to small frame houses, with little garden plots
in back and an old rowboat, now and then an outboard, tied
to a wooden dock in front. The Betters's summer place was a
long, low ranch-style structure, made of brick. It looked cool
just standing there.

The sheriff came up behind the house and turned off the
engine. Lynn's Mercedes sports car sat in the drive, in front
of one of the garage's double-doors. He waited a minute, but
there was no sign of life. Knocking on the door of the house
raised nothing, either, so he followed the flagstone walk
down around the house, then came through a small hedge
onto a patio which faced the beach and the lake. He had to
hold his hand over his eyes, momentarily, to block the glare.
There along the dock was the Betters's big new Chris Craft,
with the enclosed cabin that was the talk of Lake Eden, and
there, too, down on the beach, was Lynn Betters's body. And
what a body it was.

.She raised her head and slipped on sunglasses when his
shoes rang hollowly on the wooden dock. Then she smiled.
"Hey, sheriff," she cried, with a lilt.

He had not been prepared for the smile, nor had he been
prepared for this kind of reception. She was lying on the
beach, stomach down, tanned an even brown, as far as he
could see. The white bikini covered maybe a couple of inches
of her high saucy behind, and her little top lay slightly off to
the side on her blanket. Still smiling, conscious of her effect
and pleased with it, she reach out for the top, missed it a couple of times, said "Oh, darn," and then slipped it beneath
her, lifting her body just enough to give Whippletree a good
look. "There," she said, reaching behind and tying the thing.
"I thought you weren't going to make it. Care for a lemonade? Drink?"

"Just had a beer in town," he said.

Her face sobered a second. The Valmar? "Want another?"

"Okay, but mostly I could stand some shade."

They went inside and she led him to a glassed-in patio. It was air-conditioned, and the coolness, the low hum of the machinery, exhilarated him for a moment, then made him drowsy. She brought a couple of bottles of Lowenbrau out from the kitchen and handed one to him. No Grain Belt or Hamm's for the Betters.

"So you wanted to see me?"

He was still a little wary, but there was no doubt this young woman could turn on the charm. And why not? Lynn Betters had a lot to be charming with, and a lot to feel charming about. And, to Whippletree, she was something of a mystery. A woman like Mary Prone he could understand, even if he wouldn't care for the kind of life she led. He could understand her because she was direct, if not always scrupulously honest. What you saw on Mary's surface was pretty much what was underneath. You could count on her, and she didn't mind a hard day's work. She would be lost without it. Whippletree was a lot like that. But Lynn Betters did absolutely nothing, or what the sheriff regarded as nothing. He did not count water skiing, beach parties, kinky sex, or airplane trips to Chicago to shop at Carson-Pirie-Scott.

Mel Betters was an old Stearns County boy, but he'd tried to bring up his daughter in a different mold. He had succeeded. But only halfway. Lynn was smart, all right, with strong appetites, but she lacked her father's discipline and ambition. She had wanted a "career on the stage," and he had sent her down to the University of Minnesota, which, for Stearns County, was something like going to the far corners of the earth, or even to New York. But she came back after a semester. The people down there didn't treat her as "Mel Betters's daughter," and the Director of Theater Arts told her that if she applied herself she might develop her talents enough to capitalize on her looks. Lynn took that as an insult! All you *needed*, right, she already had: long legs, fine body, pure skin, white teeth, and eyes with a touch of deceit in them. Or was it mockery? Or simply the eyes of a reckless flirt, who is all too ready and willing to go in beyond her water level?

She had been splashing happily around out in Lake Eden for over two years, since coming back from the University. Nothing seemed to bother her very much. Now, sitting here grinning at the sheriff, with the smile of a girl who is beautiful, and knows it, she had already forgiven him entirely for hauling her in on the "creating a disturbance" charge.

Something doesn't fit here, Whippletree was thinking.

"I saw Reverend Koster this morning," she said, getting started. "He's taking this very hard."

"I know. I'm sorry. There's not much you can do . . ."

"Oh, yes there is," she interrupted. "If you will."

"Like what?"

"Do you think you could . . . not disturb him? Until things are settled? The others in our discussion group—they were with me at the hospital—all thought it would be nice if . . ."

"Miss Betters, there's nothing I'd like to do more than let everybody alone, but the Reverend's the only one who has seen the killers. You know, with politics and all, this thing is getting very complicated, and . . ."

She smiled sympathetically, a smile that meant to say *I know, I know, and I'd be on your side if it wasn't for Dad.*

". . . I've only got a few things to go on."

"Do you want to know what we think?"

"Who's we?"

156

"The girls—ah, women—in the Reverend's discussion group. We're closest to him. We know him really well."

"I bet you think it was Denny Bauch," he said, half jokingly.

Her answer, the answer itself and the quickness of it, surprised him. *"Of course it wasn't Denny Bauch,"* she said. "I wouldn't put it past Mary Prone to've been in on it, but I . . ." she paused ". . . know Denny. He wouldn't do that."

"What about that fight? All those sermons?"

"That fight is all Denny'd do, and that was enough for him. After that, he didn't care much. He was taking it as a lark."

"Reverend Koster certainly wasn't taking it that way. And he's saying it was Bauch and a young kid. Or a woman."

She looked away. "I know," she said. "He has this thing about Denny. He used to talk about it in discussion group all the time."

"What sort of things did you . . . ah . . . *discuss?*"

She poured the rest of her beer into her glass, then said, "Whatever came up. You probably heard how mad my dad was over that . . . thing with Denny. He made me go for counseling. I had to do it, and Dad gave me a choice. Either go to the Reverend, in our church out here, or I'd have to go to a shrink in Minneapolis. Isn't that something? All I do is . . . well, you *saw* . . . but, jeez, *everybody* does that nowadays. Well, don't they?"

She seemed to want some answer. He was following another train of thought.

"I suppose so," he said. "Say, personally, and on the level, what do you really think of Koster?"

On-the-level was a strange request to Lynn, demanding caution. "What do you mean, think of him?"

"Particularly, he says Denny Bauch might have been the

157

killer, and you don't think so. You know Bauch. You know Koster, at least a little. And what do these other women in the group think?"

"Well, Mrs. Hockapuk, the librarian, thinks he's . . . terrific, and so does her friend Mrs. Withers. I think the others do, too, young Mrs. Janeway and Trudy Benoit. But you'd have to ask them. I think he's . . ." she hesitated too long . . . "interesting."

"Does that mean 'weird'?" Whippletree suggested.

She bristled. "No. No! Men always say that. The men around here are so . . ." she stopped.

"Yes?" He almost smiled.

"Well, *crude*," she said. "I wouldn't have picked Koster for a minister if I'd seen him on the street, but he was sure . . ." she sought an appropriate word ". . . *dedicated,* though."

"You know this for a fact?"

"Sure. Why else would he go through all the time and trouble to convince me that what I'd done was sinful, and all that? When I don't believe it at all, but just played the game?"

"How did he take that? What did the other women think?"

"Sheriff," she said, giving him what he was sure—for just an instant—was a conspiratorial wink, "I'm a much better actress than that stuffed shirt at the university thought I was."

He finished his beer and sat back.

"So, anyway, you want me to go easy on the Reverend? But I've got to talk to him again. There were some signs of evidence that . . ."

"What kind of evidence?" she asked eagerly.

"Read about it in the *Trib*," he said, not able to keep the edge out of his voice. "But, other than the fight with Bauch and the sermons, is there *anything* about Koster that's unique? Anything you can think of that might have made somebody do what they did?"

158

"Well, he *did* sort of pry a lot," she said, after a moment. "He wasn't like most people out here. I thought that was part of his job, though. At least with me. And because of where he'd come from, and the problems he'd had, too."

"You mean he asked a lot of questions?"

She laughed. "No more than you."

"Well, how about yourself? After you went in for—what do they call it, counseling? What did he want to know?"

"It's kind of embarrassing, really. Anyway, you know about it already."

"Skim the top, anyway."

She thought it over a minute. The way he had it figured, she had some reason for wanting him to ease off on Koster, or maybe the other women had put her up to it. Would she do it to please them? He doubted it, unless she wanted something different to do. As a lark. Something to have been *in* on. He would have to talk to those other women. Jesus, he was tired, and here it was already quarter-past-four, and in St. Cloud the *Tribune* would be out on the streets.

"He was pretty angry at first," she began. "You see, Dad had had to go in and set it up. Tell the Reverend why I'd be coming in. I hadn't been in church all that much for a while. Hardly ever. So he was pretty mad. He really doesn't have all that much idea what goes on, you know. I thought it was pretty silly, all the time, but at least Matt . . ." She corrected herself, ". . . at least the Reverend was *interesting*.

"He made me part of the group sessions after a couple of weeks. I had to go in by myself at first. In that poor old dump of a house, with all the kids running in all the time. I was mad the first time. At Daddy, mostly. So I came on tough. I said, 'Okay, preacher'—something like that—'Okay, preacher, I guess you've heard. I've been giving away my behind all over town, so what's it to you?'"

"How did he react? I've heard he was very down on things like that."

"Oh, he was. He was. He was a very moral guy, almost rigid. But he didn't pick up my attack. Instead, he talked about himself. About his old man. I guess he wanted me to know I wasn't the first person to have disagreements with a parent. His life hadn't been any bed of roses."

Whippletree remembered fragments of the newspaper article his wife had showed him the morning after the killings. "Comes from Montana, as I recall?"

"Yes. Near Missoula. I've never been there, and after what he told me about it, I'll never go."

"Didn't like it much?"

"I guess the place was all right. It was his *father* he couldn't stand. He got to talking about that. The guy gave him all kinds of trouble when he was growing up. Or so he said. Things like not letting him read books, and keeping him home from school. What was absolutely forbidden was going to church with his mother. Old man Koster wouldn't stand for that. It was very unhappy for him."

Clear enough. There were really very few variations when it came to growing up. The human animal being what he is, no more than twice removed from the standard mule, all you have to do to guarantee that a person will turn out one way is to absolutely forbid him to turn out that way. It's a simple, yet complicated truth, and Koster's father had not mastered it.

"So that's why he eventually went to the seminary?"

"Yes. By that time, his mother had left his father. She had some money, a little, anyway, and gave it to him for his education. He went into the seminary right away. Never went home again."

Whippletree remembered what Elwood Fensterwald had said.

160

"Wait, I thought he went up there this summer? In fact, I thought his father visited down here?"

"I meant to say until now," Lynn said. "I was getting to that. See, that's why I admire the Reverend so much, even if I really haven't any time for religion and all that. Knowing how he felt about his father, he actually invited the guy down here."

"Why?"

"He said something about how his father had never met his wife, Bonnie, or even seen the kids."

"Maybe he thought it would improve things."

"If he did, it didn't. The guy only stayed two days. He came down here, took a look at the church, took a look at the family, took a look at some of the farms around here, grunted, and went back to Montana."

"Was Koster upset about that? Do you recall?"

"Sure. This was only, let's see, couple of weeks ago. We had group the day after he'd left. Matt . . . the Reverend . . . seemed excited."

"Upset?" Whippletree found himself at work on a new theory.

"Not so much that. More like keyed up. He said Bonnie hadn't gotten on too well with his father, but he hadn't expected that, anyway. He made some joke about his father thinking the church would make a good corn crib if it wasn't falling down."

"He made a joke about *that?*"

"It *was* funny, come to think of it. I mean odd. Maybe he'd been seeing things from the old man's point-of-view. Maybe things didn't look the same anymore. Anyway, the visit wasn't much of a success."

"Then why did he go up to Montana next week?"

"To patch things up, I guess. He didn't say."

Maybe the old man has something to do with it, the sheriff was thinking. A sudden and long-deferred meeting of father and son, who had never been close, who had virtually been enemies, radically alters a previously unpleasant but stable situation . . .

That would have to be checked. He pulled out his note pad and wrote: "Contact Montana."

Lynn Betters looked curious.

"Just a note for myself. I should get in touch with the old man. Just another thing to do."

"You have to do all that stuff?"

"Most of it. It'd be a lot easier if I had more leads. Now, do you think Koster could have irritated somebody—anybody—enough to set them off against him? To the extent of what's been done?"

She thought it over. "Maybe," she said. "He could be pretty fanatic. When he got around to talking about . . . what I was there for, he could be pretty opinionated. Like, he told me sex belonged in marriage. Can you believe it? Marriage! He called me all kinds of names once. He sort of lost control."

"Such as?"

"You know. The names men call women. Except he did it in, like, Bible talk. *Harlot. Tainted woman.* That kind of thing."

"This didn't bother you?"

"Why should it? I've been called a lot worse, even by my boyfriends. But he really got worked up. I thought it was sort of cute. Sure, when he started in on Mary Prone and the Valmar every Sunday, it got repetitious."

Whippletree recalled the change in the nature, mood, and tone of the sermon outlines, and asked if, to Lynn's knowledge, the Reverend had *himself* changed, if something might have been happening in his life, in the parish, to alter his personality. He didn't quite have the vocabulary that Nicky Rollis might have brought to the task, but she got the drift.

"Well, I really can't say. Because I didn't have much to do with him until this summer, when Dad made me."

"All right, Miss Betters. It was just a thought." He stood up and reached for his straw hat.

"Leaving? Stay for another beer. It's a drag out here, and my date's not coming by until dinner."

"No, got to get back and check on the church. Then back to St. Cloud."

"You'd go faster in a helicopter," she said, giving him a wink.

He shrugged. "You know it. One more thing. Who do you think did it? The shootings."

"You want to know? I think it was Elwood Fensterwald. Elwood and his kid."

"Why's that?"

"To get even for that choir thing. Old Fensterwald is creepy, anyway, if you ask me. Hard as nails. Next to him, Dad looks like Pollyanna."

"That's another case of father and son not getting along. They wouldn't have been in on it together."

She saw him out into the parking area. The sun was heading down a little now, and the shade trees cooled the air a little. "Why don't you think it was Denny Bauch?" he asked again.

"I told you. Denny was satisfied when he beat the hell out of Koster. Denny's no killer."

Whippletree thought of those fingerprints in the parsonage, and Bauch's convenient departure. And of his continued elusiveness.

"We'll see."

"But you'll go easy on the Reverend, right? Give him a chance to get his feet on the ground?"

"The 'girls' would appreciate it, is that right?" He got into the patrol car. She came over next to the door.

"They thought it would be nice to help him. He was really upset. And they thought I knew you. Because of Dad."

Or, he thought, *'Dad' wants to find out as much as he can.*

IV

If at first you're a damn fool, next time play it cool, Whippletree was thinking. He parked the car two blocks from the Valmar and came up on it from a side street. His .45 revolver, usually locked in the trunk, was belted on, and a few kids playing hopscotch on the hot concrete looked at him in awe. He felt a little funny with the gun on, but it was better, just in case. An old lady, rocking on her front porch, saw him, stopped dead still, and hurried off into her house. He ducked into the alley that ran behind the club. He could see the silver metallic glint of Mary's trailer and he smelled the rotting garbage and the sweet, sickly smell of the half-empties in the stacked cases of beer. *Get lucky,* he told himself, *let's hope there aren't a lot of customers,* and he slammed into the rear entrance, into the kitchen of the Valmar, crossed the floor quickly, and appeared behind the bar.

Trixie Wade was there, serving beer and shots to Clem Duckworth, gas-station Ahlers, and a couple of the crazy Laundenbush boys from St. Augusta. They looked up in surprise.

"Hey, sheriff, what's up?" Ahlers said.

"Hey, I seen Bimbo over to the church," blithered one of the Laundenbushes. "You catch them there killers yet?"

The Fields of Eden

Clem Duckworth choked on a swallow of beer. Trixie Wade looked scared. He just nodded to the boys and motioned her into the kitchen.

"Absolutely no games," he said, giving her a look that said he meant business. "Is Denny around here?"

She looked away.

"You'd better tell me."

"In the trailer," she said, "with Mary."

"All right. I'm going over there right now. You don't *say* anything. Don't *do* anything. You get right back out there and tell 'em I was in for a quick one, if they're interested. You got that?"

She nodded.

He stepped out the back door and walked quickly along the rear side of the club, turning the corner. The trailer was now about ten feet away, but the door was on the opposite side. There was a screened window looking right at him, a filmy curtain drawn across it. He could not see in, but anybody inside would have no trouble spotting him. There was no sound, so he guessed that he was unobserved. The stony gravel around the trailer, however, would be a problem. He solved it the only way he could think of—he took off his shoes. The ground, dry and sun-baked, was hotter than hell, and so were the two metal steps. He jerked open the screen door and stepped inside the trailer. There they were—Denny Bauch and Mary Prone. Stark naked.

Bauch lay on his back on the floor of what passed for the "living" area, his head braced on a pillow cushion, his knees up. Mary knelt between his legs, her head moving up and down, up and down, in a graceful flowing motion. Bauch saw the sheriff first. His eyes went wide open underneath that greasy 'Fifties Elvis Presley pompadour. He jerked away from Mary, grabbing for a T-shirt. Taking no chances, Whippletree yanked out his .45 and said, "Freeze!"

165

Denny did, his hand halfway to the couch where the T-shirt was. Mary Prone stopped, too, one hand underneath him, one hand on him—he was fading fast already—her mouth on the upstroke.

"Okay," Whippletree said, relaxed, "take it easy. Nothing's going to happen. Denny, seems I meet you quite a lot in situations like this. You two put some clothes on."

"You ain't got no right . . ." Bauch started, pulling his personality back into acceptable form.

"I got every right in the world, punk, and I could run you in right now. But I'm giving you the benefit of the doubt. I'm going to talk to you first. Now shut up and put some clothes on."

Mary Prone went back to the sleeping area, put on a robe, and came back. Bauch, grumbling indistinctly, pulled on a white T-shirt, shorts, Levi's. He slipped into his engineer boots and sat down on the tiny couch, looking sullen.

"Curl your lip some more, why don't you?" Whippletree grinned.

"Where's your warrant?"

"We're all friends here. You invited me in. Listen, Denny, you think you're so damn smart all the time. But you're in big trouble. Bigger than your brain, I'm afraid."

Whippletree pulled up a small folding chair and sat down, facing the two of them.

"What in the hell was the point of that stupid cut-out letter you sent me? Huh? You think you're so cool. What kind of idiot would pull a crazy stunt like that?"

Bauch actually looked a little abashed, and exchanged glances with Mary Prone. "Well," he grouched aggressively, "I was afraid you'd try to tie me in with that Koster thing."

"And shouldn't I?"

It didn't take much for Bauch to fly off the handle. He was one of those punks who *know their rights!*

166

"Look here, sheriff. You got nothin' on me. If you do, prove it. Me an' Mary was up camping at Gull Lake that night."

"That's your alibi?"

"You damn right. Anything ties me to Lake Eden that night is . . . is . . . hoked up, it's . . ." He found a big word, out of a mind informed by a thousand TV detective shows. ". . . *circumstantial.*" Triumphant announcement.

"So's your alibi. You think a jury is going to believe that, with your record, and your prints in the Koster house?"

Whippletree had been waiting for this moment, the surprise of it. As a technique, it worked only sometimes in getting at the truth, but it always got a very human reaction, and Whippletree could read that kind of thing.

"Denny!" Mary cried, and it seemed as if she shrank away from him. For his part, Bauch looked astounded, confused. "That can't be . . ." he said. "That can't . . . oh, wait a minute . . ." He seemed perplexed, uncertain.

"I'm waiting," Whippletree said.

"That must have been . . ." Mary began.

"Oh, I know," Bauch said, "I went there to . . ."

"Maybe you better not say anything," Mary cautioned.

"No, hell, it's . . ."

"You don't have to, you know," Whippletree said, wondering, *where in the hell is my Miranda card?*

". . . I went over there to tell him I was sorry for knocking him around like that," Bauch decided.

"Oh, now really?" The sheriff couldn't keep the amusement out of his voice. "This is something you regularly do? Apologize to the guys you beat up? Look, Bauch, I'm fed up with this. I'm going to run you in for the Koster killings, so help me . . ."

Denny took that like a slug in the gut. He half-rose from the couch, and his face went white and scared.

"N–n–now, Sheriff, we've had our run-ins, you an' me, and I ain't no angel by a long shot. But killings? No man, no *way!* I didn't . . ."

"Koster started that fight!" Mary declared.

Whippletree looked at her.

"Yeah, didn't you know that?" Bauch asked, recovering a little hope. "You mean you thought *I* picked a fight with a wimpy minister? *Me?*"

He sounded insulted.

"Now hold on a minute," Whippletree said. "You're going to sit here and tell me Koster started a fight with *you?*"

"It's the truth. I swear it." Bauch raised his right hand over an imaginary Bible. "Happened a couple months ago. I was in the club knocking back a few, but it was a slow night. Nothing doing, you know. I thought, hell, I'll go on over to Brooten, see if I can't maybe scarf up a little guide action at the Rod and Gun. So I went out back, and there he was. Koster. Right by my car. By the door. I say something like, "How you doin', Rev.' You know, I'd been hearin' all the things he'd said, and I didn't care for the guy much, truth to tell. But I had nothin' against him. So you want to know what he says? He says, 'We're goin' to have a little talk, mister.' I say, 'C'mon, man, move away from the wheels. I'm in a hurry.' So I step over and reach for the door, right? An' he pushes me. He *pushes* me. Can you believe it? An' says, 'Let's talk about what you've been doin' in this town.' I'm mad by now, so I tell him where he can shove it. I go for the door again, and kind of ease him aside, but when I do he takes a swing. I see red when that happens. Nobody takes a swing at me, and kind of like instinct I give him a shot to the gut. He doubles over. I give him one to the side of the head. Now he's screaming at me. 'Scum! Scum!' An' somehow he actually catches me one on the side of my head. That's enough, I think, and I slam him right across the hood of the car. He gets up, though, like he's ready for more. I never seen nothin' like it. I mean, here he is, a skinny guy, never did a day's work in his life, looks like, an' he's taking on the Bauch. Well, I would of stopped then, but he comes around the car kicking and screaming. By this time there's a little crowd out back. Mary. Trix. Duckworth, I think. I can't remember. Koster runs smack into me an' we both go down. Jesus. I had on my white pants. Really pissed me, I'll tell you that. Well, anyway, I get him up, stand him against the car, and shoot him the old one-two a couple of times. One to the gut, one to the head. That stops him. He drops. But he's still screaming, something about how evil I am. You know, minister talk. Only now you can't understand him too good, because of the blood. I stand him up then and shove him along toward home. He can still walk."

"You sure you're not giving me a line?"

"That's the way it was," Mary affirmed, nodding vigorously. "That's exactly the way it happened."

"Anyway, I got to thinking about it, and went on over to the Reverend's to apologize for clobbering him so bad. But you know I just don't care to be called them names."

"And exactly when did you go over there?"

Bauch looked a little doubtful now. "Early this week," he said.

"Well, seems you gave it a lot of thought. It's been about two months since that fight."

"I can explain it," Bauch said quickly. "See, we was . . . Mary wanted to . . . have the wedding there. In spite of everything. I figured if I buttered him up a little, Koster, I mean, things might go a little smoother. That's why I went there. Actually, he deserved getting the shit kicked out of him, for what he done, but . . ."

He shrugged, as if to say, *she made me go over. You know women.*

"It's not going to be an easy job convincing a jury of that

169

one, either," Whippletree said. "Anyway, get your things together. I have to take you in."

"What? *What?*" Bauch and Mary Prone were incredulous.

"Look, I have to. Just on suspicion. I doubt it'll amount to much. I don't think you got it in you to . . ."

He didn't get a chance to finish. Bauch was on his feet in a flash and covered the distance between the couch and the chair in which the sheriff was sitting. The sheriff felt himself falling backward even before he felt the impact of Denny's rush and reached to brace himself with one arm while with the other he grabbed at his holster. His fingers found it just as he hit the wall of the trailer, but it was empty. He hit the wall and rolled slightly to the side, upsetting a small table with bric-a-brac on it, found a bit of balance, got ready to jump up.

"Hold it!" Bauch warned, in a jittery voice.

Whippletree stopped and looked up. Bauch had the .45.

"Come on now, Denny. Don't be a damn fool. You're in enough trouble already."

"Dennis, put the gun down," Mary pleaded, with an effort to stay calm.

"No way." Bauch eased toward the door. "Somebody's got me set up for somethin' but I ain't buyin'. I had enough of . . ."

Abruptly, he spun sideways, crashed through the screen door, and leaped from the trailer. Whippletree, already on his feet, saw him head down the street toward . . . Ahlers's Deep Rock. The Grand Prix. He too jumped down from the trailer, and when the heat came through his socks he remembered—*Idiot!*—that he'd taken his shoes off. Instantly, he decided to put them on. "Mary, call the Koster house."

She was standing in the door, stunned. "What?"

"Call the Koster house. Come on. Tell my deputies to get down to the Deep Rock right away."

The Fields of Eden

She didn't move. He had his shoes on, not bothering to tie them. *"Please!"* he practically shouted. "Call Bimbo. *Now!"* he saw her moving dreamlike and dazed toward the Valmar as he set off at a trot for the gas station.

He wasn't meant for this kind of thing anymore, he knew. He hadn't even run half a block and, way ahead of him, Bauch was almost at the station. The jerk. He would never get away. *I'll call the highway patrol,* he thought, *they'll* . . . But his heart was pounding in his chest. It's not a pleasant sensation when you feel it banging away against your ribs. And it seemed suddenly there wasn't any air. He had to drop into a walk as Bauch was rounding the corner, heading into the back lot of the gas station.

Whippletree felt himself slow down some more. Being sixty was no picnic. People were out on the steps of their houses now, or looking through the windows, watching—so the sheriff felt—the old man drag along after the young one. He felt ridiculous and a little ashamed of the failing mechanism that was his body, but there wasn't much time for crying about it, because, up ahead, Bauch was in the car now, fumbling with the ignition. The sheriff made the edge of the parking lot just as the first blast of exhaust smoked out of the two pipes, and Bauch's big 450 engine rumbled and roared into life. The car shot backward, Bauch swinging the wheel, into a sharp curve. Whippletree, winded and panting, ducked behind one of the gas pumps. Bauch swung the wheel again, waved the gun, and slammed on the brakes, then grabbed the shift lever, slapped it into low, and stepped down on the accelerator. But he had to hit the brakes again. Bimbo Bonwit screamed up in the patrol car and shrieked to a stop directly in his path. "I knew what I was doin'," Bimbo would tell it later. "There warn't no way that boy was gonna crash outta there. I swear he loves that Grand Prix better than good old Mary Prone."

171

Bauch jumped out of his car, Bimbo out of his. The two of them stood there facing each other, Whippletree off to the side, bent over, panting and hawking, his shoelaces dangling around on the ground. Bimbo grinned and moved toward Bauch, who eased backward, still holding the gun, but undecided about what to do with it.

"Hand over that piece," Bimbo ordered. As he got closer to Bauch, he looked bigger. It didn't hurt him any. He might not have a big brain, but maybe that helped him face down a lot of things with little fear. Across the street, huddled together, fearful and expectant at the same time, as people always are in the presence of violence or disaster, were a good two dozen or so residents of Lake Eden. They saw it all. Bimbo's bravery.

The big deputy eased forward, forward, slowly forward, grinning, hands outstretched. "He never even pulled his own gun," people would say later, in awe and country wonderment. "You shouldda seen it. He went on into Bauch and he didn't even pull his own gun!" Bauch was afraid, there was no denying it, and, concentrating on watching Bimbo's advance, wondering what the hell to do with the .45—that would mean *more* trouble, if he used it—he backed himself right up against his Grand Prix. Hadn't expected that. He started to turn and Bimbo made his move—he just jumped forward and landed right on top of Bauch, pinning him against the car. With one of those arms that was as big as the leg of a medium-sized man, he twisted the gun out of Bauch's hand—broke three fingers, sprained a wrist, would be the subsequent diagnosis—and with the other, he put Bauch in a hammerlock that was more like a hanging. The punk's eyes bulged, his tongue shot out and began to swell, his face turned blue. When he gurgled and went limp, Bimbo dropped him on the hot concrete. Across the street, the people let out a cheer. Bimbo waved at them and they cheered again, louder.

"Good work, Wayne," Whippletree heard himself say, and he heard, too, the shame and resentment in it.

"Here's your gun," Bonwit grunted, handing it over. He didn't have to say any more. Anybody knows a lawman who lets his weapon be taken from him is worse than a fool. He's a goddam clown. That's what Whippletree felt like.

He had the momentary ludicrous impulse to bend down right there in the parking lot and tie his shoelaces. Instead he said, "Get the cuffs on him and take him in to St. Cloud. I want him booked on suspicion in the Koster case, and assault with a deadly weapon."

Bimbo frowned. "You goin' to mention resistin' arrest and takin' your .45 away?"

"No, we have enough on him as it is."

"All right. You're the boss." Bimbo reached down, grabbed the unconscious Bauch under the arms, and hoisted him over to the patrol car. He tossed the prisoner face down on the backseat, twisted his arms around behind, and clamped on a pair of cuffs tight enough to have brought a bellow from a bull elephant. Lucky Bauch was unconscious.

"Let's break it up," Whippletree called to the people across the street, but either he didn't put enough authority in it or he didn't have enough authority left, because nobody moved. He felt stupid, and walked over to the Grand Prix. The engine was still idling dully. He turned off the ignition and took the keys out. He stared stupidly at them for a moment, then drifted on back and opened the trunk. That woke him up a little. In back, under a couple of gunny sacks, was an old, highly-polished .22 caliber rifle. He turned it over and looked up under the trigger housing. Two tiny initials were burned into the wood. "E.F."

173

"What you got there?" Bimbo asked, coming over.

"I think we found that other gun," Whippletree replied.

V

"So you didn't find much out at the house, is that right?" Mel Betters asked. He seemed just right up to the point of breaking into a big huge grin of glee.

The three of them were in the commissioner's office in the courthouse, Betters, Whippletree, and young Nicky Rollis. It was the morning after Bauch's apprehension, and Betters had summoned the other two in order to go over the details of the case, preparatory to charges.

"No," Whippletree muttered. He was not feeling very well, neither in body nor spirit.

"What?"

"I said *no.*"

That gleeful grin bubbled up inside Betters again, from his heart or his gut, welled and swelled up inside him, quivered just behind his mouth. He didn't look as much like a ferret right now as he looked like a grinning cat. "So you had three deputies working away all afternoon, looking around the Koster house, an' the weapon used on Koster turns up inside Denny Bauch's trunk."

"It's not conclusive," Whippletree said.

Though he didn't know how to explain it, he was not convinced, just the same. Last evening, before driving back to St. Cloud, he'd gone over to the parsonage once again. Farley and Ruehle were dragging, beat out, snappish, and exhausted. They'd found nothing in the house. Whippletree himself had done a onceover while they watched and muttered

174

things he couldn't—and wasn't supposed to—hear. He checked the basement, house, choir loft, everything, stood there on the lawn and looked at the shaky clothesline poles—the ropes had already been taken back to St. Cloud as evidence for the trial—and up at the belltower. Well, that seemed to be it. They had two weapons. One shotgun with Ruthie Koster's blood on it, and one rifle, which, under painful "questioning" by Bimbo, Denny Bauch admitted having taken from the Fensterwald farm. The questioning took place in the basement of the jail, where nobody could hear Bauch screaming, not even Whippletree, who was home consoling Sarah at the time. Bimbo tied Bauch in a chair and twisted his broken hand whenever he wanted to know something. Bauch *had* taken a number of guns, and certain other items—fishing rods, tackle, a pair of hip boots—from the Fensterwald home. But he denied taking the shotgun, he denied doing the killings, and he denied having a "partner." He passed out denying these things, and had to be taken back to the St. Cloud hospital to have his hand reset.

"We can get this guy," Nicky Rollis was saying. "If he's protecting an accomplice, let him. We'll nail him and get the case over with before election. I don't see why we shouldn't."

Whippletree, tired and discouraged, rubbed his chin and demurred. "I'm not satisfied," he said.

Betters sat forward in his swivel chair, sarcastic and aggressive. "Aw, hell, Emil, you're full of shit," he said.

"It will take me no more than five minutes to get an indictment from the grand jury," Rollis put in, "and with a Stearns County jury, even F. Lee Bailey couldn't pull it out for Bauch now."

"That's what I'm worried about," the sheriff said.

"You got a right to be," Betters guffawed. Nicky Rollis smiled appreciatively at his mentor's wit.

"Well, if it wasn't Bauch, who was it?" Betters wanted to know. "Fensterwald? The old man or the young one? Mary Prone?"

Whippletree tried something: "Maybe your daughter was in on it," he said.

The other two stared at him, Betters reddening. "Why you . . ."

"There may have been a woman involved," Whippletree explained. "That's what Koster said first, and . . . "

"Hell, don't you try nothing like that, Emil, or we'll really take care of you. Won't we, Nick?"

"Oh, yessir, we surely will . . ."

"Dammit, Emil, you might just as well sit here and tell me it was Koster himself who did it."

"I've thought of that myself."

This time they were more alarmed than angry. "What the hell's gotten into you? How can you say a damnfool thing like that."

"I can because it's a possibility. I've heard some rather strange things about the guy, both good and bad, but mostly contradictory. And it seems he's been going through some kind of a change this summer. Acting different than he used to . . ."

"Well, now, everybody has a different way of looking at things," Nicky Rollis said, "and you can't just go and . . . oh, that's idiotic. He was a well-known family-type guy, from what I've heard. There's not one iota of evidence to support *that* one. Look, Emil, your image is bad enough after the paper came out yesterday afternoon. You don't have to go and commit public suicide for us. It's unnecessary."

"I still say Koster's in this somewhere," Whippletree maintained stubbornly, as the other two hooted. "Naw," Mel Betters concluded. "We got Bauch and we'll nail him. An', Emil,

176

if you don't get the second man . . . or woman, or child, whatever, we'll do it for you. Now, you follow up everything. Everything. Hell, I bet it *was* Mary Prone. They got no alibi can stand up, right Nick?"

"Looks that way to me, all right."

"Okay. You get going on that grand jury. Emil, we goin' to be readin' about you again in the paper?"

"You're the one who ought to know, Mel," Whippletree said. "But I'll tell you one thing, if it makes any difference to you. You're really giving Sarah a hard time."

Betters let a trace of sympathy cross his face, then took it back. "Can't be helped," he said. "Can't be helped. That's the news business. People have got a right to know."

"It may be news, but it's also politics."

Rollis chortled. "What would you know about that, Emil?"

Betters sneered. "Look, you play ball on this case, an' we'll go easy on you this election." He winked. "Might even be able to get you some kind of special pension. Not full by any means, but something can be . . . ah . . . worked out, know what I mean."

Whippletree felt beaten, being spoken to like that, having it assumed that he could be so easily trounced in the election, and so crudely bought off.

"Drop dead," he snapped.

Betters just laughed.

VI

He drove over to the hospital faster than he should have, worried about Sarah, angered at himself. Things were falling apart.

177

On the seat beside him was the offending issue of the *Tribune*. They had done a job on him, all right, but a lot of it had been his own fault. He was going around passing out ammo for them to use against him. *At least you're giving the folks something to laugh about,* he thought.

BONWIT APPREHENDS SUSPECT IN KOSTER CASE

Sheriff Whippletree's Weapon Taken by
Bauch
Procedural Errors Abound, Attorney
Rollis Says

St. Cloud. Several developments occurred today in the ongoing investigation of the slayings of the Matthew Koster family in Lake Eden. Most important was the apprehension and arraignment on charges of suspicion of Mr. Dennis Bauch, a Lake Eden resident. Bauch was also brought in on charges of resisting arrest. A number of Lake Eden residents observed the collaring of the suspect by sheriff's deputy Wayne "Bimbo" Bonwit. After eluding Sheriff Whippletree, taking his weapon from him without a fight, and leaving the county's chief lawman shoeless, Bauch raced for his vehicle, a 1976 Pontiac, along the hot streets of this western Stearns County resort area. Deputy Bonwit, busy at work supervising . . .

Supervising! Whippletree snorted to himself.

178

. . . an on-site inspection of the murder site, raced to the scene, and faced down and disarmed the suspect, taking Whippletree's weapon from him in the process. "It was just about the gutsiest thing I ever did see," stated Floyd Rosha, carwash operator at Ahlers's Deep Rock Station. "He didn't flinch once." Dana Cook, short order chef at Rehnquist's lunch counter said, "It was too hot to move, almost, but Bimbo took the man, fair and square." After subduing the violent Bauch, Bonwit looked on with alarm as Sheriff Whippletree searched the Bauch vehicle. "There was a weapon found in the search," county attorney Rollis informed the *Tribune* later, "but in spite of the fact that it would appear to be the gun used to shoot Reverend Koster, Whippletree's failure to obtain a warrant seriously jeopardizes our efforts to put this alleged killer away, where he won't do more harm to society . . ."

You bastard! Whippletree groaned, driving the car.

. . . Later it was learned from Mary Prone, proprietor of the Club Valmar, a Lake Eden place of recreation, that Whippletree engaged in a long conversation with the suspect, Bauch, on the Koster case, without informing him of his rights, and then sought to take him into custody. It was at this time that Mr.

Bauch apparently disabled the sheriff
and fled toward his vehicle. "The Miranda Rules are quite clear," Attorney
Rollis commented, "and I had
hoped—as the people of Stearns County
have a right to expect—that their sheriff
would know how to read a man his
rights. After all, it is on technicalities
that murderers go free . . ."

And it went on pretty much in that vein. There he was, a
dunderhead sheriff, too trusting, if not in fact stupid, disarmed, "shoeless"! Good God. He turned into the hospital
parking lot, found a space at the far end, switched off the engine, and leaned back, eyes closed.

"Is this *true?*" Sarah had wanted to know, the pained look
all over, her voice more worried than ever and shivery, too.

He had not looked at her, just forked in the shepherd's pie
and said nothing.

She'd been quiet a little, roaming around the kitchen, trying to find things to do, and, finding nothing, doing things
that had already been done. Wiping the dishes a second time.
Then: "What are we going to do if . . . ?"

There was a long silence. He continued to eat.

She began to cry softly. He knew what it was. She had never really recovered from the loss of Susie, nor from the loss
of the farm. It was a memory, like the memory of the Great
Depression, an inexpurgable knowledge of disaster and despair.

"It won't be that bad," he gritted, sounding as cheerful as
he could. "I might still pull it out . . ."

"Oh, Emil . . ."

"No, look." He set down his fork. She faced him. "What

180

would you say if I told you Koster killed his whole family and then shot himself?"

Her face held a flurry of passing emotions, some mixed together, but none there for long: disbelief, ridicule, anger, hope, befuddlement.

"I know you're desperate," she began, "but . . ."

"Then let's drop it, okay?"

"Have you talked to his people? Anybody who really knew him?"

"Not the real parishioners yet. I haven't had the time . . ."

She said nothing, tried to stop crying, failed, and went upstairs. *What the hell am I doing?* he started to wonder. His continuing failure to get anywhere, and a combination of circumstances, seemed to be robbing him not only of confidence but of simple integrity as well. *It's your own antipathy to the clergy that's doing this,* he thought. *You're killing yourself on your own bitter juices.* Or maybe it was simply that he'd lost touch with the way things were supposed to be done. Had relied too much on the old county man-to-man traditions. Imminent danger, too, from another *Trib* article:

> Dr. Paul Petly, director of residency at St. Cloud Hospital, indicated today that it was his predisposition to seek a warrant against Mr. Elwood Fensterwald of Lake Eden, on charges of child abuse. Mr. Fensterwald allegedly beat his son, Abner, seventeen, with a horsewhip. There may be some connection to the Koster case, but at this time it cannot be determined. "I'll give Whippletree this much," Petly said. "He got this boy to the hospital. I know the barbaric ways of this county, and I've opposed them

whenever I could, as quietly as I could, but I'm sick of it. Any of a thousand people in Stearns County could have killed the Kosters. I'm sick of suffering imposed simply because someone has the power to inflict it."

"Hey, Petly," Whippletree said, seeing him in the hospital corridor, "I don't know if I should thank you or not."

"Don't," the doctor said. He had an uncharacteristically bitter tightness around the cheekbones. "You didn't bring old Fensterwald up on charges, so I get stuck with it."

"But I've known Elwood for . . . "

"Two hundred years," Petley finished, exaggerating bitterly. "Look, Emil, it's obvious they're out to get you. But could you possibly refrain from playing into their hands? They're using the new techniques. Political hardball. And there you are, back in left field, an old barnyard gladhander. Look, I've got an offer from Mount Sinai in Chicago. I'm taking it. I'm getting out of this Neanderthal town. But, Jesus, why don't you call a spade a spade, as long as they're going to get you anyway."

Whippletree said nothing, and Petly noted his crestfallen look. He softened his tone.

"Emil, you're all right," he said, reaching out and touching Whippletree's shoulder gently. "You're too all right. You really are."

"How's Koster?" Whippletree asked.

"Improving. He's a lucky man, I'll say that."

"I think he's the killer," said the sheriff.

Petly looked startled.

"That's a spade," Whippletree said.

Petly let out a breath. "I don't like Koster," he said, "but he's got God on his side. That bullet was meant for his heart or his gut. The rope marks on his wrists had blood on them. We've got him on Librium for depression, and on Valium so he can relax. The guy is wild with desolation." He paused. "Look," he said, in a softer tone, "anything I can do for you? Tranquilizers? Anything? It can be taken care of, and nobody will know."

Whippletree recognized the sincerity of the offer, but he was offended.

"No, thanks. Can I see him?"

"I guess so. If you have to."

"Is he sober?"

"You mean of drugs? More or less. It's morning, and he's had some breakfast. But he's down. The only time I've seen him really himself was when those women were here."

"The ones from his church? What did they talk about?"

"Nothing. They avoided subjects. They talked around everything. It cheered him up, though."

"They tell you anything?"

"How much they love him. At least the older ones did, a Mrs. Hockapuk, said she was a librarian. Betters's daughter was with them. Why is that?"

"The old man made her get moral counseling. Because of some of her behavior earlier this summer."

Petly grinned. "She certainly has plenty to behave with."

"She told me to lay off Koster. That's why I wondered if anything special happened."

"Well, I was only in the room with them for a little while. She treated him like a wounded puppy. Personally, I think she's slicker than old Mel."

"Yeah, I've talked to her. She gave me a couple of ideas. About who did the job on the Kosters." He shrugged, unable to buy it still. "She thinks it was old Fensterwald. Along with his kid."

"They must've had a falling out since then. The kid, by the way, is three doors down from Koster, if you want to check in with him."

"Maybe I will. See you later."

He took the elevator up to Koster's floor. A couple of men and a few women were in the elevator with him, but nobody said anything, not even 'Good morning, sheriff,' and he thought he spotted a sly smile on the face of one of the men. A *Tribune* reader. No doubt. He could imagine the stories at the Courthouse Bar-and-Grill, "Hey, old Emil is going out in glory. You see the story in the paper? Lost his shoes an' his gun! Probably getting a quickie from Mary Prone when Bauch interrupted. *Hoo-boy!*"—and so on and so forth. And this morning at the office, dumb, loyal old Alyce Pelser asked him point blank if he could put in a good word for her with Bimbo 'cause when Bimbo got to be sheriff, she still wanted to answer the phones just like she was doing now.

Koster was awake and staring at the ceiling. There were a lot of flowers in the room, and they smelled. The hose had been removed from his mid-section, and the bottle of blood no longer hung from the metal arm at the side of the bed. Whippletree said, "Goodmornin', Reverend," and Koster looked over at him, moved his head indeterminately in what might have been a greeting, and looked back at the ceiling. Whippletree knew it for sure, now. He did not like the guy. That's probably why he suspected him, that and the fact that he had no real suspects, at least not in his own mind. Anyway, it was pretty clear that Koster didn't like him, either. The *Trib*, rumpled and read, sprawled across a bed tray.

"You've been having an exciting time, I understand," Koster said dully. His lips tightened horizontally in what might have passed for a smile.

Whippletree took a deep breath. If he got the guy upset

184

again, he'd have to come back and go through it all later. On the other hand, he had to know a few things.

"How you feelin'?" he asked, in a conscious effort to put the guy off-guard.

"Wonderful."

"Just about like you felt after that fight with Denny Bauch, huh?"

Bingo! Koster almost shot up off the pillow, remembered his wound—or the pain reminded him—and fell back, flushed and sputtering. "How . . . how did you find about about . . . that?"

"You told me Bauch did the killings. That's a serious charge. So I started asking questions around town. You might have had a reason to pin it on him."

Koster looked at him, his expression full of anger and pity. "You poor man," he said quietly. "You don't believe anyone, do you?"

"That's the wrong way. I believe too many people, I think. So tell me about that big fight."

Koster had a little trouble collecting himself, and the sheriff was afraid for a moment that he was going to reach for the little button and summon a nurse. "That *animal*," he hissed. "That vicious *animal*."

"I thought you were in the forgiveness business."

Koster gave him that look again. "If thy eye offends thee, pluck it out," he said. "An eye for an eye. My family's been . . . been destroyed . . . everything . . . everything I . . ." and he had to turn away for a couple of minutes. Whippletree looked away, kept on hearing the muted sobbing, and felt like a jerk. After a while, Koster turned back to him. "I feel differently now," he said quietly, resolved. "I want my pound of flesh now, just like everybody else."

What was this? A temporary change, brought on by the

shock of what had happened? Or yet another Koster? So far, as the sheriff calculated, there was the gentle, beloved Jesus-like Koster, then there was the half-awed, half-calculating Koster that Elwood Fensterwald had described, then there was the moral Koster of Biblical vengeance, fighting sin— represented by Denny Bauch—in alleys in back of bars. And here was a new one: cold, bitter, bent on settling a score. The sheriff wavered. The man in the bed in front of him was absolutely not the ineffectual, somewhat effeminate young man he had envisioned just a few days ago, but neither did he seem, in this new manifestation, the kind of person who would kill his family. *You're crazy, Emil,* he told himself. *You're slipping badly.* Simultaneously, he remembered Ruthie Koster and the notes from the minister's sermon: "talk of love . . . Bonnie and I in the early days . . . try to recapture. Bonnie and I and the children, and our poor, poor life together . . ."

"Sorry, Reverend," he heard himself saying. "Didn't mean to get you upset. You have to understand I'm just a crude old country boy, and I want to help you find the killers just as much as you want to settle with them yourself."

Koster didn't give. He stayed cold. What had been done was sufficient: There wasn't much tenderness left.

"You want to tell me about that fight?"

"All right." The minister licked his pale lips. "Well, I'd been concerned for some time about the kinds of things that were going on at that place . . ."

"Valmar?"

Koster nodded, apparently unable to bring himself to say the name. "And one day it just got to be too much. Some of the women in the parish had been complaining about it to me, and wondering if there wasn't anything we could do."

186

"Who were they? The women, I mean?"

"Well, the members of my discussion group, mostly Mrs. Withers, Mrs. Hockapuk. Young Mrs. Janeway—she lived only two houses away, and the noise, the cursing . . ."

He clenched his fists.

" . . . and after a while, Miss Betters, too."

Lynn Betters! Whippletree tried not to smile and succeeded. *She contributed on many an occasion to the noise and the cursing.* Apparently she was a pretty good actress, after all—she'd certainly pulled the old wool over Koster's eyes.

"I didn't know Miss Betters was a regular church participant," he said, checking out the angle.

Koster responded quickly. "That was because of her father. She'd done . . ." he flushed and seemed to be on the verge of some strong emotion. "I can't talk about it. It's personal. All I can say is that she improved considerably during the course of counseling and group discussions . . ."

"Anyway, the women wanted you to go over and clean it all out? Lynn Betters and the rest?"

"No. I didn't know Miss Betters then. At first it was the others. They told me the kinds of things that were going on there."

"What things *were* going on there?"

Koster looked at him. "Sheriff, you *know.*"

"Tell me. I'm working on a theory that you offended somebody, who waited for the right moment to strike back in full force."

"Well, there was intemperate drinking. And lewd jokes. And a perversion of love."

"You mean the sodomy case that got covered up?"

Koster flushed deeply and a vein stood out on his forehead.

187

"That *animal*," he mumbled again, bringing his fist to his mouth, looking at it. "Yes, that, but I'm speaking of what love should be, something pure and holy, between two people who were meant for one another. Then nothing can stand in the way. But there, at *that* place, it was only . . . only lascivious, gutter-rotten, *perverted*. There those people did it for . . . for the pleasure of the body. For their own greed and sensual selfishness. They didn't care!"

He pronounced *care* with the strange, soft emphasis, like the final word in a eulogy, like a dedication.

"I suppose I sound a little strange to you, sheriff?"

"Nope, can't say as you do, 'cause that's your line of work, after all, an' I understand that. So . . ."

"So I had been thinking of speaking out from the pulpit. Speaking out against the den of sin in our village, when my sons came to me with a story of their own. They'd been coming back from Little League, and took a short cut through the alley in back of . . . that place, and they . . . they saw an act of sexual copulation!"

For some reason, he raised his chin defiantly and looked at Whippletree accusingly.

"What? In the trailer?"

"Yes."

"Well, if that's true, they must have had to stand on each other's heads, because no kids that age can see in through the window."

Koster was angered. "You don't believe me? They saw it through the door."

"Was it open?"

"Of course it was open."

Whippletree remembered how the trailer was positioned. "Then they would have had to go around to get a look," he said. "I know about that trailer."

188

"So do I," the minister såid. "I read the paper. But, whatever, the boys came home and told me they'd seen a man and woman with no clothes on, and the man was on top of the woman and *beating her with his body.* That's the way Paul put it. I had to explain to them about sex . . . I didn't want to yet . . . about good sex and bad sex so I . . ."

"Is that why your sermons started to change?"

"What do you mean?"

"This summer. I had to take the liberty of looking over your things, you understand, and I couldn't help but notice that your sermons got more . . . tough, I guess you'd say . . . since June. Other people mentioned it, too. Was it that thing your boys saw that set you off?"

Koster seized it aggressively. "Yes, that was it," he cried, "and I went over to the bar, all by myself, to . . . " he searched for a reason, as if it were hard to find.

"To what?" Whippletree prodded.

"I don't know . . . now." Koster seemed momentarily confused. "I . . . . I guess it was anger. I guess I just wanted to . . . to tell them what they'd done and what I thought of them."

"Who was in the trailer? The ones your boys saw."

"It must have been Bauch and Mary Prone."

"That bothered you? They were going to be married. In your church."

"I didn't know that then. They hadn't published banns then. And it doesn't *matter*, don't you see? The sexual act is forbidden outside marriage, and they . . . they couldn't possibly do it . . . for . . . for love. They're . . ."

"That's a little judgmental, if you ask me . . ."

"They're *not the type*," the minister declared. "They're . . . *vile*."

"Could have been somebody else in there, couldn't it?" He

189

was thinking, among others, Clem Duckworth and Trixie Wade, old Clem getting his rocks off and thinking himself a lover boy, Trixie supplementing her income.

"No, it was Bauch. Just as it was Bauch with the shotgun the night of the . . . this is very painful for me."

"Reverend, it's no picnic for me, either."

Koster paused, then resumed: "So I went up into the bar . . . "

"Front steps or back steps?"

"Front steps, I went . . . "

So now there were three versions of the fight, Whippletree thought. First, Bauch had come down on his own and beaten Koster in back of the Valmar. Second, Koster had obstructed Bauch's access to his Grand Prix, and picked the fight, and third . . .

" . . . inside and walked up to him at the bar. He was drinking something. It smelled terrible. The place was full of tobacco smoke and the smell of grease. When he saw me, he laughed . . . oh, God, I know that laugh. That night. That's why I know he did it, if you'd just *believe* me . . ."

"I've got an open mind." *Haven't I? I do have, don't I?*

" . . . and I asked him to step outside with me. That I wanted to talk to him. He laughed again and said what about? I said it's private. There were maybe a dozen people in the place, and he waved his arm around, including them all, and said, 'These people know all about me, and I don't want secrets,' or something like that, and, 'Now you come on out with it and tell old Denny what's on your little mind? God, the tone of voice he uses . . .'"

"I know."

"So I told him I didn't want my children having to see sinful acts going on right under their noses. You know what he *said*? He said tell them not to look then, and he hit me."

"Right there in the bar?"

190

"As God is my witness. Of course, I wouldn't expect any of those others to support me. To give the same story. They were on his side the whole time . . ."

His jaw tightened, and he worked the upper row of teeth against the lower, full of pain at the memory of his humiliation. " . . . and they cheered while he was punching me around. I tried to get out the front, but they wouldn't let me, and finally I . . . " his voice was breaking " . . . struggled to the back, but he followed me out and kept hitting me. At last I staggered away . . ." Whippletree took it in. He recalled Lynn Betters's observations about Bauch.

"Then why, if he beat you up," he asked, "would he have also waited all summer to attack your family?"

The answer was immediate. "Because that's the way he *is*, don't you see? He won't let a thing rest."

"And, of course, you'd been giving your sermons all summer. The tough ones. At least until the one you were supposed to give this Sunday."

Koster looked puzzled, then remembered: "Yes, 'The Lord Shall Give Acceptance and Grant Us Rest.' "

"That doesn't sound too tough to me. Why the change back to the old way?"

"I was . . . I guess I . . . well, after I saw my father, things kind of fell into place, and I felt better."

"Well, you know, Reverend, I don't mean to pry, but I've heard things didn't go very well . . . between your wife and your father, in particular, and then I've heard stories about your life with your father in Montana . . ."

Koster looked at him with an expression much like that of surprise, but it was more than surprise, something else. A cool appraisal, wary and alert.

"You sure have been asking questions. Only, please ask people who *really* know me. Like Mrs. Hockapuk."

"What I just told you I heard from Lynn Betters."

Koster looked shocked, stunned. "No . . . " he murmured, "No, she . . . anyway, I went to Montana alone," he said, "after my father visited us here. We patched things up then. I felt better after that."

"Yet in the same week you did a pretty hard piece of business to a young boy."

"Fensterwald," Koster said, biting it off unpleasantly. He thought about it a moment, then spoke vehemently. "I can't abide a person who cannot control himself sexually. There is a time and a place for . . ."

"Well, granted, the choir loft is probably neither, but you really didn't have to go and broadcast it all over."

"I wouldn't put it that way. I was safeguarding the morals of my church. That's my responsibility."

Whippletree sat back in his chair and said nothing for a little while, looking out the window and at the same time trying to keep an eye on Koster. It didn't take long before he realized Koster was doing the same thing to him, pretending to rest, but watching him all the while behind slitted eyes. *Well,* he thought, *I really don't believe it's Bauch, and he can sense it. Got a right to treat me a little suspicious.*

"I'll be leaving in a minute," he said then, "but I've got to know something. How come when you told me the fight story this time it had more details? You didn't go into this kind of thing before?"

Koster opened his eyes and gave the sheriff a level look that pleaded for understanding.

"I didn't . . . I didn't want to admit that I'd ever been inside that place. And I couldn't bring myself to talk about— what my boys had seen. They were *babies!* So young! And to have seen . . ."

"Nothing especially wrong with it, in my view."

"No, no, you *misunderstand.* It's beautiful. It's lovely, the *feeling* . . . but not when it's *them*, not when it's seen by . . ."

"You have anything in particular against Mary Prone?"

"Why?"

"You've been telling me the second one was either Abner Fensterwald or Mary Prone. How come you can't make up your mind? Maybe it was two other people entirely. How about old man Fensterwald, maybe, and his kid? Together?"

Koster considered it. "No," he said after a while. "I don't think so. Mr. Fensterwald is built differently than Bauch. But the young one . . . it . . . it could have been a boy or a woman . . . I . . . you have to remember there were no lights and I was scared."

"Right." Whippletree stood up, ran the rim of his hat through his big, gnarled fingers. Koster seemed to be relieved that he was going.

"So, anyway, you got things patched up with your father?"

Koster nodded.

"I like to see that. It's a hard thing, family. Family life. Problems." He thought it over, and although it was something he never talked about with anyone, not even Sarah anymore—it upset her too much—he said now, "You know, Reverend, when you lose a child, anywhere along the line, you lose everything."

Koster looked at him. Tears began to form in his eyes. They hovered on the long lashes, and pearled in the corners. "It might seem so," he said gently, as one would counsel another, "but we must remember . . . we must keep in our minds . . . that they have gone on to a fuller life."

Sure, Whippletree was thinking. He shouldn't have brought it up, shouldn't have reminded himself again. In his mind he saw the stone over the grave at the cemetery in Clearwater and the name Susan Whippletree chiseled on it—

Clearwater, oh, that was a good one, wasn't it, that was a joke—and how the sun had been out on that spring morning long ago, and how he had stood there at the side of the grave, hearing the far-off, diminished booming of the Mississippi, thinking *you killer, you bastard, you goddam killer* and they lowered the tiny coffin into Minnesota earth and his heart along with it.

"Well, Reverend, if I had my druthers, I'd just as soon of had that fuller life this time around."

Koster was sympathetic. "You must decide to have it," he said. "You can have it if you try."

Whippletree stepped out of the room, into the corridor. For some reason, he was thinking of one of the phrases on Koster's sermon outline. *Set your face like flint.*

The Reverend seemed startled when Whippletree reappeared in the doorway. "Why, sheriff, I . . ."

"Nothing much. Just one last thing. I just wondered what were those numbers?"

"Numbers? What numbers?"

"In your Bible with the sermon outline. There was another sheet of paper with some numbers on it."

Koster's eyes darkened suddenly, as his memory placed and found. "Oh, that's . . . those were references," he said wearily.

"From the Bible, right?"

"Yes."

"That's what I thought. For your sermon."

Koster nodded, closed his eyes.

"Take it easy now, hear?" the sheriff said. "We'll wrap this up yet."

Abner Fensterwald looked in a lot worse shape than Koster, both physically and mentally.

"He's all yours," Nicky Rollis said, smiling a little and getting up. He'd been sitting on one side of young Fensterwald's bed, and on the other side, shorthand pad out and at the ready, was one of Rollis's pneumatic secretaries. A disgusted-looking staff physician leaned against the wall by the window, arms crossed.

"Except he can't say anything," Rollis added, suppressing a laugh. "Okay, Barbie. Get back to the office, type that up, and shoot a copy over to Mel."

"There be any point in asking what's going on here?"

"You can always ask, sheriff. It's up to the defendant, I guess. See you." Rollis swaggered out, preceded by the rump-twitching amanuensis.

The doctor said nothing, put his hands out, palms upward, in a what-can-you-do gesture.

Rollis stuck his head back in the door. "Oh, Emil, the kid's waived his right to an attorney. It's all set with his old man, too."

Defendant? Right to an attorney? What the hell was going on? But before he could shape a question, the counsel was gone.

"It's a rotten business," the doctor said quietly. "You need me here for anything?"

"Is he all right?" the sheriff asked, meaning Fensterwald.

"Better than he's got any right to expect, after what's happened to him. And what's going to."

"Can I talk to him?"

"No harm in trying. Do you need me?"

Whippletree shook his head, and the doctor eased out. "How you doin', son?" the sheriff asked.

195

Pointless question. Young Fensterwald lay face downward on the hospital bed, and under the thin white gown Whippletree could see the gauzy strips of bandage. Abner's face was sallow and his complexion a blank, save for acne scars. He was a scarred kid, all right, and it was going to get worse.

"Son, you haven't let them talk you into anything, have you?"

No response, not a motion for a minute, then: "What the hell difference does it make? I don't give a damn what happens to me."

Adolescent despair, but real. "You should," Whippletree said. "Now, did they sell you a bill of goods?"

"A lot you could do about it, even if they did."

"Where's your father?"

"I don't know."

"Has he been here?"

"No. And I don't want him, either."

"You should have somebody. How about your mother?"

"He won't let her come. Anyway, I don't care. It's better this way. I'll be out in five years, and then I'll go someplace where nobody can . . . "

Whippletree did not want to believe what he knew he was going to hear.

"What are you talking about? Five years?"

"That's what that guy promised. That Rollis guy. He said if I fingered Denny Bauch as my partner, I wouldn't get no more than five years, and the first two down in Red Wing, instead of the adult prison."

The sheriff felt his breath go out of him, and a sick hollow formed down in his stomach.

"Son, do you know what you're saying?"

"Yeah," said Abner dully. "And it doesn't make a bit of difference. It's a good thing, really. I'll get away from home."

Whippletree thought it over. *So, you did it again.* So insistent had he been with Rollis and Betters earlier this morning that they had paid heed to his warning. The case could not stand without the alleged accomplice, especially not now, after the story of two killers had been in all the *Tribune* stories. So they'd gotten themselves another person from Lake Eden, who had a motive, who had access to the shotgun, and who, moreover, had already admitted bringing it to the church. *You've got to find out about those shells,* he thought. *It's one of the only leads left, along with that missing .22 rifle.*

Whippletree was probably the only man, woman or child in Stearns County who didn't believe the weapon found in Bauch's trunk to be the one used in shooting Koster.

"It wasn't a good idea to agree to that," the sheriff told Abner gently.

"I don't care. It doesn't make any difference."

"Yes, it does. It's your *life*."

"Then I don't want it."

He thought for a moment. "You only took that one weapon from your father's collection?"

"One was enough, wasn't it?" Grimly.

"And you filed off the initials? Why?"

"Because I knew they were *there*, that's why. What else do you think?"

"When you took it, the shotgun, were any of the others missing?"

Abner thought a minute. "Yeah. But I didn't pay much attention."

So, that meant Bauch had been down there, doing his business sometime previously. He must have taken several guns, and unloaded all but the rifle. Did the fact that he'd kept it mean simply that he'd forgotten about it? Or did it mean he was absolutely not one of the killers? Or was it a trick? Bauch had that rude intelligence one finds in punks and petty thieves. No one would say he was smart, but nobody would say he was stupid, either. The kind of brain that has a maze of tricky grooves, and is always two steps to the right and one step up from where a normal, straight-thinking person would be if he were in the same situation.

"You didn't do it, did you?" Whippletree asked.

"No," Abner spat. "But who cares? What difference does it make, anyway? I don't even give a damn."

"Now, when . . . "

"I don't want to talk to anybody anymore, either." Fensterwald turned his face down into the pillow. In a moment, Whippletree could see his shoulders quivering rhythmically, but heard no sound.

"Don't worry, son," he said, putting his hand gently on the kid. "It's not over yet."

But, as if to signify the opposite, Abner shrugged him off, still buried in his own young hopelessness and innocent despair.

VIII

Back at his office, Whippletree made a few phone calls. All they proved was that things were no longer slipping away from him, they were being yanked away.

"Look," rasped old man Fensterwald over the wire. "They want to hang an abuse charge, or some such, on me. And that ain't true, dammit. I just did what had to be done under the circumstances. Discipline, I call it."

"But I thought you were satisfied that Abner wasn't the one who . . ."

"Yeah, but Emil, look. You got to consider how it's going to look to a jury. That Rollis told me about it. Mighty sharp boy. Going to go places. It's what they call "circumstantial," know what I mean? Abs has admitted everything but pulling the damn trigger."

"Where'd he get the shells?"

"That would be easy. He got 'em from Bauch. Bauch has got easy access to all that kind of stuff, being with the Rod and Gun . . ."

"It's your own *kid*, dammit!"

"That's what I'm thinking of, can't you see? Hell, Emil, you're an old farm boy just like me. You know the score. You got the horse sense you were born with, or at least I used to think you did. This way they give him a couple of years, and it's all over. Pleading guilty is the only way. He's in it up to his ass, if not higher."

Whippletree remembered what Lynn Betters had said about Elwood. That he was "creepy." It was true that people out here in this part of Minnesota, many of them not so far removed from the iron exigencies of the frontier, could be extremely matter-of-fact about suffering and pain, even life and death. Many of them were still alive, and Elwood Fensterwald was one, who knew what it was like to awaken before dawn in a log and plank building, laughingly called a "house," with the temperature at forty degrees below and the January wind blowing snow under the eaves and even through the minute cracks in the chinks of the walls, who knew what it was like to shake the snow off your clothes before you dressed, to light a feeble fire in a small round metal stove, and shiver until you were warm. To live on salt pork during the winter, and not much else, and to see people die, children, women, men, because it was impossible to get through the snow and into town, impossible to get a doctor.

People died. It was a fact of life. Things happened, or things had to be done, and they had to be accepted. You could change them about as much as you could alter the necessity for twelve-, fourteen-, sixteen-hour days behind a team of horses, breaking sod in the humid summers of the Mississippi Valley, with the temperature at a hundred and four in the shade, and no time even to stand under it. There were still people who remembered the days when you fished and hunted to eat, and if you didn't have any luck, you would be hungry that day. Elwood Fensterwald had known these things, and so had the sheriff, and neither had forgotten. Oh, it was true that they were mellowed some, especially Whippletree, but the memory of those things, those days, was never far away, and with Elwood it was an outlook bleak and inflexible, that had at once led to his perfervid acquisitiveness, his prosperity, and to his unyielding, unsentimental regard for men, even his own flesh and blood.

Things happened, and things had to be done, and that was that.

"But did you know Abner *ever* to have anything doing with Denny Bauch?"

"How would I know? The kid never told me nothing. But he run that pickup all around. He had plenty of time and opportunity. Anyway, it's no matter. The powers that be, Rollis and Betters, have it locked up, and the kid went ahead and agreed to it. He'll testify it was Bauch who used the shotgun and he was the one shot Koster with the rifle. He agreed to do it. Maybe it'll make a man of him."

"But do *you* think he did it?"

There was a long silence on the line. "You know, Emil, I been thinking about that. And if he did it, it must have been Abs, because he's the only one I can think of out here who would miss at point-blank range."

200

And he was serious!

Whippletree was desperate now. He wasn't even thinking of himself anymore, or the election, or his pension. He was frightened, thinking instead of a giant pincers that had suddenly and inexplicably begun to close around him, and he was powerless not only to stop it but even to understand it. The Koster case. With Koster at the center, an enigma, and the ripples circling further and further, undiminishing, as in a pond, but sweeping into a mean red tide in the drowning pool that was Stearns County.

"And so what did Bauch do with the rest of your guns and stuff?"

"Where you been, Emil? He fenced them through a connection at the Brooten Rod and Gun. Bimbo was over there and found it out. Just stopped by here at the farm, on his way back to St. Cloud. He figures he can even get some of the stuff back for me. How about that Bimbo for you, hey?"

Yeah, how about that Bimbo!

"Well, Elwood, if anything else comes up, let me know."

"You'll be the first," rasped the older farmer, hanging up.

The sheriff put the phone down, too, leaned back in his chair, and put his feet on the office desk.

"Hey, Alyce, did they bring Bauch back from the courthouse yet?" The punk had been scheduled for arraignment before Judge Reisinger this morning.

Alyce, busy eating a cheese danish and reading *Modern Romances,* took a minute to register the question.

"Oh, yeah. The courthouse. Right. Lugosch and Farley took him over while you were at the hospital. Him and his lawyer."

So, Bauch had a lawyer. That meant, of course, a not-guilty plea. The circumstantial aspects of the case were all against Bauch, though, and Fensterwald would drive the nails into the coffin. But it would be a contested trial, a good hard-driving, *newsy* trial, and Betters would milk it for every drop of publicity. People of the county would eat it up.

"I wonder why they didn't bring Mary Prone into this?"

"Can't," said Deputy Ruehle, over-the-shoulder, from his place near the radio. "Bauch's lawyer is claiming Denny and Mary Prone are common-law, so she can't testify against him. They're going to stick with that Gull Lake camping trip story, though."

Whippletree was almost amused at the common-law ploy. How tricky and how stupid. That would hardly get much sympathetic response in St. Cloud or around the county, where people took the public appearance of strict morality very seriously, whatever else they might do behind closed doors. It could only be one lawyer.

"So he got Steinbrone, huh?"

Ruehle nodded.

Tricky Ricky Steinbrone. From Holdingford, a little town out in the country famous for "Red" Fritsch, Stearns County's greatest athlete, who had played one year of class "C" ball for a Yankee franchised team in North Dakota. And now famous for Steinbrone. It would be quite a trial, if you could call it that. Rollis would take him apart.

"How did Bauch pick him?"

"He was here when they brought Denny back from the hospital. The second time. After Bimbo "questioned" him. He offered his services and Denny bought it. You know, Denny doesn't look too hot."

"I believe it," Whippletree said. "Now you two try and keep it quiet for a couple minutes, will you? I got to go through my files."

They tried to cooperate, and he pulled out "The Koster Case," with his early jottings. He checked his list again.

Maybe he had something in there to explain everything, something he'd missed before. After all, they'd told him in Chicago that it often went that way, and in Chicago they ought to know.

1. A goody two-shoes murder? *Could still be that,* he thought, and unless there was a suspect who had not been uncovered, this item still left Bauch very much in the running. Who else might have resented the Reverend? He thought of the young minister, slim and sort of like—there was a word for it, "androgynous," but the sheriff didn't know it— both a young boy and a young woman. Who would most resent something like that? A he-man type?

2. Koster said something in a sermon that bugged somebody? That left Bauch, added Mary Prone, and did not exclude young Abner Fensterwald. And how many other people? *Jesus, if I only had more time. . . .*

3. Where is it? Something in the Koster house? Whippletree pretty much ruled this one out. It didn't hold water. The only thing he needed to find was the .22 used in shooting Koster, and if he found it, he might be capable of putting together an entirely new theory. He was still convinced it must be somewhere in or adjacent to the parsonage and church, because the shotgun had been left right where Abner had hidden it in the first place. *Had* some of those women seen him up there in the choir loft that afternoon? Checked and found the gun? What women had been there, at the Ladies' Auxiliary? *Check on this,* he noted for himself. And as he did, the possibility that another woman was involved dawned on him quite slowly, yet with definite shape. Bauch and another woman. He had been stupid! *Lynn Betters.* He could float this one easily enough as soon as they brought Denny back from the courthouse.

4. Koster in some unknown conflict with somebody? Same

answer here as with Items #1 and #2. If there was somebody, other than the handful of people stirred up around
Lake Eden, Whippletree didn't know it yet. Talk to more
people. Ask more questions. Talk to the guy's father in Montana . . . *Hey, that's something, but.* . . . But strange things
happen in life, and after Elwood Fensterwald, strange things
were not so difficult to believe.

Then he took out his old ball-point and wrote down another one: *Koster did it himself.* He did not trust the man, nor like
him, and he did not feel comfortable in his presence. Koster
had education, which the sheriff regarded as an agent pro-
ducing artificial subtlety, which in turn complicates the rela-
tionships between one person and another. Besides, *how*
could he have done it? And not only that, *why?* In order to do
what had been done, Koster would have had to kill his wife,
his love for whom there was ample evidence, and his children, his love for whom there was likewise proof, and then
not only shoot himself, but conceal a weapon he'd used (the
shotgun could have been returned to the music seat with no
trouble), and, wounded and bleeding, *tie himself to the laundry
poles, spread-eagled, hand and foot.*

It was the kind of thing Tricky Ricky Steinbrone might
dream up, thinking to get a client off the hook, which would
backfire, putting him away for a hundred years instead.

Or, it suddenly occurred to him, *maybe it was suicide, an attempt.* The minister, judging by his sermons, *was* going
through some kind of change during the summer.

He checked the notes for the sermons again, and the other
sheet of paper with the numbers on it.

QM 23 B46   QM 23.2 E48   QM 23 F713

Couldn't make head nor tail, hide nor hair, out of them.
"Alyce," he called. "We have a Bible in here?"

She looked up, a little dazed, as always. "A what?"

"A Bible. You know, with all those battles and begots in it."

"Oh. Oh. I don't know." She looked around among the procedural manuals and assorted bureaucratic debris. "Nope, don't look like it."

"Well, go on over to the JP in the courthouse and see if he has one."

She shuffled out, and he saw her cross the street and slowly climb the courthouse steps. Somebody she apparently knew stopped and started to talk to her, and the two of them sat down in the sun. Whippletree sighed, told the deputy to call over there and see if they had the Good Book.

"Which one's that?" Ruehle asked.

Whippletree told him. "And just get me the damn thing, will you? I might need it."

Ruehle, offended, muttered something about the sheriff needing more than that, but made the call anyway. Meantime, the sheriff's mind was busy on the guns. To prove that Elwood Fensterwald's .22 had *not* been used, or at least to cast doubt on what had by now become conventional wisdom, there would have to be and *have to be found* another .22, somewhere near the scene. It seemed impossible, since the place had been scoured twice. Well, let that wait. The other problem was the shotgun. Okay, so Abner had taken it into the church. Now, if he had not been the one to come back and use it, then it had been taken from the music seat by someone who knew it was there, used, and returned. Abner had been less than lucky, having been found up there with shells and gun, a discovery that had complicated the case no end. He thought of Abner, hopeless and despondent in the hospital, thinking his life over! Seventeen, and he thought his life was over! Ruthie Koster and Susan Whippletree had had just five years, too young to have known much else but happiness. It wasn't fair. The thought saddened and confused him, as always, and he put it out of his mind.

So, he thought, *if Abner came along and fouled up the possibility of a good clean logical solution . . .*

. . . *that* would mean whoever the murderer was knew about the shotgun, somehow, and unless someone else had entered the church that afternoon or evening, the only thing left to work on was the Ladies' Auxiliary. He knew *they* had been inside during the afternoon. On an impulse, he picked up the phone himself and called the hospital. He asked for Koster's room.

Surprisingly, the voice was eager, expectant, but when Whippletree gave his name, the minister could not quite conceal his disappointment.

"Who were you expecting?" Whippletree heard himself blurt.

Pause. "No one. It's just I like to get calls, cooped up in here."

Except from me. "I see. Just a quick question. Were you inside the church on the afternoon or evening of . . . of that day?"

"No. No, I . . . I was out . . . ah . . ."

He seemed about to say something, then decided against it.

"Where?"

"I had to visit some . . . counselees."

"I see. Who?" Whippletree persisted. Koster's distress was evident, but he was partially successful in maintaining the cool, even tone of his voice.

"Well, really sheriff, it's . . ."

"Confidential? But didn't you usually attend the Auxiliary meetings?"

"Sometimes. But if it happened that I had other duties . . . now, don't misread me, sheriff. I just didn't want to embarrass . . . no, it's all right. I did make a visit that afternoon, and it was to Miss Betters."

A switch clicked in Whippletree's mind, and the circuits of the Koster case brightened and hummed in his head.

"Didn't she normally have her sessions with the Tuesday group?"

Another pause. "Not that Tuesday. I had . . . had noticed some . . . ah . . . increased *laxity* in her . . . ah . . . behavior, and she hadn't been there that Tuesday. So I decided to make sure everything was . . . ."

This was taking a new turn. "Where did you meet her?"

"Oh, I went out to the house."

"Mel's house? On the lake."

"That's right."

"When was this?"

"Look, sheriff. I told you. It was in the afternoon. In fact, you may speak to Miss Betters about this. She was there . . . with a friend."

"What kind of a friend?"

"A . . . a man."

The circuits flashed and jumped. More connections were made. "Why didn't you tell me this before?"

"I . . . I didn't think . . . think of it, frankly, until you asked. It didn't seem . . . of particular significance . . . ."

"So, anyway, then you came back to the parsonage. What happened then?"

"Nothing. The afternoon and evening were entirely routine."

"And you didn't go into the church? For anything?"

"No. If there isn't a meeting, or choir practice, I generally stay in the house. The people know that's where my desk is."

"Okay, thanks, Reverend."

207

"Has this helped you any?" It seemed Koster really wanted to know.

"I don't know yet."

A good-looking young girl, her blonde hair pigtailed charmingly against the heat, was coming into the office, carrying a heavy book.

"Did you find the other .22 yet?" Koster was asking.

"No, no," the sheriff said, saying "Put it over here," to the girl.

"What?" the Reverend asked, confused.

"Got to go," Whippletree said, "somebody's here. Now, take it easy, Reverend," he said, hanging up. "An' what have we got here, young lady?"

"I hope this isn't some joke," she giggled, a little uncertainly, "but did you people need a Bible over here?"

"We sure as hell do," Whippletree boomed, and the girl laughed.

It made him feel good. He glanced at the numbers again, all those QM's and letters, and began to turn the pages of the Bible. Genesis, Exodus, Leviticus, Numbers, Deuteronomy, Joshua, Judges, Samuel, Kings, Ecclesiastes, Isaiah, Jeremiah, and so on all the way to Revelations. Nope, there was nothing in there that started with a "Q."

Wondering, he leaned back in his chair and scratched his head. "Hey, Alvin, you know much about this here Bible?"

"Can't say as I do, sheriff. I'm a Catholic. You better ask somebody who's a Protestant. They read the Bible all the time, I hear."

Bimbo was a Protestant, but the sheriff counted him out, along with Alyce Pelser, whom he saw now getting up and coming *down* the courthouse steps, saying good-bye to her friend. Hadn't even been inside! Probably'd forgotten what the hell she was over there for.

He turned idly through the pages once more, going backward, and checked the chunks of italicized abbreviations on the bottoms of the pages. Couldn't find much there either. He debated calling Koster again—the minister had said the numbers were references for sermons—but he didn't want to give him the satisfaction of knowing the Stearns County sheriff was buffaloed by a couple of jottings. Anyway, what the hell difference could it make?

Alyce Pelser came in. "They ain't got one, sheriff."

Whippletree sighed. The pigtailed girl had gone back to the courthouse, so he said, "No, Alyce, you got it all wrong. The Bible's right *here,* an' I wanted you to take it over *there.* You forgot it, is all. Understand?"

She turned that around for a while, sort of like a cow waiting for the cud to come up. "Oh," she cried finally, "I see," and started back across the street again. The sheriff watched her for a little ways, and then out of a side door of the courthouse, on street level, came a hustling body of men. The arraignment of Denny Bauch was concluded, and he was on his way back to jail. In front came Bimbo, who was wearing his prize hat. It made him look like a state trooper or a Canadian Mountie. Bimbo didn't even look as he started across the street. Why should he? What car could withstand the impact? And behind him, hunched and manacled, in spite of the big white bandage on his hand, was Denny Bauch. The heavyset guy beside him, walking with a chin-in-the-air swagger, would be his lawyer, "Tricky " Ricky Steinbrone, whose law degree, Whippletree felt, was little more than a license to steal from his hapless clients. Behind client and attorney were Lugosch and Pollock, proud and alert with their hands on pistolbelts, and then a couple of guys from the *Tribune,* one writing in a note pad, the other trying to get in a good angle for a picture. Just then, the photographer ran on out ahead and knelt in front of the little caravan. The sheriff could see the flash of the bulb in spite of the raw morning sun. He could also see the caption underneath the picture this afternoon: "'Bimbo' Bonwit Escorts Suspected Killer."

Well, nothing to do but go on down to the cell block and see if Bauch would know anything.

"I'm afraid my client will not be answering any questions," Attorney Steinbrone pronounced. He said everything in a slow, deliberate way, and in a very deep voice. Where Nicky Rollis was verbose, Steinbrone was baroque. Where Rollis was babbling or dazzling, depending upon your taste in rhetoric, "Tricky" Ricky was portentous, heavy with false drama. He could make ordering a cup of coffee at the bar-and-grill an act of weight and wonder. Now he lifted his chin—chins, actually: he had three—and veiled his eyes and repeated, "I'm afraid my client will not be answering any questions. As you know, *Sher-iff Whip-pull-tree,* many of his rights have already been *vi-o-lat-ed,* and even should, through some egregious mischance, a conviction occur, I have assured my client that an appeal will almost certainly reverse . . ."

"Hey, Denny ," Whippletree called through the bars to the hangdog Bauch, "can I talk to ya a minute?"

Bauch spat in the commode and nodded.

Tricky Ricky hadn't missed a beat. ". . . however, if, on his own *vo-lit-shun* and absence of duress, the client wishes to . . ."

"Open the cell, Bimbo, then go over and handle the office. Ricky, you stick around. I want you to hear every damn thing, so it doesn't get changed around later on."

"But . . . but," Bimbo put in, "them reporters upstairs want a chance to interview Denny."

"That seems to me a fine idea, Mr. Bauch," Steinbrone said. "It will give us a wonderful opportunity to win public sympathy in the face of . . ."

"Denny, you can do what you want," Whippletree advised curtly, "but you know who runs the *Trib,* don't you?"

Bauch, who didn't exactly look scared, except when Bimbo got close to him, but who did look a little sick and disgusted, spat again, this time on the floor.

"Fuck the paper," he said. "I ain't goin' to be no freak. An' take off these damn cuffs, will ya? I don't intend on goin' nowhere."

The manacles were removed, and the sheriff and Steinbrone were let inside the cell.

"You can think what you want of me, Denny," Whippletree began, "but I'm probably one of the only people in the county who figures you didn't do it. They're gonna do a job on you, you know that?"

"Now, I beg to differ . . . " Steinbrone said.

Bauch just nodded and lit up a cigarette.

"You know why?"

"Yeah, 'cause of me an' that Betters bitch."

"Tell me a few things. You know young Fensterwald? Elwood's kid?"

"I guess I'm supposed to," the punk said cynically, French-inhaling, " 'cause me an' him did the killing."

He eased a look at Whippletree out of slitted eyes, trying to read him.

"I'm serious. Do you know him? Ever met him?"

Bauch gave a straight look now. "Sheriff, I was up near Brainerd the night Koster was hit. With Mary. An' that's the goddamn truth. I wouldn't know Abner Fensterwald from a used rubber."

Whippletree nodded. "See?" said Steinbrone triumphantly. "See!"

"Do you know a couple of kids saw you banging Mary in the trailer once, last June? Koster's kids, they were."

Bauch put his head back and puffed reflectively, trying to sort out this one time from all the other times. Then a slow smile. "Yeah, I remember. The little bastards came snoopin'

211

around. I knew they was there, titterin' an' hangin' around the door." He grinned. "I gave them quite a show."

"Did Mary know they were watching?"

"Huh? What?" He grinned again. "Hell, sheriff, I wasn't with Mary. That was Lynn Betters I was puttin' it to."

It was the sheriff's turn to be surprised. "Was this before or after that time I got called out to pick you up because of the Grand Prix thing?"

"Oh, this was a couple of weeks *before*. We had a thing goin', Lynn an' me, just a little somethin' on the side, see? After you got us that time in the car, Mary slammed the lid down, an' I had enough sense not to mess with Betters anymore."

"Mel or Lynn?"

"Both."

"Where were you afternoon of the killings?"

"In the club. Knockin' 'em back."

"Until?"

"Until around suppertime. When we headed north for Brainerd."

"Then you weren't at Lynn's place on the lake at any time that afternoon?"

Bauch tossed his cigarette into the john in the corner of the cell. "What's this anyway, sheriff? What the hell . . ."

"I believe he's trying to implicate you . . ." Steinbrone started.

"Screw off," Bauch told him, "and spend your time thinking of something to get me out of this. No," he said to the sheriff. "I swear it. After that time in my car, that was it. The old endo, man."

He made a pass with his hand, palm down, a semi-circle in front of him, the "cool" gesture for negative, no way, etc. Whippletree believed him. Yet, Koster had said, there was a "man" friend of Lynn's, one Whippletree didn't know about, who *had* been at the lake on the afternoon of the killings. Who was he? And what, if anything, would it have to do with Bauch? After all, Lynn had been almost adamant in her assertion that Denny could not have been involved. Was this something new? Or merely another dead-end lead, like most of the others seemed to have been.

"My client assures you that he is totally in-no-cent," Steinbrone orated, leaning back against the concrete wall of the cell. A four-letter obscenity, misspelled "FUKE" emblazoned the wall on one side of his head, and part of a telephone number trailed out from behind the other side. "When the case is called, you and the rest of the county can be firmly confident that . . ."

"When's the case going up?"

"Right after Labor Day."

Whippletree was astounded. "A murder trial that still hasn't got rhyme or reason, and they're giving you less than three weeks to get ready for it?"

"We shall prevail, withal," Tricky Ricky said, sounding, for once, less than confident. "There are cases in one's life when time is not of the essence . . ."

"Bullshit," Bauch spat, lighting up again, with some difficulty because of his hand. "They're gonna put me away for plenty of time. I wish they had the chair, or somethin', in this here state."

He blew out some smoke and thought it over.

"But that poor son-of-a-bitch Fensterwald kid," he said then. "He's the one who's gonna get it in the balls."

They all stood there in the cell for a moment, not looking at each other.

"I wonder why," Bauch said.

"I know a lot of men," Lynn smiled. Her eyes teased and mocked. "I like them. In *all* ways. Why, don't you like women, sheriff?"

Whippletree, through something close to divine inspiration, had checked in St. Cloud before taking another long drive to Lake Eden. Well, it wasn't all that hard, either. He'd just checked the bars. He tracked her down to a back table in the dimly lit Griffin cocktail lounge in the Germain Hotel in St. Cloud. She was with a sleek, slick-haired smoothie named Butler, from Duluth. His manners were perfect, his grammar correct, his clothing quiet and expensive. He was even polite when Whippletree interrupted his *tête-à-tête* with Lynn.

The sheriff looked at Butler and wondered why all he could think of was Denny Bauch.

"Women are fine," he said, feeling uncomfortable. He had the suspicion that he was being used in some kind of teasing game the couple had been playing just before he showed up.

"See?" Lynn said, giving Butler a playfully provocative nudge. The man gave a male grimace of a smile. *Touché.* "Would you care for something, sheriff? Drink? A beer?"

"No, thanks, I've got to get out to Lake Eden again, and this won't take long . . ."

"If you had a . . . let's see now . . . maybe a . . . I know, a *helicopter,*" Lynn said gleefully, "it would take only fifteen minutes to . . ."

"I know. But I don't. There are only two questions this time."

Butler looked interested, but impassive. Lynn toyed with her swizzle stick, waiting.

"We can talk alone," the sheriff offered, with an apologetic glance at Butler, who smiled as if he could care less.

"It's all right," Lynn assured.

Okay. Here goes. "On the afternoon of the Koster shootings," Whippletree asked, "you were with some man, out at the Lake house. Who was it?"

Miss Betters looked surprised. "Why . . . ?"

"It was I," Butler said. "Can I be of help in any way?"

"No . . . ah, no," the sheriff replied, a little nonplussed. "But, tell me, did the Reverend show up while you were there?"

Lynn gave her low, gurgling conspiratorial laugh that both let you into the plot and left you out of it.

"Poor old Matt," she said. "He was worried that Daddy would be after me, because I'd been slacking off on my 'treatment.' But," she went on, leaning into Butler suggestively and squeezing his biceps, "I'd just been unable to *make it* that week . . ."

Butler smiled.

"And where were the two of you that night?"

"Down in Bloomington, at the Twins game," Butler said smoothly.

Lynn nodded.

Okay. Okay. Alibi.

"When the Reverend was there, at your lake place, how did he seem?"

"I don't get you,"Lynn said.

"I mean, was he any . . . any different? How did he act?"

"He seemed like a nice guy to me, sheriff," Butler volunteered. "Just like anyone else. He might not even have been a clergyman."

"Well," Lynn said. "He seemed about normal, maybe a little more worried than usual."

"Worried?"

"Oh, I know that's not the right word. That's as close as I can get, but . . ."

"I would say," Butler put in, "that the man was under some kind of strain."

"What do you do for a living, Mr. Butler, if I can ask?"

"You can. You have," Butler said. "I don't do anything, frankly."

"That's why you can recognize 'strain' in others, is that it?"

Whippletree was unable to keep a tone of distaste out of his voice. Butler caught it, but didn't care, and laughed pleasantly.

"I thought he was a little tense, sheriff, that's all."

"He was the same as ever," Lynn said again.

"How long did he stay at the house?"

They both laughed. "About a half-hour," Lynn said."He kept worrying about whether I was coming in again, and when, and if maybe we could set up another kind of schedule. So Dad wouldn't throw a fit. He talked to Paul a lot . . ." nodding towards Butler " . . . wanting to know what he did, and all that . . ."

"His reaction was about the same as yours, sheriff," Butler said.

" . . . and we laughed just before because, well, when he showed up, we were . . . busy . . ."

They smiled at each other.

"Just like you were in Mary Prone's trailer last June?"

Lynn's face went stiff and blank in an instant.

"Oh, Bauch," Butler said easily, in a throwaway manner. "I know all about him. That's in the past, isn't it?"

She didn't miss a lead or a trick, leaned against him and cooed that yes, yes, it was in the past, and that well, really now gee, hadn't she all of her past to bring to him, and didn't he think it was worthwhile?

Whippletree left them there, in the cocktail lounge, busy with nothing but their pleasure, past, present, and to come.

It was difficult for him to understand, and when he crawled into the sun-heated oven of his parked patrol car, he suddenly remembered a county fair he'd gone to, when he was nine or ten and his father was still alive. All he had had to spend was a quarter, and it had been a fortune to him then, because it had been needed dearly by the family, had been given him by his father at great sacrifice. And then he remembered the barn dances of his later youth, when there was nothing but a two-bit band who would play for corn whiskey, the corn whiskey itself stimulant, entertainment, and medium of exchange, and he remembered meeting Sarah and finally, after months, getting her to go off alone with him into the stand of birch out behind the dance hall. He didn't even kiss her then, of course. It was much too soon, and besides he was scared. Getting her out there alone with him in the first place was courage enough and proof of love enough.

He remembered these things, and he remembered the county when it had been another world. Not any better, probably, and certainly less comfortable, but cleaner, newer, purer. Or was that only the trick of age, enticing him against his will to the happy thoughts, and away from the grave in Clearwater, on the green rising banks against which the killer Mississippi rolled? He shook his head. No, it was a true memory, and not a trick. There had been the good times, too.

He thought of the slick, idle young couple in the Griffin Room, bright and aimless, empty of need or desire. He thought of himself as a ragged young man who had once, once at least, possessed a sense of wonder.

And he knew how lucky he had been.

X

"Yes, sheriff, I've been waiting for you," the little lady announced primly. "In fact, I wondered why you haven't been around sooner. I *am* the social chairman of the Auxiliary, you know."

The sheriff stood out there on the screened-in front porch, his hat in his hand, contriving to look contrite.

"Well, you'd best come in, I guess," she chirped. "I cleaned the whole house just on account of it. Your visit, I mean."

He stepped into a shocking parlor. Never in his life had he seen so much furniture, so many toy plastic animals, so many lamps. And so *clean!*

"You should have come sooner," she was saying. "You see, I was waiting for you. I didn't dare tell a soul."

Whippletree gave her a look of interest. *Another little old church lady with a life of great importance. Sure.*

"You see," she said, chirping on unhindered, "I'm the one who saw young Fensterwald with the gun."

Just a little stunned by this news, Whippletree felt his way in among a maze of love seats and ottomans and found a place on an overstuffed chair. Mrs. Withers—wife of old Pete Withers, who ran the sawmill in Fair Haven—sat down in front of him, beaming.

"When exactly was this?" he heard himself asking. "I mean, if you'd let me know . . ."

"Oh, I didn't know it *then,*" she said quickly, still beaming. "*Then* I thought he was fixing the organ."

"*What?*"

"Maybe I'd better tell you about it."

"That would be nice."

"Well," she sputtered, fluffing her feathers a little and

ready to get into it, "It was on the day of the . . . on the day of that horrible thing . . ."

They had all been in the church, the Ladies' Auxiliary Group, to discuss plans for the annual picnic, raffle, and bazaar later in the summer. Mrs. Hockapuk had chaired the meeting. She was the president of the Auxiliary. Did the sheriff know that? He knew it now. Anyway, that afternoon the Reverend hadn't been able to make it—out on a call, or something, Bonnie had said—and they all went into the church and sat down. Now, they sat in the back of the church, kind of informal, you know? And, as it happened, most of them were sitting beneath the overhang of the choir loft. All except Mrs. Hockapuk, chairing the meeting out in front, and herself, Mrs. Withers.

"So I kept hearing this faint noise," she said, "like somebody was up there, moving around. I didn't want to say anything—might have been my imagination—and anyway I didn't want to interrupt the meeting. So what I did was this. I took out my compact, with the little mirror in it, and pretended to check my face. And there in the reflection I saw the Fensterwald boy holding what seemed to be a length of pipe!"

Her voice rose as she ended her sentence, and she looked at Whippletree shrewdly, waiting for applause.

"And that's all?" he said, before he could stop himself.

She looked hurt. "Isn't that enough? I saw him *there*. With the *gun*."

"I'm sorry, maybe I'm missing something here. You just said it was a piece of pipe."

"Of course, that's what I thought it was at the time. A piece of pipe. But don't you see, it was *actually* the barrel of the gun!"

"Ah . . . yes."

"And the reason I didn't report it to you was that I didn't know it was the gun until later, after I heard about the murders. I thought the young man was repairing the organ. I thought it was an *organ* pipe, you see, and . . ."

Now he understood. In her compact mirror, she had seen young Abs, with the shotgun broken down, holding only the barrel part of it in his hand. "Now I get it," he said.

"I was sure you would. Isn't that something, how a nice young boy can suddenly go berserk, and . . . ?"

"But didn't it surprise you? To see him in church? I thought everybody knew that the Reverend had removed him as organist."

"Hortense told me that later," she said, blushing, and looking away. "I was visiting my sister in Kandiyohi County when it happened, and later, after the meeting, I told Mildred . . ."

"Who is Mildred?"

"Why, Mrs. Hockapuk, the librarian, of course. Sheriff, you're slipping a little, aren't you, now . . ."

I'll say.

" . . . when I told her, she said now, Bernice, I'm glad you saw him because he shouldn't be up there at all. He did a filthy thing and the Reverend had to take action, *had to take action,* she said, I recall her very words, and he shouldn't be up there. We'll have to tell the Reverend the next time we see him, she said. And we did, that first time we visited the hospital. But by then it was too late . . ."

She lowered her eyes sadly. Whippletree was remembering Koster's initial confusion over the possible identity of the second attacker: Mary Prone or Abner Fensterwald. Maybe these women, with their story of Abner in the choir loft, had confused the minister, swayed him, during a moment of panic and despair, to put the finger on the young man. If so, the sheriff thought he might be able to fashion a way to help Fensterwald, but it was too early yet.

"Who were the women at the meeting?" he asked.

"Why, the whole group. Mildred. Myself. Mrs. Janeway and Trudy Benoit and Mrs. Rehnquist. Mrs. Ahlers was there, too, and Florence Duckworth. Her boy Clem is such a nice young man, don't you think?"

Whippletree nodded politely, and his mind ran out ahead of him, picturing long red skinny Clem and his big Adam's apple atop raunchy little Trixie Wade.

"What about Lynn Betters?"

Mrs. Withers paused. "No, she wasn't there, come to think of it. She was pretty good about coming all summer, but that day she wasn't . . ."

"What do you think of Miss Betters?"

Mrs. Withers ducked her head, half-embarrassed, half-coy. "People can change, you know, sheriff. I'd heard many a nasty story about that young lady, but I think the Reverend brought her around."

"Brought her around?"

"Helped her, you know, *change.* Here she'd been running around for a couple of years, mother gone, father too busy, and too much money and boys, besides, but Reverend Koster, he helped her. We thought he did *so* well."

"Just with Lynn?"

"Oh, no, you don't understand, you don't understand." She stopped and then made her big pronouncement. "Reverend Koster is one of the finest men I've ever had the privilege to know. I'd do *anything* for him."

She was very heavy on the anything.

He had a sudden suspicion. "Mrs. Withers . . ."

"Call me Bernice."

"Bernice, will you be testifying at the trial?"

"Oh, yes, of course," she said happily. "I'll be there. County Attorney Rollis spoke to me on the phone just before you came. I'll tell him just what I told you. It was Abner Fensterwald who did it, don't you see? Abner and that wicked Dennis Bauch. High time somebody put him away, going down and up Main Street in that car . . ."

"Can you think of anybody else who might have had reason to attack the Kosters?"

"Only that woman from the tavern. But that can't be, because I *saw* the young man with the gun on the *day* of the killings!"

Again, she waited for applause. He gave her a big smile and she seemed satisfied. The circle was closing on the Koster case, and there didn't seem to be much he could do about it.

"Do you think Mrs. Hockapuk would be over at the library right about now?"

Bernice checked her kitchen clock. "Yes, until five-thirty, but why?"

"I thought I'd talk to her. Never know what you might find out."

This activated Mrs. Withers's competitive instincts. "But *she* didn't see anything. *I* did."

"It's just my job," he hastened to soothe. "I just have to check almost everything I can think of."

"Oh. Oh, *yes,*" she said doubtfully.

"*Yas?*" asked Mrs. Hockapuk, the librarian, in a dry, nasal, imperial tone. She was a large, stern-faced, white-haired lady who dominated the Lake Eden branch of the Stearns County library, a one-story beige-brick structure behind lilac hedges, just off the road to the lake. A frequent recipient of the Andrew Carnegie Service Award, for never having lost a book or missed the collection of a late-penalty fine, her suspicious, piercing stare and the belligerent cast of her jaw tended to discourage circulation, and had pretty well reduced her pale skinny assistant, Miss Vivian Whippet, to quivering neurosis.

"*Yas?*" demanded Mrs. Hockapuk once more.

"I'd like to ask you a couple of questions," Whippletree said, realizing that he had actually whispered. There was no one in the library, except Miss Whippet, who, upon seeing him, flashed a terrified smile and scurried off among the stacks.

"Speak up, sheriff," Mrs. Hockapuk encouraged. "What about?"

"The Reverend Koster." His voice was almost normal now.

She nodded curtly and came out from behind the semi-circular desk. "Miss Whippet, take charge of the desk," she commanded, and although there seemed little to be done, the furtive assistant reappeared and hurried over, in a kind of ducking slouch, as if waiting to be struck.

"We shall sit here," Mrs. Hockapuk directed, leading the sheriff to a sturdy, polished table among ranks of file cabinets. Everything from A to Z, the sheriff figured, getting in a surreptitious look. He always felt overwhelmed and ill-at-ease in places like libraries and schools, rather like he'd once felt as a kid in church. He figured it was because of his lack of formal education.

"What do you wish to know?" he was asked.

"Just a few things, actually. I understand you're President of the Ladies' Auxiliary?"

"I certainly am."

"And you know the Reverend pretty well, do you?"

"I certainly do. I have worked closely with him from the time he arrived in Lake Eden. A fine man. No finer."

"Who do you think did . . . ?"

She interrupted him. She surprised him. "Sheriff," she said, "as far as I'm concerned, there is no way to know for sure. Yet."

His glance must have been astonished. She went on.

"I make it a point to wait and get the facts straight. That is a result of my education and rigorous training. Detail. When you are in my line of work, you must be *obsessed* with detail. To my way of thinking, there are not enough details yet to make a judgment."

Whippletree found himself liking her. Of course, it is hard not to like somebody who shares your opinions.

"Mrs. Withers told me she saw the Fensterwald boy . . ."

"Oh, *Bernice!*" said Mrs. Hockapuk, waving it away. "She gets so excited. I had to tell the Reverend Koster about the boy in the choir loft, had to do it myself. I couldn't trust her not to get everything all upset . . ."

"You told him in the hospital?"

"No, I called him on the phone. Later that afternoon, on the day of the Auxiliary meeting. I told him Bernice thought that she had seen young Fensterwald up in the loft with an organ pipe. Now, isn't that absurd?"

"When was this?"

"Just at closingtime, five-thirty, on that same day."

"He was at home?"

"Of course, he was at home. He had been out on a call, but he had returned."

"How did he react when you told him?"

"He seemed very interested. Not upset. Almost amused. He said he would check on it, but that it was surely nothing to worry about—Abner Fensterwald was not a malicious boy, whatever other faults he may have had."

"What did you think when you learned there was a gun found up there? Which had been used in the killings?"

"I didn't think anything. Anyone might have put the gun there. Or, if Fensterwald's story is true, it is still quite possible that someone else used the weapon. It remains to be proven in court."

"You'll testify?"

"That's ridiculous. What about?"

He saw her attitude. It was all hearsay to her, at least so far. "Well, if I might ask, what is your personal . . ." he didn't want to say something vague, like "opinion," so he said, " . . . *appraisal* of Reverend Koster?"

"As I indicated previously, a fine man, intelligent. Well-read. He was a regular here, and read widely in many areas. It showed in the depths of his sermons. An astounding accomplishment for one of his age and origins. I had occasion to meet his father, who was, in my estimation, a cave dweller. He came from Montana on a visit, did you know?"

"I've been told."

"A cave dweller. At any rate, his son was superior. Clearly superior. Personally, just between the two of us, I didn't care for his wife."

"Bonnie? You didn't?"

"No, I didn't. She was too slow for him. Of course, Koster is young, too. He'll develop. If he has one fault at present, it is that he is not really a good judge of people. He does poorly in reading their motives. And even here, in Lake Eden," she said, smiling for the first time, but smiling with an edge to it, "people have their motives."

"You're right there." She affirmed her own wisdom. "Now if there's anything else? It *is* almost five-thirty . . ."

"When was the last time you saw the Reverend?" he asked, while she guided him out.

"At the hospital yesterday. He is taking this very, very hard."

"I know, but I meant before it happened?"

"Well, let's see. He couldn't make the meeting that afternoon, because of a call."

"Do you know who it was he had to see?"

"He didn't have to see her—but I do know. It was Miss Betters."

She spoke the name with intense, but refined distaste.

"Don't care for the young lady?"

"Sheriff, I am not in the business of making moral judgments. If a young woman wishes to offer herself to whomsoever comes down the pike, that is her business, but when she corrupts the purposes of the church, which is a serious institution, then I say she has gone too far."

They were standing by the door now. The sheriff could smell the odor of lilac leaves baking in the sun. "She corrupted the church?"

"Well, she was pretending to all of us, so that, apparently, her father would restore certain privileges. That was what I thought, at any rate. And when I saw her car outside the church on my walk home from work that night, I . . ."

"What night?"

"The night of the shootings. It was about six-forty-five. I had had a bite to eat at Rehnquist's, and I was walking home as usual."

"Her car was there?"

"Yes, and she was, too. They were standing by the door of the church. She and a man."

Whippletree felt excited, for some unknown reason. This was something he had not known, but how it fitted into the framework—or even *if* it did—remained vague and elusive.

"Could you describe the man?"

"I certainly could. He was fairly tall, of good build. He was

226

dark, had dark hair. The two of them were dressed in tennis regalia. At church!"

Butler, Whippletree thought. *But why . . . ?*

"Then you went home?"

"I certainly did. I went right home and called the Reverend again, and told him two *individuals* were hanging around out in front of the church."

"What did he say?"

"He didn't say anything."

"Why not?"

"Because he wasn't there. He was out on another call."

"You talked to Bonnie? Where was he?"

"Yes. She didn't say. All she said was that he'd been called out again. I asked her to look out the window and see if those people were still in front of the church, and she did, or she said she did, and told me no, they weren't."

"You're certain it was Lynn Betters?"

"Yes, Lynn and a man."

"Would you be able to identify him again?"

"I am sure of it. He gave me one of those idiot grins that silly young men who think they are smart and good-looking give to women like me. They think it will melt us down."

The sheriff did not have to ask if Butler's grin had been successful.

"So that was the last contact, or attempted contact, I had with the parsonage before the murders," Mrs. Hockapuk concluded.

The seed of a possibility began to send tender shoots into the soil of Whippletree's mind. "Would you testify to what you've just told me?"

Mrs. Hockapuk raised her chin. "I don't see how it is of much importance. Lynn Betters is a jack rabbit and so, I assume, are her companions, but . . ."

227

"Well, let that lie, for now. But would you? Testify?"

"As I indicated, I am not sure I have . . ."

"Bernice Withers is testifying. Nicky Rollis apparently called her earlier today."

Mrs. Hockapuk crossed her formidable arms and thought that over. "If called," she pronounced slowly, "I will most certainly do my duty."

XI

When Whippletree stopped in at the office, everybody was pretty quiet, and when he saw the headlines in the *Tribune,* he understood why. At home, Sarah was too dispirited to say much either, but at least there weren't any tears. "You'll just have to do the best you can," was all she said. "I'm sure you will," she added.

He just read the headlines; he already knew what the assorted stories would contain.

GRAND JURY INDICTS FENSTERWALD, BAUCH, IN KOSTER CASE;

ATTORNEY ROLLIS TO DEMAND LIFE SENTENCES FOR BOTH

Trial Set to Begin on September 8

Fensterwald to plead Guilty;
Waives Right to Counsel.

Koster to Testify at Trial;
Lake Eden Minister "Better."

The Fields of Eden

But Mel Betters was not just a one-word man, and he said more than just "silly." Unfortunately, he said it in a page-one black-margined editorial, such as he usually reserved for great events, like presidential assassinations, the victory of any local sports team, or the imminent failure of the soybean crop.

Time To Call It Quits?

Call For An Act Of Leadership

Public life and publishing are alike in one transcendent respect: they possess duties and responsibilities that are at once painful and necessary. More often than we realize, the passage of time and the infrequency of actual crisis in an area as blessed as Stearns County can give the illusion, both to individuals and to the citizenry at large, that all is well in their government. Such is usually, but not always, the case, and it is not the case now. To wit: the Koster affair.

Now, let's be frank. The Koster case is a crisis, and in such a crisis, the people of Stearns County have a right to expect that their sheriff move quickly, perceive facts, exert power, bring charges, and jail suspects. Sheriff Whippletree not only did *none* of these things, except un-

229

der duress or the pressure of events,
and even now he continues to pursue
some will-o'-the-wisp investigation of his
own deriving and imagination. It is not
our intention to criticize Sheriff Whippletree's many fine years of service . . .

Yeah, sure.

. . . nor to impugn the judgment and
integrity of those who have supported
him in the past. (Readers will, in fact, recall that the *Tribune* itself has endorsed
his candidacy on occasion.) But there
comes a time in the life of any man, and
especially in the life of a public man,
when, if he can no longer perform the
duties required of the office, he ought to
step aside. The sheriff may do this via an
immediate resignation, or he may, if he
so chooses, not place his name on the
November ballot. Either way . . ."

And so on and so forth. *Either way, I'm out*, the sheriff
thought. He walked into the dining room and picked up the
phone. "Bimbo, take over," he said. "Yeah, that's right.
You're in charge. I'm taking some of that annual leave I've
been meaning to. Right. But I'll be back in time for the trial.
What? If something comes up? Don't worry, I read in the papers that you and Mel can handle the whole thing. See you in
September."

He hung up, walked slowly upstairs, where Sarah was putting her hair up in those green curlers that looked like sec-
tions of pipeline.

"Where are the suitcases?"

"What?" she asked, looking up, her face a mass of cold
cream.

230

"I said where are the suitcases?"

"In the attic, like always. Why?"

"Because we're going on a vacation trip," he said. "You ever seen Montana this time of year?"

XII

Whippletree never got away much. He was always too busy. He had been to that Chicago conference, true, and a couple of law enforcement things in St. Paul, and a fishing trip maybe once every three years up to Lake of the Woods, but never, like this, a couple of weeks, with past and future both held in abeyance. It wasn't a bad feeling, all things considered.

He had, however, been out to the Dakotas and Montana once, years before. That was the year they'd lost both Susan and the farm, and he'd needed money. He hadn't known anything then but farming, so he'd signed on with a harvesting crew, riding the big trucks behind the long file of mechanized combines that moved across plains and prairies, from the Red River in Minnesota, into the Dakotas, North and South, and then on into Montana.

Things had changed over the years. The land was as empty and as vast, but the old rutted roads he remembered that snaked forever into the mocking horizon had been replaced by hard, flat superexpressways that shot him savage and clean, untouched, over the trail of his youth, through windravaged towns and brave small cities and across the timeless rolling plains. At the Minnesota border, he was still tense, and muttered a curse at some hapless driver at a Grand Forks street corner. Sarah told him to calm down. But midway through Dakota, the poison began to seep away, and when they crossed over into Montana on the morning of the second day, he was thinking about nothing in particular and actually enjoying himself. He could feel his wife relax, as well. They were not an especially talkative couple, and this trip was no exception in that respect, but they felt together, comfortable, close.

"We should do this more often," Sarah said, at least four or five times.

Well, why not? Maybe they should. *At least every time there's a mass murder in Stearns County.*

After the second night, in Great Falls, Whippletree turned the car toward Augusta, northeast of Missoula, and once in the town he stopped at a gas station.

"Caleb Koster?" repeated the attendant. His voice drawled. His eyes were glinty with laconic suspicion. "Name sounds familiar, but can't seem to place him. You say he's got a spread hereabouts?"

"I heard it was up in this neighborhood somewhere."

"What you want him for?"

The guy must have been a native of Stearns County.

"Used to know his boy. Figured I'd look him up, now that I was in the area."

The man's face twisted with the effort of memory. "His boy? His *boy*! Why, you must mean that kid, the one went down to college in Missoula."

"Right, that's the one."

The man spat. "Never could figure him," he muttered. "Whatever happened to him? Say, where you from, anyway?" He glanced at the license plate. "Minnesota, huh? So the kid went east."

He made a noise somewhere between a snicker and a snort, a combination of resentment and derision.

"So you knew him?"

232

"I wouldn't say that. He wouldn't even talk to me. How's he doing?"

"Oh, fine. He's doing just fine. So you do know where I can get in touch with his pa?"

The attendant finished filling the tank, replaced the cap. "Sure," he said, as Whippletree handed him some bills, "you take this here road due north of town, maybe about twenty, twenty-five miles, till you come to a place has two windmills. That's Cal Koster's place."

The man was as good as his word, and a little more than half-an-hour later, Whippletree turned the car down a long driveway toward a set of sprawling, ramshackle machine sheds and a weather-beaten, lonesome house. The house was set on a slight rise, making it seem even more bleak and solitary. A runty mongrel scrambled out from beneath the tilting porch when the car pulled into the yard, but otherwise there was no sign of life.

"This is where the Reverend grew up?" Sarah asked quietly. The implication was obvious. Who would *not* leave?

The mongrel kept on yapping away, but its tail was going a mile-a-minute, so Whippletree climbed out of the car and looked around. He could make out the angular shapes of machinery in some of the sheds—wheat harvest was pretty well over, by now—and to the west the dim blue mist of the mountains braced the sweeping sky. He looked at the house; the house looked back at him.

"Well, I guess . . ." he started, stepping back toward the car, the dog jumping at him manically, crazy for company, when Sarah said, "Emil, down there," and pointed to a range of low hills out behind the sheds.

Whippletree looked, and saw a figure moving toward them over the bristling wheat-stubble of the fields, moving slowly, steadily, a dark figure who grew larger as he came.

Not as big as Bimbo, when he got up close. More about the sheriff's size, but older—or at least he looked it—and far more weathered. He did not so much look unfriendly as he did guarded; his suspicious glance was so slitted that he appeared not to have eyes at all. He carried a shotgun, crooked in his arm.

"Pheasant," was his first word, and, as if it were a handshake, he broke open the weapon and removed the shells. "What can I do fer yuh?"

"I'm Emil Whippletree, sheriff of Stearns County, from down in Minnesota. You Caleb Koster?"

The man's eyes widened slightly at the mention of "sheriff" and a little more at the mention of "Minnesota."

"I could be," he said.

Whippletree knew then, knew that Koster did not know what had happened to his son and his son's family, and he felt the guilty, sinking feeling that goes with the bearer of bad news.

"I'm afraid I've got something to tell you," he said slowly, "and it's none too good."

But even before he got started, the old man's face changed, took on a cast of something that was not quite fear, not quite sadness. It looked oddly like acceptance and resignation, as if the expression formed the words "all right now, finally . . ."

"Something happen to Matt?" he asked, and Whippletree sensed the tautness in the drawl.

"Is there someplace we can sit down?" Whippletree asked. "It might be better."

Caleb Koster took them into the house, and made apologies neither for the dusty squalor of the ancient furnishings, nor for the strong, rank coffee he brewed by dumping the smashed beans into a saucepan of boiling water. Whippletree talked for about fifteen, twenty minutes, telling exactly what had happened back in Stearns County, and that the case was coming up for trial. Then he stopped.

"Then you didn't come up here to tell me this?" Koster asked.

"I thought you knew."

Koster set down the big coffee mug he was holding and lowered his eyes. Then he looked away to the wall, his shoulders hunched so that he was suddenly smaller. At that moment, he looked like a sad and very beaten man.

"He never told me nothing," he said, after a time, very quietly, full of regret and loss. "He never told me nothing, and now . . ." His voice trailed off.

"We're very sorry," Sarah said, sounding hollow and vaguely alarmed in the old house.

"Yeah," Koster said.

"Here's the thing," Whippletree began. "I don't know how to figure it, and I'm trying to. I don't have much time before the trial starts, and they're fixing to send away a young kid who's no more the killer than I am. I guess . . . I guess I'm up here to see if you can help me any."

Koster looked up with faint interest.

"Do you have any idea the kind of person who might do something like that to your boy?"

The other man's laugh was shuddering and icy. "I reckon there's plenty," he gritted. "Leastways around here. Matt had a knack for doin' that to folks. Makin' 'em wild, ah, what the hell . . ."

He leaned forward, elbows on the table. "You got a kid," he muttered, "you got a kid, and then . . ."

And then nothing is ever the same again.

"Maybe if it hadn'ta been for my wife," he said, voice full of wishing and sadness, lost hope and regret, "Or maybe if it hadn'ta been for me, the way I am, an' all . . ."

He told his story, and it was not that of the "barbarian"

235

Whippletree had heard about from Mrs. Hockapuk and the others. It was just the story of a plain, hard, simple man who had not known what to do. The wife had been "high strung" and "clever" and "restless." The boy had been "a little puny as a kid, couldn't take him on a hunt, say, or even if I could of, his ma wouldn'ta had none of it," and then when he got older, "seemed nothin' was right about me. Wouldn't talk to me, that kind of thing. It hurts a man. And he an' the missus was always sending away for things, books, pictures, things from the Montgomery Ward's catalogue. Like for clothes that nobody else ever wore up here, or even could wear. An' after a while he got like his Ma, who was gettin' worse all along, anyway, lookin' down on everybody. An' over in Augusta, when I'd go into town, the guys would say 'Hey, Caleb, where's that wonder boy of your'n?" It'd make me mad an' I'd come on home an' storm around like a durn fool, an' the woman and the kid would, you know, just smile at each other, like *see*! See how he is! It don't set right. It don't set right. There was nothin' I could do for him, because I didn't know how to go about it, know what I mean? I didn't have it in me."

He shrugged, seemed about to bury his face in his hands, resisted the impulse.

"Maybe it wouldda turned out different if I'da had the time earlier on, time to get out in the hills with him, an' show him how to track a deer, or fix a rabbit snare, an' how to sight a pheasant on the fly come autumn . . ."

His voice trailed off into the unrecapturable sadness of lost years, lost time.

"That's the kind of thing I *am* good at," he said. "Where you don't have to go an' talk so much."

He laughed, not bitterly. "An' so what does he go off an' do, first chance he gets? Becomes a *preacher*!"

He laughed again at the thought of it.

Whippletree sat back and listened. He liked the man. He liked his way and understood it, and he saw how things had happened to him. He understood Koster because there was much of the man in himself, and understood his feeling for the son who had never really been his own, because he knew what it was like to have that kind of loss, even if the loss of Susan had been more final.

"I understand you were down to Lake Eden a while back?"

"That's right."

"Well, how'd you like it?"

"I think I would have liked it fine except I didn't know what I was supposed to do. You see, I'm an old man, alone, and been alone for a long time. An' I figured I'd go down an' see Matt at least one last time. I'm not gettin' any younger . . ."

"You went down to Minnesota? I thought he *invited* you."

"Nope." Koster shook his head sadly. "Nope, I went by myself. An' I didn't know how to handle it. The grandkids was fine, but I got to feelin' their mother was tellin' 'em not to mess with me too much. Had never met her before, an' I can just about imagine what she'd heard of me. Matt hardly talked to me at all. It was upsetting, that's what it was. Here he is, the kingpin of the place, an' all the women flocking around and callin' him Reverend this and Reverend that, an' there I sit a big old dumb bastard, can't hardly read . . ."

"I also understand your son came back here to see you a little later on?"

"Yep. That he did."

"Why?"

"Don't know. Don't know at all. He hardly stayed a day, hardly said anything. 'Course, he never did. Not to me."

The three of them sat there, not looking at one another,

237

and trying to think of what to say next. And, as usual, with each passing moment, it got harder and harder to say anything at all. The old man's loneliness weighed on Whippletree. Finally, he glanced at Sarah and said, "Mr. Koster, how'd you like to join us in town? I figure they must have a pretty good steak place up here, an' maybe a little bourbon, too. An' tell you what, we'll talk about hunting. I might have a little time on my hands come November, and it looks like up here might be the place to come."

Koster liked the idea, and it turned out well. And he had been wrong about himself, in what he'd told Sarah and the sheriff. When he got started on hunts of the old days, or his pride in Montana, or his skill at marksmanship—great shots he'd made in the past—he spoke very well, indeed.

A couple of days later, when Whippletree turned the car around and headed back across the flatlands toward Minnesota, a few more elements of the puzzle had come together, taken shape in his mind.

The Bauch-Fensterwald trial would be in for a surprise witness.

XIII

Clearwater, the town, is set high on the bluffs above the Mississippi, south of St. Cloud. The farmland is rich down in the valley, rich because of the river, and deadly, too, because of it. Whippletree knew.

He and Sarah had returned to St. Cloud, tired, but feeling better for the trip. The sheriff's mind was busy with the case again, and many times during the long drive Sarah would say "Did you hear me?" or "Emil, are you listening?" Actually, he had not been. He was a man whose whole intellectual life—if that is what you would call it; he wouldn't—had been based more or less on instinct, intuition, the "hunch." Now, he had to work something out in detail, point by point, with no certainty of getting an answer, at least not a definite answer. He was distracted.

St. Cloud was practically deserted that Labor Day, the people out at the lakes for one last time, the kids poised for another year of school, and in only three more weeks, maybe a little longer, the snap of the imminent winter would already be in the air at dawn or nightfall. Sarah made a lunch of tomatoes and cheese, sliced salami and rye bread and said that she was going to take a nap on the porch. Whippletree, restless, still thinking, said he was going for a little drive, left the house, and ten minutes later found himself on old Route 52, headed south toward the little town near which he'd grown up, been married, had a child, and come to disaster. When had he been there last? Fifteen, maybe twenty years ago?

The killer may return to the scene of the crime, he was thinking, *but a man seldom goes back to battlefields on which he has been defeated.*

Was there some kind of truth in that? He doubted it. As far as he knew, no killer had returned to the parsonage, and right now he was driving down in the valley, on a road that went through land which had once been his. It was owned now by somebody named Bellwether. He wished Bellwether luck, driving past the place. There was a new house now, and new buildings, or, more accurately, different buildings. When he had left the place, there had been none at all. The flood.

While they slept . . .

March of 1941. Night. He and Sarah slept downstairs, in

the big bedroom just off the porch. Upstairs, in a room with a window overlooking the porch and the river valley, Susan had her little bed, her toys, her pictures on the wall, and boxes of mysterious treasure that only she could properly evaluate. He had come into the house, dead tired and with the rain still on him, and had said, "It's crested. I think it's over," too tired to do anything but fall into sleep.

And while they slept the river rose and went on rising. He awoke to a strange gurgling sound, juxtaposed against the distant, steady thunder of the river itself. He fumbled for matches to light the lamp—they'd had no electricity in those days—and when he failed to find them he sat up and swung his feet over the edge of the bed.

Into water. The house was flooding.

He could not remember if he screamed or not, but suddenly Sarah was awake and they had lit the lamp, which cast strange, frightening shadows on the water that was already rising in their room.

Upstairs, Susan slept.

He was a strong man then, and Sarah a young woman. They waded through the bedroom—not thinking for the moment of ruined furniture, clothes, not even thinking of financial loss—and raced upstairs. Susan was asleep, and as they stayed in her room, trying to gauge the progress of the flood, she stirred, rubbed her eyes, and sat up.

"It's nothing, honey," he said. "Go back to sleep."

And she did, for a time, but it was not nothing. The water was coming up the stairs now, and a strong current washed against the sides of the old farmhouse. If it reached the second story, they would have to get out. But where could they go?

Whippletree thought of these things now, all these years later, driving over the same land, in warm September. Memory. Whether you want it or not, it holds you to the past.

The Fields of Eden

On the wooden shingles of the roof, the rain battered. Outside, the ebb and sob of the throbbing wind drove against the house. And the river kept on rising. What came next had been reduced in the sheriff's brain, compressed to a set of events, one thing after another, that he could neither forget nor keep himself from remembering. When the water reached the second floor, they had dressed and climbed out onto the porch. Surely, it would rise no further, and morning would come, or perhaps the rain would stop. (Would have been nice to have helicopters in those days, too.)

The water kept on rising, and after a time, against the darkness, he had hoisted Sarah onto the roof, then handed Susan up to her, then climbed up himself. They huddled there for a long time, listening to the water, bracing against the wind, clinging to the steep and slippery shingles. His arm was around Susan, his arm was around Susan, his arm was around Susan . . .

When she twisted, or moved, or only shivered, or *what?* Even now, all these years later, he remembered—his body remembered, his muscles remembered, his very *nerves* remembered—the precise quivering movement of her tiny body, and she was *sliding away down the shingles* . . .

Ah, don't think of the rest of it, don't think of the rest of it, the river or God or whatever, who did this . . .

And in a while he was in the Clearwater Cemetery. Over the iron gate at the entrance, in scrollwork, were the words: I AM THE BEGINNING AND THE END.

He stood over the small grave and waited for the feelings to come, the old feelings that had always come before. The sun was warm, the day was still and calm, and the grass was green and soft against the stones. Maybe that was it: a peaceful day. Or maybe it was something else, a gift of luck or chance. But he did not remember his outrage, or the numb grief of 1941, or even the loneliness and despair of all the years since then. Instead, he remembered Caleb Koster, alone and desolate in faraway Montana, still seeking some meaning in the fact that, biologically at least, he had a son. And he thought of Abner Fensterwald, alone and deeply depressed, in his cell now in the Stearns County jail, doomed and abandoned. It was not right, *it is not right,* he thought, and he remembered now not the terrible night on the roof, nor the dark, hopeless dive into the swirling waters of the flood, seeking a tiny hand that was gone, but the smile on Susan's face in the morning, and the way she laughed, and the feel of her small, totally-trusting arms around him, and he thought *I had that once, at least I had that once,* and he thought, *I'll repay that, anyway,* but he did not know how until he walked out of the cemetery, beneath: I AM THE BEGINNING AND THE END.

From A to Z, he thought suddenly. *Mrs. Hockapuk's library!*

"Whippletree's Folly"

I

Judge Alphonse Reisinger did not take any guff in his courtroom. He had been around so long, been Chief Judge so long, that even his idiosyncrasies had come to be regarded as Solomon-like. In bad weather, twinges of rheumatism tended to enhance his natural irascibility, and then he yelled at counsel if he felt like it. (Nicky Rollis and Ricky Steinbrone were grateful for a warm September day.) But he was very fair, very slow to overrule an objection if it meant that certain evidence would not be heard, and his courtroom was often as casual and freewheeling as a gathering of old friends. Or at least acquaintances, which it was, since everybody knew each other.

"All rise!" the bailiff bellowed. "Stearns County Court now in session. Judge Alphonse T. Reisinger presiding!"

And with this the judge strolled in from his chambers off to the side of the courtroom, the long black robe setting off his silvery hair. He took his seat on the high bench, scowled down at the assembled throng, adjusted his hearing aid, and bent to study a sheaf of papers before him. Everybody sat down.

Sheriff Whippletree took a look around and tried to make it casual. In truth, he was nervous. He wasn't quite sure if he would be allowed to go ahead with his plan at all, and even if Reisinger growled "Okay, Emil, it's all right by me," he wasn't sure if he could elude the tricks of Nicky Rollis, while at the same time avoiding the obstacles Steinbrone was sure to throw in his path, if only by sheer accident. And he would have to do both if he meant to save Abner Fensterwald, to show the court what had really happened in Lake Eden on that bloody August night.

"Case of Dennis Bauch and Abner Fensterwald versus the People of the State of Minnesota," moaned the bailiff, reading from a sheet of paper.

The charges had been arranged in this manner by county attorney Rollis, who reasoned that, since Bauch was pleading innocent, but Fensterwald, as his accomplice, was to acknowledge guilt, he might just as well knock off the second bird with a single throw of the stone. And Fensterwald had no lawyer to complicate procedure.

Or so Rollis thought.

The sheriff saw Fensterwald at the defense table now, his hair a little too long for court, his face sallow and thin from confinement and depression. The boy did not look good, he seemed to be trembling slightly, and Whippletree was worried about that, too. It meant things were even less certain than they'd been when he'd visited Abner in his cell.

Next to Fensterwald, bulky Steinbrone was moving his

244

finger theatrically down a long sheet of yellow legal paper, leaning slightly toward his client Dennis Bauch. Now and then his finger would stop and he would glance significantly at Bauch, who stared impassively at the paper or the finger, and then he would give the jury a confident glance before his finger started moving again.

Whippletree, seated in the front row of the spectators' gallery, could see that the sheet of paper was blank. The sheriff figured Bauch must be plenty scared not to laugh, unless he recognized in his attorney a kindred soul, attuned either to the lucky break or the double shuffle. Bauch was dressed up in a suit and tie, maybe for the first time in his life. The pompadour was matted down, low profile for that proud plumage, and when he looked at the jury, he ducked his head, an effort at boyish innocence. It didn't work too well. Most of the jury had heard of Denny before, or read about him in the *Trib* from time to time. Whippletree saw them looking back at the prize defendant, studying him. There was Ben Beumer from Elrosa, and Mrs. Alma Richter, from the southside of St. Cloud, and Harry Bellows, and Mavis Tuckerman and the rest: all good sober Stearns County souls. The sheriff saw them look at Denny Bauch, and he almost heard them saying to one another: "So that's Bauch, huh? *That's* the guy that kicked the commode in the Press Bar and broke it and caused a flood, and that got clocked at 115 on the Mississippi Bridge, and that would have got locked up for raping MarySue Hull, Myron's old lady, if she hadn't been so willing. Why, he don't look like much!"

At the prosecution table, Nicky Rollis, in a blue pin-stripe suit, a gleaming white shirt, and a red- and maroon-striped tie, eyes lidded in feigned sleepiness, leaned back in the leather chair and crossed his arms, waiting. Now and then he glanced at a leather-bound folder on the table, a momentary

insouciant glance that was like a yawn. On the bench, Reisinger shuffled papers, and in the gallery the spectators whispered expectantly: the courthouse regulars who showed up
for every case, relatives and next of kin to those involved in
the trial—Elwood Fensterwald was there, looking upset and
ill-at-ease: *Second thoughts?* Whippletree hoped—and even a
reporter from the Minneapolis paper, up here to find out
what was happening in the boondocks. He would get an illus-
tration.

"All right," the Judge said, looking up. "Let's get this thing
started. Defendants rise. Bailiff, read the charges against accused."

The bailiff seized the moment. "Against Dennis LeRoy
Bauch, murder in the first degree, five counts. Against Abner Reuben Fensterwald, attempted homicide, one count,
and accessory to murder."

"How do the defendants plead?"

Attorney Steinbrone stood up, squared his shoulders,
cleared his throat. "Your honor, my client, Dennis Bauch,
pleads *not guilty.*"

"Mr. Fensterwald?" said the judge, looking down at the
young man. "You are represented by counsel?"

That was for form's sake. As far as Reisinger knew, everything had been arranged before the trial even started, and
Abner was going to do little more than enter his plea and
then testify on the State's behalf.

Abner said something nobody could hear. Reisinger
reached for the knob on the panel in his coat pocket, which
would increase the receptivity of his hearing aid.

"Speak up, will you?" he ordered.

Whippletree waited, and he saw Abner's jaw quiver, and
his body bend forward, as though he were bracing against a
strong wind. *Well,* the sheriff was thinking, *you tried anyway,*

but he's not going to make it, when the young man found something left way down inside, something not beaten or humiliated or frozen out of him.

"*I am,*" Abner said, in a voice that seemed surprised at its sudden unnatural loudness.

Whippletree had a moment of faith in the presence of human courage, however quavering, then wondered if he himself would be up to it.

"Who?" asked the judge in surprise, bending over the bench, and fingering his hearing aid, as if he might not have heard correctly.

Sheriff Whippletree stood up, right behind the gallery rail. He had been in the public eye a long time, and he enjoyed a casual chat with a group of people he knew, but standing here with all eyes on him, and having to go ahead and do a lot of complicated speaking, well, that was not so pleasant, and he didn't care for the feeling. But if Abner could go through his little crisis of courage, then Emil Whippletree could do it, too.

He felt Sarah, taut and rigid in the seat beside him.

He saw Nicky Rollis, partially turned, his face a mixture of bafflement and anger that slowly became surprise, then actual delight.

Well, the son of a bitch, Whippletree thought.

"I am, judge," he heard himself saying. "I'm representing Mr. Fensterwald."

The courtroom went up for grabs. *Tribune* men were scribbling wildly on small steno pads. Judge Reisinger's gavel tapped away somewhere down among the swell and roar. At first, the sheriff was stunned, a little dazed by his own declaration, then by the excitement it had unleashed. He almost wished that Mel Betters had shown up to see it.

Finally, the judge started yelling and people calmed down.

"All right," he said, setting the gavel down. "All right. Counsel will approach the bench. We got to figure out how this is going to work."

II

Whippletree had figured it out as best he could, and then fixed it up with Abner Fensterwald in his cell in the Stearns County jail. Abner was just a little—but not much—better than he had been in the hospital. The cell was dirty and dark gray, with a commode grown yellow through time and misdirection, a cracked sink, a metallic mirror bolted to the wall, and a swing-down cot, hinged to concrete blocks. The place cooked in a late-summer blaze. Abner was on the cot, unmoving, not looking at anything.

The sheriff had given quite a bit of thought to his approach. The main problem, as he figured it, was that he himself didn't really know how to talk to young people. If he wanted to persuade Abs to go along with his plan, it had, first, to sound good, and second, to *be* the kind of thing that would shake Fensterwald out of his lethargy, at least long enough to stand up in the courtroom and say, "Not guilty, Your Honor."

And then, of course, he would need the courage to face down Nicky Rollis, who would go into everything in loving detail, right up to and including the verbal picture of Fensterwald hunched over himself in the choir loft. *But,* Whippletree reasoned, *if he has the guts to make the first step, he just might stumble along well enough later for me to take care of the rest.*

Entering the cell, he'd intended to tell Abner about his own child, and what had happened, and to win his sympathy and cooperation in that way, but seeing the boy on the cot, he changed his mind. Abner was almost a man, but he was also an adolescent boy, with all that implied of ambition and fury, confusion, anger and resentment. And pride.

"You know, son, you and I may be the only two people in the whole county who know for a damn sure fact that you didn't fire that rifle."

Silence.

"Because you didn't have a rifle."

No response.

"And, of course, we know that you brought the shotgun to church, but you didn't fire that, either."

Blank.

"Because you didn't have any shells."

Quiet.

"But I know who got the shells and I know where from."

Fensterwald didn't move, but he stopped breathing and blinked once.

"That's a fact, I do."

Blink, blink.

"And I know who did the killings, and how they were done, and how they used you."

Head turned slightly.

"Now, I'm not saying it doesn't look bad for you, and I know you feel you've been abandoned by a couple of people . . ."

The mouth tightened.

". . . but they're just weak people, scared, and we shouldn't blame 'em too much just yet, even your pa."

Real anger now.

"He's a good man, and I figure he's plenty worried about a lot of things, like his business and his reputation . . ."

More anger, suppressed with effort.

249

". . . when he should have been worried more about you. But it's not the first time a man was weak when what he considered his whole life is about to be put up in the spotlights. It's just that he made some mistakes, and he's not fighting like I figured a Fensterwald would . . ."

Now fully aware, Abner turned around and looked directly at Whippletree.

". . . and I figure, son, you got the fight to make a horse race out of this."

There was a long pause, then with a voice hoarse from disuse, Abner asked, "How?"

"You go up in that courtroom and tell 'em you're not guilty of what they're accusing you of. Sure, you brought the gun in, and you were a damn fool, but they're saying you shot a man, and aided in the murder of five people. You didn't do that, and no combination of anything should make you say you did. I know, I know, Rollis got to you and said you'd get off easy if you played along, and if you didn't he'd put you away for a hundred years, but . . ."

"You know something nobody else does?"

"I sure do, son. At least I think I do. I know who fired that .22 at the Reverend, and why, and I know where it is."

"Where?"

"Son, it's a hunch. I can't tell anybody now, and I can't even go and check it myself lest I jeopardize the case I'm going to make, and the surprise of it. We got to have that. The surprise. Otherwise nobody in the world is going to believe it. But I need your help."

There was a long, long silence.

"You got to fight them, son," the sheriff said quietly. "You got to fight 'em all your life. Nobody says it's easy, *but the bastards got to know when not to mess around with a peaceable fellow.* You can see that, can't you?"

Abner could.

III

The first day of the trial was spent getting Whippletree's position as advocate straightened out. Judge Reisinger scratched his head a while, and finally turned off his hearing aid entirely while he thought it over. The issue, on its face, was this: whether to have two trials, or one. Rollis, whose entire case was based upon Fensterwald, argued for a single, joint effort, confident that he could easily handle the young man, in spite of the complications of his not-guilty plea. Steinbrone, excited, orated pompously for the opposite conclusion—it was at this point Reisinger turned off the hearing aid—smiling at the jury and at Bauch, who himself had the wit to see this might be a stroke of luck for him, too. If, as the Reverend told it, there had been *two* men in the house, and now *one* of them said he had not been there at all, in spite of hearsay, somebody was going to have to produce that second man to make the story hold together. Rollis immediately began to wonder if he could fit Mary Prone back into the affair.

For his part, the sheriff supported Rollis. He *wanted* a joint trial.

"It's this way, judge," he said, feeling a little funny up there at the front of the courtroom, "they're saying, that is, Nicky and the prosecution, that the boy . . ."

"You ought to call him your client, Emil."

". . . that my client was in on this with Bauch . . . ah . . . the other client . . ."

"Defendant, Emil."

". . . right, Bauch, the other defendant. Now, if they're saying that, I figure it's only fair to let me paint an opposite picture with the same characters, see what I mean?"

In the end, the judge did. He set down the procedure to be followed: opening argument for the prosecution by county attorney Rollis, defense argument by Steinbrone, in behalf of Bauch, and finally Whippletree's defense of Abner. The prosecution would built its case and call its witnesses, as would the defense counsels. Then the cross-examination would come, and it was here that Emil hoped to make his case, the only thing he could think of, the only thing that made sense to him. The *Tribune*, that afternoon, did not take a sanguine view of his decision.

SHERIFF TO DEFEND YOUTH ACCUSED IN KOSTER CASE: MOVE STUNS COURTROOM

Effort is "Patently Political," Rollis Claims

The Koster murder trial got underway today at Stearns County Court, after a morning spent in jury selection and attendant preparations. In the afternoon, however, when pleas were entered, Sheriff Emil Whippletree stepped forward to represent Abner Fensterwald, one of the two accused in the case. It was a surprise move to all concerned, as it had been widely known that the Fensterwald youth intended to enter a guilty plea. "It is more than a surprise," said county attorney Nicholas Rollis, "it is a farce. Theater. What does the sheriff know of advocacy? Clearly this is a grandstand attempt on his part to showcase his election hopes in November. Well, it won't work. What Whippletree has done is folly . . .

Even Sarah, always so supportive, was doubtful. "Are you sure you know what you're doing?" she worried.

"Sure, sure," he lied. "I've been in those courtrooms a long time. All you have to do is say, 'I object, I object.' Didn't you ever see it on Perry Mason?"

"Oh, Emil."

"Look," he said, "I may not know all the right moves, and I may not talk so well, either, but I figure I've got the key to this whole thing. Except I've got to go through the trial to bring it out."

"Why don't you just come out and tell everybody, if, like you say, you know?"

"It's just a hunch. I've got to let everybody talk first, and bring everything out. Otherwise it won't fit. Nobody would believe me, especially not now, with things going so badly and the election coming up."

"Oh, Emil, I hope you know what you're doing."

Me, too, he thought. *That damn .22 rifle better be where it's supposed to.*

IV

"And so the State will prove," said Nicky Rollis confidently, leaning over the rail and looking at each juror in turn, "that this . . ." he pointed at Denny Bauch, who was clearly restraining himself from jumping up and punching Rollis out ". . . this savage, this obscenity, this *thug,* offended by the righteous judgment of a minister of God, of *God,* my fellow citizens, did deliberately, knowingly, and with malice aforethought, enter the Koster home and kill, *kill,* a mother and her four children, one of them a tiny baby, and then, having enlisted in his disgusting schemes a vicious young man . . ." here he pointed at red-faced, tight-lipped Abner Fensterwald ". . . who was also bent upon revenge, this young man,

253

a companion in ignominy and savagery, did himself shoot Reverend Koster with the intent to kill him as well. This the State will prove, and, my fellow citizens, since we no longer have capital punishment, unfortunately, the State will ask you to send these . . . these *murderers* away for the rest of their natural . . . or ought I say unnatural . . . lives."

With that, he stepped back dramatically, spun around in a military fashion, and marched to his table.

The spectators' gallery exploded in sudden applause, and Judge Reisinger had to use his gavel. The noise died slowly; the spectators' gallery was packed. The case itself was widely known, and last night's issue of the *Tribune,* with its news of Whippletree, added a dimension of drama that had not been there before. Mel Betters himself was there, and Lynn seated next to him, wearing a subdued but provocative pantsuit, and holding hands with slick-haired Butler, who followed developments with amused lassitude, or so it seemed. The ladies of the Lake Eden Seventh Reformed Auxiliary sat together, close to the jury rail, surrounding Reverend Koster, who was pale and still a little shaky. Due to depression and lack of ability or desire to take solid foods, he had had to remain in the St. Cloud hospital far longer than anticipated, right up until the time of the trial. He seemed locked into himself, and paid little attention to Rollis's opening attack. A figure of pity, a broken, lost man. Courtroom cynics claimed that his seat close to the jury box was no accident, not by a damn sight, and didn't Nicky Rollis think of everything? Even Bimbo Bonwit was there, slouching against the wall beside the door in the back of the courtroom, ducking his crew cut and his tiny head, giving his big broad country-boy grin and shaking hands with everybody as they entered or departed. Mel Betters had told him to do that. No sense wasting a chance to meet the public, right?

Tricky Ricky Steinbrone was up next, giving Bauch's story,

which was, at the beginning, just what everybody had expected. Steinbrone took up his position in front of the jurors, who regarded him with interest, raised his chins, and cleared his throat.

"I will prove, beyond the shadow of a doubt," he pronounced, "that Dennis Bauch did not, could not, and would not commit the crimes of which he is accused. Because on the night in question he was . . ." glancing around and finding Mary Prone in the gallery, her face set stiff against what had to come ". . . with a woman, his fiancée, a hundred miles from the scene of the crime. Moreover, I will show he had no motive for a crime as brutal as that which has been committed, and I will show that others had greater motive . . ."

Whippletree grimaced. Steinbrone was going to throw the weight of it on Abner Fensterwald and the shotgun, in an effort to distract the jury from Bauch. The sheriff got angry, thinking about it. He was always too fair, too decent. He would never use that same tactic, making Bauch the decoy. Maybe he really shouldn't be here at all. .

There wasn't much time to think about it. Steinbrone made his case for Denny Bauch and sat down.

Emil found himself shuffling around awkwardly in front of the jury. They *seemed* sympathetic, or were they just trying pretty hard not to laugh. *What the hell, here goes . . .*

"Well, folks," he heard his voice saying, "I guess you know me, an' I know most of you, just like I know this boy sitting here behind me. Abner Fensterwald. I'm going to . . ." What was the phrase? "I'm going to *attempt to prove*, no, I'm *going* to prove that this boy wasn't in the Koster house on the night of the killings. And he didn't shoot the Reverend with any .22 rifle, because he wasn't there, and he didn't have a rifle." He stopped. "But he did bring a shotgun to the church . . ."

The jury looked up with sudden alertness; the gallery

stirred. *Shouldn't have put it that way. Shouldn't have said that just now . . .*

". . . but that was just to scare him . . ."

Again, a low mumbling from the people. He felt his face reddening. In the corner of his eye, he saw Nicky Rollis grinning broadly. *Got to plug on . . .*

". . . because of having been kicked out as organist of the church. He was mad at the Reverend, you see . . ."

Oh, you damn fool, give it up, he thought, hearing, "An' he just wanted to . . . uh . . scare him . . ." come out of his mouth again.

It was about what he had meant to say, but somehow it sounded a lot different when set against the way he had planned it. Now, too, was the time he was going to say: And I am going to show how the murders were actually performed and tell you who did them; but he felt so uncertain standing up there—a couple of jurors were staring at him with a mixture of pity and embarrassment—and the safety of his chair at the defense table seemed so attractive that he just shuffled once or twice, and said, "That's about it, for now, I guess." And sat down, wiping his forehead.

Judge Reisinger shook his head and cleared his throat. Abner Fensterwald looked as if he'd been betrayed. The sheriff felt sick.

V

The give-and-take of the trial started when the Reverend Matthew Koster came forward and took the stand to give his story. He made a striking appearance, like a wounded crusader, his regular, almost delicate features set off by his paleness, light hair, and the simple black suit he wore.

"I know this is going to be difficult for you, Reverend," Nicky Rollis confided, "but we must get it on the record to see that justice will be done. There is God's law and judgment, and that takes time. Man's justice, to work when it should and as it should, has to proceed according to the rules of evidence. We cannot see what God does, but what we have seen we must put down. Do you understand?"

The Reverend understood. With a pained expression, in a quiet voice that often broke as he fought tears, he told his story. It *had* been Dennis Bauch. He was also sure it *had* been Abner Fensterwald. Bauch's fingerprints in the parsonage were duly discussed and put down in the record, and Mrs. Withers was very sure Abner had been up in the choir loft with the murder weapon.

"And so *there* are your circumstances," Rollis roared triumphantly at the jury, "and *there* are your motives! A tragedy of double revenge perpetrated by two sick and vicious animals . . ."

"Well, then, how did they get together in this?" Emil said, standing up.

"Your Honor!" Rollis complained.

"Emil, you can't do it that way. You have to bring it out by asking questions. The clerk will strike the sheriff's question and the jury will disregard it."

"But hold on a minute . . ."

"Emil, it's not your turn yet."

The people in the gallery were snickering; Rollis was grinning broadly.

"Well, then, when do I get my turn?"

"Later."

He sat down, furious and humiliated. "Don't worry, son," he said to Fensterwald, "something's bound to happen."

Abner did not look so certain. In fact, he looked just about as certain as the sheriff felt.

Nevertheless, as Rollis went on, leading the minister through the events of the fateful night, and through the different motivations of Bauch and Fensterwald—the sermons, the fight behind the bar, the "sin of self-abuse" in the choir loft, Emil's point stood out. However Rollis might finesse it, there was no way to present anything factual, anything circumstantial, to demonstrate that Abner and Denny had ever planned anything together. Of course, Rollis claimed that their relationship was to be simply *assumed,* and obviously they must have been together in conspiracy since they are, by *demonstrated* proof, together in crime.

"The one assumes the other," Rollis said. "It is as clear as Lake Eden in April."

The trial went very badly for the defendants. Steinbrone erred grievously by putting Bauch on the stand. Restraint was alien to Denny, and, if Tricky had coached his man to beware Rollis's goading, the training hadn't taken.

"And so, Mr. Bauch," Rollis taunted, swaggering before the jury, stopping occasionally to smirk at Bauch, hunching in the witness chair, "and so you expect us to believe that you were *shacking up* on the night in question?"

"I was out campin'," Bauch said sullenly.

"Oh, camping, yes, of course. Of course. We all believe that. I believe that. And I'm sure the jury believes that, too. But the problem is, Mr. Bauch, is that no one, with the exception of your . . . ah . . . wife-to-be . . ."

"I don't like your tone none, you . . ."

". . . with the exception of your *friend,* Ms. Prone, can support that, and your shrewd attorney has arranged that she may not testify because . . ."

"Object!" Steinbrone shouted.

"Okay, okay," Judge Reisinger growled. "Drop it, Nick."

"Sure, judge. Anyway, Mr. Bauch, the fact remains that

your fingerprints were in the Koster house . . ." he paraded before the jury with Denny's prints and photos of the Koster house, just as, previously, he had paraded before them with the bloody picture Sheriff Whippletree had taken back in August ". . . and we know your record. You have been a thief, a liar, a no-good bum . . ."

"Object! Object!"

". . . a fornicator, a con man, and a rapist . . ."

"Object! Object!"

"Sustained," the judge said. "Now, Nick . . ."

"I wasn't *ever* no rapist, you goddam son of a bitch," Bauch snarled, doing an instinctive one-armed vault over the rail of the witness box and fixing Rollis for good—he thought—with a jab to the gut and a roundhouse to the side of the head.

Rollis went down—Bauch had a damn good punch—and lay stunned for about a minute, while Farley and Pollock grabbed Bauch from behind and pinioned his arms.

"He's a goddam skinny queer lawyer," Bauch roared to the jury. "If these goons let me go, I'll take the bastard apart!"

Slowly, Rollis came around and got to his feet.

"Do you see what I mean?" he asked the jury. "Do you see what we have here?"

Then he dropped to his knees for a couple of minutes, and the trial had to be adjourned temporarily. Until Tricky Ricky Steinbrone, attempting to salvage lost ground, recalled the Reverend Koster to the stand, and, after recapitulating several points previously covered by Rollis, asked suddenly:

• "Reverend, are you a heterosexual?"

If you have ever seen, say, a boxing match, in which a knockdown occurs, you may have noticed a strange, somewhat ludicrous phenomenon. The first fighter will score a blow; the second fighter will hit the canvas. But between these two events, there will be a delayed reaction. The second fighter, already hit, begins to throw his counterpunch as if nothing has happened, as if he has not even been struck, when all of a sudden the blow registers, like something disastrous from the past come crashing right up into your immediate present.

What happened in Reisinger's courtroom when Steinbrone asked his question was much like that. Koster, serious and undismayed, leaning forward, his mouth already shaping an answer, the judge, leaning sideways, the better to hear, Nicky Rollis, making notes, pen poised in mid-air, and all the rest of the people in the place were caught in a momentary delayed reaction, in which everything still seemed fine. And then they all, as one, rocked back and reeled from the blow. Tricky Ricky Steinbrone had done it again.

Some were silent. Some were astounded. Some were amused or scornful. Many were shocked.

Koster blanched, swayed. "I beg your pardon?" he quavered.

Steinbrone had captured the trial, at least for the moment, and he knew it. He thought he had figured out a way to get Bauch off the hook.

"I asked," he repeated proudly, "if you are a heterosexual?"

No one quite knew what to do. Up on the high bench, Judge Reisinger looked as if he were trying to figure out what was going on. He knew Steinbrone, of course, and the things he might come up with.

"Ah, Rick," he managed to say, before Koster recovered enough from the question to fashion a reply, "ah . . . maybe we ought to talk this over."

Steinbrone, radiant, especially since he seemed to have the whole courtroom buffaloed, now deigned to give his point.

"It's this way, judge," he said. "I don't mean to offend anybody. But it seems to me there's something else in this somewhere. And I think it's the ugly head of sex that has been reared . . ."

By now the courtroom cognoscenti were straining forward, shushing one another, or passing shrewd nods and winks above the heads of the gallery crowd. Tricky Ricky was at it again. If Bauch's neck wasn't in a noose already, it sure *would* be by the time Steinbrone finished his ploy. The blow, the surprise, had now been absorbed and shaken off by the spectators; amazement and amusement vied for supremacy.

". . . and, if the court will permit, I'll explain."

He put his hands on his hips and waited, while Reisinger swiveled in his big chair, shut off his hearing aid again, and scratched his head.

"Okay," he grunted at length, "but the bailiff is going to have to escort the jury out until we can draw a bead on this."

The twelve looked disappointed as they trooped out, then:

"It was *someone else*," Steinbrone began, "someone else and Fensterwald at the house that night. My client wasn't even there. You see, what we have here is a lovers' quarrel."

Koster, on the stand, looked dazed, as if he'd been hit in the gut with another kind of slug.

"You want to explain that?" Reisinger droned skeptically.

"Sure. Easy. Let's look at the facts. All summer long the minister has been giving harangues from the pulpit. And what was he denouncing? He was denouncing *sex*, my friends. You know what that means. It was on his mind. He was obsessed by it . . ."

"No," Koster croaked.

". . . but it wasn't like it seems. He was denouncing my client, Mr. Bauch here, not because of sex itself—my client's prowess is well known, as some of you have heard—but because of the *kind* of sex involved. Now, it's on the record that the other defendant was dismissed from his position as church organist because of a sexual practice of another kind. What I'm suggesting is that . . ." and here he paused dramatically ". . . the key to this whole case is *whatever was going on between Mr. Fensterwald and the Reverend!*"

Koster stammered, and looked about ready to faint.

"And then, Mr. Steinbrone," asked the judge, "*who* was the second man in the house that night? With the rifle?"

Steinbrone smiled. "We don't know that, Your Honor. But we do know it couldn't have been my client. He's not that kind of a guy, and that's why I asked the Reverend if he was a hetero. Now . . ."

But he didn't get a chance to finish, because Koster shot to his feet and responded as no one expected he would, with a trembling outrage that was scornful and excessive, even under the circumstances.

"I am *not!*" he yelled. "I love women. They are . . . for me . . . I have known plenty of women . . ."

And then he realized what he was saying, had said, and his face went blank and ashen.

"I resent and deplore what this man has said," he pronounced coolly, pointing at Steinbrone, "and I want it stopped now. Your Honor?"

"You got anything to say to that?" Reisinger asked Tricky Ricky.

Steinbrone, usually too shrewd by a half, did something that, for him, had a small measure of aplomb.

"Judge, it just seems to me there's a lot missing in all this. All I was trying to do was get a few possibilities. It seems logical enough to me, since we've got the freedom of two men at stake."

His Honor considered that, then asked, "What is your feeling about this, Mr. Rollis?"

The county attorney, who had been following the contretemps with considerable enjoyment, which he had not bothered to conceal, stood up and gave his opinion.

"The prosecution has no doubt whatever that the two accused did knowingly and with malice aforethought carry out the foul deeds for which they have been brought to this trial. However, so certain are we in the ineffable veracity of our case, that we welcome any efforts to challenge it. The outcome will be the same. Conviction of the two accused."

He fixed Bauch and Fensterwald with a glare of theatrical menace and sat down.

"Well, Emil, what have you got to say about this?" the judge said. "It involves your client, you know."

Whippletree, whose mind had been working fast throughout Steinbrone's performance, now had an idea of how he might proceed.

"Can I ask some questions now?"

The judge looked at Steinbrone, who nodded, then at Rollis, who likewise acquiesced.

"Bailiff," ordered the judge, "get the jury back in here. Emil, you want the Reverend to stay on the stand?"

"No," Whippletree said. "Maybe he can help me out a little later on. But first I'd like to get Mrs. Withers up here, if I could?"

"You're a lawyer now, sheriff, defending a client. You can get anybody up here you want."

That didn't sound so bad to Whippletree, and he noted that a number of people in the gallery who had previously been having a good time mocking his efforts no longer looked so pert and saucy. He started hauling the ones he wanted, one after another, up to the stand. The swearing in. The questions. He went at it step by step, heading toward something he only suspected. At first, nothing really happened, except that certain generally known facts got "on the record," as he understood they were supposed to.

Mrs. Withers told about seeing Abner in the choir loft on the day of the killings.

Mrs. Hockapuk, stern and formidable, affirmed that she had warned Reverend Koster of this fact, and that he had said he would take care of it.

The Reverend, already sworn in, was allowed to reply from his seat in the gallery. "Yes, Mrs. Hockapuk *had* said that, but I didn't expect . . . not . . . not then, that anything could happen. After all, ah . . . Abner was . . . just a boy . . . and I had two calls that day."

"Who'd you call on?" asked the judge.

"It is . . . ah . . . somewhat confidential. I could . . . if I might . . . simply give the locations, and then if, later on, you need . . ."

"Okay."

"I had one call at a home on Lake Eden, and another in Paynesville."

Nobody noticed the sheriff write "Paynesville" in his note pad, and the few who paid any attention as he passed a note to Deputy Lugosch, seated by the gallery rail, quickly turned their attention back to the trial. On his part, Whippletree tried to stay calm. He was convinced, now, that he had the final key. If it would just work out that way . . .

"And you never did go into the church, then?" he asked Koster.

"Of course, I did. When I got back from Paynesville. It was late. And obviously there was no one inside."

"Thanks, Reverend," Emil said, turning around to face the

gallery. "And now I'd like to get Mr. Butler up here for a minute."

A stricken look appeared on the smooth handsome face of Lynn Betters's latest boyfriend, and his smooth, even tan did not hide it. Lynn looked at him quickly, alarmed, and tried to smile. He recovered a little, though, and strode up to the witness stand confidently, taking the oath in a deep voice.

Whippletree asked him who he was, where he was from, and that necessary sort of thing. Then: "Where were you on the afternoon of the murders?"

"Out at Miss Betters's place, on Lake Eden."

"All afternoon?"

Butler, as if sensing a trap: "That is correct. All afternoon."

"And where were you that night?"

"In Minneapolis. We went to see the ball game in Bloomington, the Minnesota Twins, and we stayed over in Minneapolis."

"Where, in Minneapolis?"

"At the Radisson Hotel."

"I see, I see," Whippletree said slowly. He was making a few points that might come in handy. He caught a glimpse of Lynn, her chin raised defiantly.

"And, Mr. Butler, can you prove you were there that night?"

"Well, I . . . uh . . ." Butler saw the problem. "Well, you see, sheriff, we're . . ."

"You're telling me the two of you stayed in separate rooms, aren't you? On account of you're not married?"

There was a juicy titter among the spectators, and in the stand before him Whippletree saw Butler trying to think his way out of this one.

"Now, don't you worry about that," the sheriff said, reaching inside his old suit-coat pocket and pulling out a number of photocopied sheets of paper. "Now, don't you worry, because, you see, I don't think you were down there at the Radisson at all."

"But I . . . we were . . ." Butler protested, half-rising, all his composure gone. "I . . ."

"Because you see I took the trouble to get the registration pages for that night from the Radisson, and lo and behold your name isn't on it, and *neither is Lynn's.*"

Butler let out a breath, sank back, and looked profoundly relieved. The court room silenced. Tension had been building, it looked like Whippletree was about to spring a trap, but now Butler's reaction was puzzling.

"Of course, I didn't use my own name," he said, with great relief.

"Which one did you use?" Whippletree handed him the pages. Butler ran on down the list of registrants. "Here," he pointed.

"Well, well," said the sheriff, "if it isn't Mr. and Mrs. Smith."

Everybody laughed, except Butler and the Betters, Lynn and her father. *Got old Mel on that one,* Whippletree thought, with no little satisfaction.

"You're sure this is you?" he asked Butler.

"Yes," the witness acknowledged grudgingly.

"Well, no matter, we can always get back to that later. What I want to know now is, when you were out at the lake house that afternoon, did anybody stop by?"

Pause. "Yes, Reverend Koster did."

"What for?"

"To see Lynn, he said."

"Why?"

266

"She was . . . she was supposed to have been in to some kind of a counseling session earlier in the week or something . . . I don't know . . ."

"And he wondered why she hadn't shown up?"

"Yes. I guess so. That's what he said."

"This was at the lake home?"

"Yes."

"Had you met him before?"

"No."

"What was your reaction? To him?"

Butler looked nervous now and seemed to be trying not to look at Koster, who watched from the gallery rail.

"It was . . . was a little . . . ah . . . awkward," he said. "I didn't really notice too much . . ." He swallowed. "I guess . . . guess he was a little nervous, or like that."

"Why didn't you notice much? Why was he nervous?"

"Well, Lynn and I were . . . had just been, that is . . . and . . . anyway, the Reverend interrupted us."

"I see. So maybe he was a little nervous, seeing the two of you in, maybe, an obvious state?"

"Could have been. I think so."

Whippletree had watched Nicky Rollis in court for a lot of years, and now, with these questions going pretty well and feeling confident, he tried a little Rollis trick. He walked slowly away from Butler, seeming to go back to the defense table, then suddenly he turned and shot the question:

"An' what were you and Lynn doing around the Seventh Reformed Church at about suppertime, like Mrs. Hockapuk told me?"

Butler looked confused. "What . . . when was that?"

"That was at suppertime, Mr. Butler. The evening of the murders. What were you doing . . ."

267

"Oh, *that.* That was just before we left for Bloomington and the ball game. We had to bring something over there. Something the Reverend had left at the house."

"What?"

"I don't know. I didn't look. A notebook, or something."

"It was my sermon notebook," Koster said, when the judge had given the sheriff permission to ask. "I often take it with me on calls, in case I have an idea for a sermon. It's not easy to keep thinking of new ideas . . ."

"Anyway," Whippletree queried Butler, "did you give it to him?"

"No, Lynn gave it to Mrs. Koster. The Reverend wasn't there."

He had been out on his Paynesville call at the time. Paynesville was a small town about fifteen miles away. Several of its residents were parishioners of the church in Lake Eden.

"Okay, Mr. Butler, that'll be all. Thanks a lot."

Butler, trying to stay cool, could not keep a flash of contempt from his face as he came down from the witness stand.

Too bad, Whippletree thought, *and now comes the hard part.*

"I want to talk to Lynn Betters," he said.

He was right. It was not easy. In the first place, she was hostile and charming and devious all at the same time, and, in the second, hardly anybody, with the possible exception of Sarah—and that was only *possible*—thought that what he was doing was anything but a shabby, dirty political ploy.

"You once told me, when I saw you in the Griffin Room, Miss Betters, that you liked men."

She smiled. "Yes I do. Don't you like women?"

Laughter, and not on the sheriff's side. *Things really have changed,* the sheriff felt. *Today you can mess around, and if you're brazen enough, people will applaud. In the old days, things were right and wrong. Wrong might have been fun, but people still knew what it was.*

"I do," Whippletree defended himself. "I do. But the question is how many men do you like?"

That might have been a fine, tough question to ask somebody like Mary Prone, who had no clout. But this was Commissioner Betters's daughter.

Rollis was on his feet. "Hey, come on now, Emil! Hey, judge . . ."

"Emil, have you got something in mind? Otherwise . . ."

"Yes, I do. I want to establish something here. Now, before, Steinbrone brought up a . . . well, a *sex* angle on this, and I want to follow it a little ways."

Reisinger thought that over. "Well that's legitimate, all right, but I'll have to warn you to mind your manners."

"Okay, Your Honor."

Lynn, in a huff, regarded him angrily.

"About how many men have you known?" he asked.

She laughed scornfully. "Quite a few."

"I meant in a Biblical sense," he said.

She stopped laughing.

Rollis was on his feet again, and they went through the whole business they'd just gone through before.

"Look," Whippletree explained. "She's already been Mrs. Smith down in the Radisson Hotel in Minneapolis and we know she and her boyfriend—*Mr.* Smith!—were at the church at the same time the shotgun was in there. Did one of them go in? Did they find the gun? What happened? My client . . ." He indicated young Fensterwald, who was beginning to look a little encouraged. "My client isn't going to have to spend a bunch of years in Red Wing on account of I didn't try to find out what happened."

"Okay, Emil," said the judge, warning him again to go easy.

Whippletree walked around up there a little, thinking of what to ask next. He was starting to feel comfortable, and he thought of his younger brother, whom he'd put through school, now a lawyer in Des Moines. *Well, it must run in the family,* he joked to himself. Anyway, there was no point in horsing around with this. He had to get it all out in front right away, or they would eventually nickel-and-dime him to death with Rollis's objections. And if he lost Reisinger's good graces he would be up shit's creek.

"Miss Betters, did you ever *know* Reverend Koster?"

There was no doubt what he meant. The crowd remembered Koster's own passionate outburst. Once again, the place went up for grabs.

"Shocking! Disturbing!" were a few of the milder things Whippletree heard, as Reisinger pounded away with his gavel.

"It's my last question along this line," he pleaded. "Just this one, no more."

"It better be, Emil. Okay, Miss Betters, go ahead and answer that one."

Lynn lowered her eyes, as counterfeit as anything the sheriff had ever seen. What modesty! What a show.

"No," she said softly. "No, but he wanted to. I could tell."

The Reverend, called to answer by Whippletree, reluctantly admitted, without embarrassment, that, yes, he was tempted, just like other men, and that Lynn Betters was an attractive woman. In fact, he seemed greatly relieved, to talk about it, after what Steinbrone had tried to do to him earlier in the day.

"Well, it's getting pretty late," said the judge, as four

o'clock came around. "What say we break it off for today and . . ."

Whippletree had a proposal, though.

"I think I can wrap this up tomorrow," he said. "If we all go out and finish this trial in Lake Eden."

"What? How can you think that . . . ?"

The sheriff had thought it through already.

"Nothing to it. There's that big lawn next to the parsonage. I'll have Bimbo and the boys put up one of those big beer-picnic tents. We can all get inside there, easy. It'll be bigger than this courtroom, and fresh air, too."

Rollis said it was a trick. Steinbrone didn't care. The judge thought it over.

"And you'll tie it up tomorrow?"

"Unless I'm off by a mile," Whippletree said, "by this time tomorrow, we'll know who the killers are."

The spectators quieted. There were a few tentative snickers, then nothing.

"Okay by me," Reisinger decided. "Bailiff, you make the travel arrangements. Lake Eden in September isn't all that hard to take. Court's adjourned until ten tomorrow."

The doors opened and the people poured out.

"Are you sure?" Sarah hissed.

The sheriff barely heard her. He was listening to the dull murmuring conversations of the people, trying to gauge their tone. They thought it was interesting, but they thought it was a gamble. He had surprised them a little and they were no longer as willing as the bar-and-grill crowd to write him off as an old incompetent, soon to be on the skids.

Mel Betters sidled up to him, malevolent and ferret-like.

"Now I don't even care how this winds up," the commissioner snarled. "You're through in this county."

271

Just at that moment a *Tribune* photographer knelt in front of the two, and Betters transformed his face. In the picture, when it was printed, Betters was grinning away, not a care in the world, and the sheriff wore a tired, hangdog expression.

"Commissioner encourages quixotic sheriff after a difficult day in the courthouse," read the caption.

VI

The tent was roomy and cool, and a morning breeze came in off the lake and across the grass. Bimbo, complaining all the while, had made sure there were plenty of tables and folding chairs. Everything was set. Whippletree was nervous again. It was not that he didn't think he was right; it was more that he wasn't sure he could do the right things at the right time in order to get the truth out. Above all, he wished that he'd had more education.

At around ten, Judge Reisinger's big black Chrysler pulled up and the judge got out, slow and a little stiff, but dignified. He glanced at the tent and the arrangements inside it, told the bailiff to bring him a pitcher of water and a glass, sat down and banged his gavel.

The participants, who were just about adjusted to being in the courthouse, seemed edgy again, not knowing what to expect. Fensterwald stared at the belltower of the church, with an expression of disgust and pain. Bauch looked mean today—meaner than usual—avoiding the parsonage, not looking at the church, poised at the edge of his folding chair as though about to make a break for it. This was his home town and a large group of spectators, overflowing the tent, seated on the grass, kept an eye on him. He didn't like it, and now

and then he glared back halfheartedly. Tricky Ricky Steinbrone, however, was in an excessively good mood.

"You're all right, Emil," he'd said, arriving in Lake Eden
that morning and giving the sheriff a big slam across the
shoulder blades. "God, but you picked up my tactic like nobody's business!"

"What?"

"Ho ho, now don't go playin' possum on old Tricky Ricky.
I know what you were up to when you got Lynn Betters on
the stand and started asking her who's she's been letting in.
You were just getting in on my coattails. Hell, you and I both
know the Fensterwald kid is probably okay, and so's the Rev,
but I had to set up a diversion, see what I mean, to separate
Denny from the case."

Whippletree said nothing.

In the folding-chair "gallery," behind a taut length of
clotheslines—the fateful clotheslines and laundry poles were
no more than ten yards outside the tent—sat Mary Prone,
overdressed and chain smoking, with Trixie Wade at her
side. Now and then she and Bauch looked at each other, al-
lowing themselves no expression that anyone could read.
Never can tell about love, Whippletree figured. The Betters
were there, of course, and Elwood Fensterwald. Last night
he'd called Emil and pleaded, "Jesus, what an ass I've been.
Now they're calling him a queer. I never figured on this. It
ain't fair, even to him. Ain't there something you can do?"

"I hope so," was all he could say.

Reisinger banged the gavel down and said, "What the hell
is this?" picking up a Gideon's Bible from the table. In fact,
each principal at the trial had a Bible in front of him, courtesy of Schwagum's Motel in St. Cloud, courtesy of Emil Whippletree.

"Well, you see, judge," Whippletree began, standing up

273

and walking around a little—it felt much better on the soft grass under the tent than it had yesterday in St. Cloud—"it's been a suspicion of mine for a long time that whoever was in on this, the murders, was a regular participant of the Seventh Reformed, or at least knew the Reverend's sermons pretty well. What's been done, if you ask me, has something to do with those sermons. Now, I'd like to get the Reverend up here for a little to explain a few things to us."

Reisinger nodded, and Koster, looking a little more relaxed today, wearing a short-sleeved white shirt and a black tie, took the chair in front. The bailiff reminded him that he was already sworn.

The sheriff picked up his Bible and turned to a page he had marked with a ripped corner of the *Tribune.*

"All right, Reverend. Let's take Isaiah, 41."

He waited until everyone had found the passage, then read it: "'I will open the rivers on the bare heights . . .'"

When he had finished, Koster and the others looked up at him with curiosity.

"Now, what does this have to do with anything?" Nicky Rollis felt compelled to complain.

"We'll see," Whippletree said.

The judge shrugged and said go ahead.

"Reverend," asked the sheriff, "what does that mean?"

He detected something in Koster's eyes just then, something that he had seen in the eyes of a lot of people during his life: the very smug, pleasant, just ever-so-slightly intolerant hint of assumed superiority.

"It's really quite simple," Koster said. "This is really a pæan of hope for fertility."

"A what? *Pe-on?*"

Koster smiled. "*Pay-on.* A celebration. An expression of joy."

"I see. And you gave this sermon, as I see by your notes, on January 11. Pretty cold to be talking about 'fountains in the valleys' that time of year, isn't it? 'Specially in Minnesota."

Whippletree got a little chuckle out of the crowd with that one, but it was ambivalent. They were waiting. Koster smiled again. "No, sheriff. In the first place, the beginning of the year is precisely the time for celebration. And, secondly, it's not literal."

"What?"

"Literal. It doesn't mean exactly what it says. It's symbolic. As a verse, it stands for something else. Not myrtle and olive and acacia, but a private meaning, close to the heart, a hope that all will go well throughout the year and that everyone will thrive."

Whippletree took that in. "I see," he said, walking slowly up and down. "I see. Then, here on March 28, you say"— he found the passage and read—"'Wait for the Lord, and keep his way, and he will exalt you to possess the land.' That's from Psalm 37. Now, are you telling me this is . . . ah . . . *literal* too?"

Koster looked slightly exasperated now, as though trying to explain something quite elemental to a rather dull-witted child.

"No, *not* literal. Symbolic. Representative. That verse is full of hope, as, for example, hope for a good harvest, something like that."

"Oh, I think I get it now," Whippletree said. "Let's see, let me try a couple of these others."

He turned more pages to another of his makeshift bookmarks, and directed the others to follow him to the next Psalm, Number 38.

"For my loins are filled with burning," he read. "This is the sermon you gave on June 20, Reverend. 'There is no

275

soundness in my flesh . . . and I groan at the tumult of my heart.'"

He looked directly at Koster.

"Now what does *that* mean?"

The Reverend looked vaguely uneasy now. "As I told you, these things are symbolic."

"So? Of what? This is pretty different than the other sermons you gave earlier in the year."

"Well, really, sheriff, one can't give the same sermons every Sunday."

"Anything happen just before June 20 to make you feel so bad?" He read again: "'I am utterly spent and crushed. . . .'"

Koster said nothing, and in his glance now there was, not superiority, but an uneasy hostility.

It's going to work, Whippletree allowed himself to hope. He said nothing for a moment, but studied the spectators, as far back as the edge of the tent. Everything was ready.

"Well, now, Reverend, let's take a look at the sermon you gave just before the tragedy. You talk about love and will. Now, that's very nice. And here in your notes you have written, 'to reach love we must be willing to suffer.' Well. All right . . ."

Then, one after another, Whippletree read the court the passages from Isaiah: "'Therefore, I have set my face like flint . . .'" and from Psalm 66, "'If I had cherished iniquity in my heart, the Lord would not have listened . . .'" and from Corinthians: "'He who sows bountifully will also reap bountifully.'"

Then he stopped. Koster, on the witness chair, was motionless, waiting, alert. The judge looked perplexed. The spectators leaned forward. Rollis had a look of distaste around his mouth and eyes, as though just on the verge of deciding the sheriff was really nuts.

"Did you reap bountifully?" Whippletree asked.

"What is this?" Koster smiled.

"You must have expected to," the sheriff went on. "The topic of your sermon on the Sunday after the murders was going on to be 'The Lord Grant Us Acceptance and Rest.' Isn't that right?"

"Why, yes, of course, but . . ."

Whippletree raised his arm, half-facing Koster, half-facing the watching crowd. This would be it.

"Reverend Koster, *you* murdered your family and shot yourself!"

It took at least fifteen minutes before everything calmed down again, and during that time Whippletree knew he had failed. At first, Koster turned livid, angry, and confused, but then he seemed to exercise a last reserve of restraint, and by the time Reisinger stopped pounding the table, he was composed agian.

"Emil, you better watch it," advised the judge. "Maybe you just better sit down."

"No, Your Honor, I can prove it."

Reisinger thought it over. "Well, now, Emil, I'm going to allow that, but only because after what you've said, I don't want any doubts remaining about this man here."

By now everybody had assimilated the situation, and they waited eagerly for the show. That Whippletree, what a card . . .

No sense being nice now. "Reverend, those sermons you gave this summer may be literal or symbolic or whatever you call them, but to my way of thinking they show a man who is pretty unhappy. Under a lot of pressure. You want me to tell you why?"

Koster stared back at him coldly. "Tell me why, sheriff."

"Because you fell in love with a woman, didn't you."

Koster took that, not too well, but he took it.

"And what you couldn't stand, absolutely couldn't stand, was not that you loved somebody else besides your wife, but that the woman you loved was giving it away free. To everybody but *you!*"

Koster shot to his feet. "It's not true, it's not true!" he said. "She . . ." And then he stood there, hand in the air, as though gesticulating behind some pulpit made of insubstantial air. He did not have the will power to control his eyes, and Whippletree saw, as did many others, his glance travel across the gallery, until his eyes found Lynn. A look of sick horror came into her face, and stayed there, like a crushed flower, slowly decomposing. Beside her, Butler seemed to shrink away.

Koster sagged into his chair.

Rollis was on his feet. "Your Honor, this is all . . ."

"I call Caleb Koster to the stand," Whippletree yelled above the tumult, and as he spoke, the minister's father, his hair cut and slicked down, wearing a shiny old blue serge suit, ambled embarrassedly up the aisle through the folding chairs.

"Now, what is this?" Rollis was asking.

"Judge, I need only this witness and another one, and I'm through."

Reisinger, who had followed the drift of the sheriff's attack better than most, nodded his concurrence. He, too, was watching the spectators' gallery; he, too, was waiting.

Caleb Koster was sworn in. Father and son crossed as the minister returned to his seat. The father looked at his son, something of sadness in the glance. The son dipped his head in greeting, face expressionless.

"Did your son visit you on your ranch in Montana, short while ago?" asked the sheriff.

"Yes, that he did."

"Was anything missing when he left?"

"Yes."

"What was it?"

"An old .22 rifle, used to belong to *my* daddy."

"Thank you, Mr. Koster."

Whippletree turned around and stared straight at the Reverend. "That true? You take it?"

Koster was on his feet, and this time he gave it his best. "It is not true! None of this is true! It is a damnable lie. Why, for as long as I can remember, that man"—he pointed at his father—"has attempted to hinder me in whatever way he could. We never had *anything!* We barely had a decent life! Why, I was forced to leave home as soon as I was able . . ."

"Calm down, son," Judge Reisinger commanded. "Emil?"

Whippletree got ready. "This is the way he did it," he began. "It's all on the record, so let me take it one point at a time. He did it, first, for love. What he thought was love. But how he did it is what we need to know. If that doesn't stand, two innocent men, Bauch and Fensterwald, are going to have to suffer more than they already have, and that's not justice. Now, we know the shotgun was in church on the afternoon and evening of the killings, and we know the Reverend knew it was there. We also know he was very upset, that day in particular, because he'd found Lynn with another man, *flagrante delicto*, the way I read it. He already had the rifle from Montana, and maybe he was thinking of using it, maybe not, but now he saw his opportunity. The shotgun was perfect. Now, remember when Lynn and Mr. Butler came to the church around suppertime? And Koster was away to Paynesville on a call? Well, it was a call, all right."

From his breast pocket, he withdrew a piece of stationery. "The Reverend isn't on trial, right now, so this deposition should do it. It's from Dirk Kreuger, of Paynesville Sporting

279

Goods. You want to know who came in and bought what on the afternoon of the murders?"

"This is outrageous!" screamed the Reverend. "This is—"

"Shut up," said the judge.

"But, of course, there are other things. Abner, attempting to get his gun back, saw Koster pacing up and down in his house, the mark of a man who is thinking, or who is tense, or both. And in this case I would expect it would be both. When we found the Reverend, bloody and roped to the poles, he had on clothes and shoes. It doesn't sound likely that murderers would allow a man to dress and put on his shoes before they killed his family and shot him, now does it?"

He stopped.

"Who tied him, then? Who *shot* him?" Rollis wanted to know.

"He tied himself. And he shot himself."

"Suicide?"

"No, a plan. He thought it was perfect."

"Aw, Emil, you're full of . . ."

"Calm down, everybody," said the judge.

"Judge," said Whippletree, "let me take you over here to the laundry lines and give a little demonstration."

Several minutes later, the judge, defendants, crowd, and Koster were gathered around. The minister had assumed an air of cold outrage, but he was conscious of the fact that even the Ladies' Auxiliary members were keeping shy of him, and that, behind him, Bimbo Bonwit kept a sharp eye.

"Look," said the sheriff. He cut a short length of rope from the clothesline, knotted it to one wrist. Did the same with the other. Then, on the dangling ends, he fashioned slipknots.

"Okay," he said. "I'm Koster. I've already returned the shotgun and the shells to the music seat in the church. Now all I have to do is shoot myself with the .22, toss the slipknots over the tops of the laundry poles . . ."

"You're losing me, there, Emil. Where's the gun?"

"Right here," Whippletree said. He bent to the base of one of the laundry poles, shaky in the ground, and yanked it up. It was nothing more than a hollow piece of metal. It was also empty.

The crowd let out an exhalation.

"More to go," Whippletree said and yanked the other one out, too.

There it was. A small weapon, quite old, and rusted now from the weeks underground. The stock had been sawed down so it would fit inside the pole. Caleb Koster would identify it as his missing weapon.

But still, it had to be a suicide attempt, didn't it?

Back under the tent, Whippletree called his last witness, Mrs. Hockapuk.

"Did the Reverend use the library much?"

"Yes. Quite a lot."

"And did he ever withdraw books with the numbers QM 23 B46, QM 23.2 E48, and QM 23 F713?"

"Yes, he did."

"What are the names of those books?"

"I have them right here," the librarian said, taking them from a shopping bag, holding them up in turn. "Berger's *Elementary Human Anatomy,* Edwards's *Concise Anatomy,* and Francis's *Introduction to Human Anatomy.*"

"Had the Reverend ever indicated an interest in anatomy before?"

"No, sir. Not until this summer."

"Is there anything unusual about any of these books?"

"Yes, one is marked."

281

"Could you show us, please."

Mrs. Hockapuk certainly could. Smiling happily at Mrs. Withers and the rest, she opened one of the books to a full-page diagram of the human physique, showing the position of all internal organs. On the diagram, just a notch up and to the side of the stomach sac, just a little below the lung sac, and just out of reach of rib and spine, there was a small, barely perceptible pencil mark, in the shape of a cross. It was the exact spot, give a jot or tittle for nervousness maybe, in which Koster had wounded himself.

"And so you see . . ." Whippletree began.

Bimbo Bonwit, seated directly behind Koster, had been leaning forward, his attention focused on the picture ("Wow, is *that* what I look like inside!"), waiting to see what would happen, what the point was. Koster did not have to do this. He already knew. So now, as Whippletree got ready to pound the final nail, the minister ducked forward under the piece of rope that separated the gallery from the "court" pro-per, dashed right past the jurors' chairs, and cut under the edge of the tent, on the run.

Everything stopped.

Except Bimbo, who lurched forward, knocked the rope down, and with it the tent braces on either side of the huge canopy. The canvas above the crowd began to sway, and the sheriff had the wit to yell "Take it easy, take it easy. Bimbo, get him."

Whippletree had assigned his gigantic deputy to watch Koster, not knowing what to expect from the minister. From the start he had admitted to himself that he did not like the man, but he had been willing to ascribe at least a part of that feeling to his own resentment. Then there had been the al-teration in the story of the fight with Bauch, and the too-abrupt switch in his accusation from Mary Prone to Abner

282

Fensterwald. And then there had been the sermons. But now, standing under the collapsing tent, Whippletree felt only fatigue and sorrow, sorrow mostly for Caleb Koster, who slumped now in a chair, oblivious to everything. He had needed the man, used him, and that need and use had brought the elder Koster to the edge of a despair at least as acute as the panic toward which his son now rushed.

Bimbo was fast for a big man, but not fast enough. Koster got into the church, as the crowd fanned out of the tent, some frightened, some weeping, some excited. Koster locked himself in. Bimbo slammed against the door a couple times, then ripped it off its hinges. Lugosch and Pollock followed him inside, with Pollock quickly coming out again.

"He's gone up the tower, sheriff," he said. "He's got the door locked."

"Well?"

"Bimbo's breaking it down."

Whippletree felt a hand on his shoulder. He turned around. It was Denny Bauch.

"Let me at 'im, Whip. C'mon, whaddya say? I can get the bastard for ya, and it'll be a pleasure. For me an' Mary, both."

Whippletree had to say thanks a lot.

Too late anyway. Another door crashed open, victim of Bimbo's prowess, at the same time Koster appeared in the belltower, high above the green grass below. The sheriff knew what was going to happen now, and he felt a sick, sinking feeling. *After all this death, please, not another . . .*

Koster, arms wide, eyes afire, stood in the tower and started over the railing. His eyes found Lynn Betters far below. She buried her head in Butler's shoulder, which seemed to disturb the minister all the more.

"Lynn, darling," he cried, "I did it for you. For *us*. For what could have been. All my . . . all my life I've had

. . . *nothing* .   don't you *see*! Nothing! I had to
. . . to start too young, marry . . . too young . . . I want
things, too, just like everybody else . . . all I ever wanted
was love . . ."

His whole body was on the flimsy railing of the belltower
now, both feet, one arm bracing, one arm balancing in thin
air.

Whippletree knew it was over.

". . . Bonnie and the kids," he called, his voice thin and
unreal way up there, "they're all right. They're saved now
. . . at . . . at peace . . ." He twisted on the rail, and one
foot left it. "They'll never have to suffer or be poor again,
and . . ."

And then he jumped.

"Going Home"

Lynn Betters had had nothing to do with it, she said. She had known how he felt, because she had seen the same symptoms in other men. But she had not led him on, she said.

Some people believed her. Some people didn't. As always.

There on the green, after it was all over, Mel sidled up to the sheriff. "Whip," he said. "You and me's always been able to work out a deal. I know we've had our differences, an', well, what the hell . . . you got that helicopter tomorrow or sooner, long's you don't, you know, hit me too hard on that patronage setup. Got to take care of my boys, you know how it is."

"What about Bimbo?"

"Well, Whip, you know, I think Bimbo'll be withdrawing from that race for sheriff. No point in it now. Just be wasting his talents, really. I figure I'll make a re-think of his career for him. They'll be needing a police chief in Sauk Centre pretty soon—old Elmer Rosha went insane on us—and, after what happened here this morning, I figure Bimbo'd be a natural."

Could very well be.

The sun was climbing toward September noon, and the white tower of the old church stood against the deep green leaves of late summer. The sheriff saw it all again in his mind. Reverend Koster's white shirt flashed against the sky. His feet kicked off the railing of the belltower, and he pushed off with his hand, toward death. Then he was in the air, and his arms spread like wings to meet his peace. All over, lost, done.

Then Bimbo Bonwit crashed onto the tower—the whole structure seemed to bend and sway under his bulk—and lashed out one gigantic arm, catching the slender Koster around the waist.

Bimbo grunted and drew him back. To safety, and the law. Below, the crowd watched, quiet, as if in prayer.

II

Everybody had lunch at the Valmar. Plenty of beer and not a little bourbon went around. Denny Bauch kissed Mary Prone in front of the whole assemblage, then yelled, *"The hell with all of you!"* Everybody cheered. Trixie Wade gave the sheriff a big kiss on the forehead. Elwood Fensterwald told everybody what a stupid damn fool he had been and he had one of the gutsiest kids in the county, and if the kid could just stand him, well, they could make a go of it, all right. And Mel Betters came over to apologize to Sarah, just as the sheriff had demanded if Mel didn't want to get his ass run out of politics altogether come November.

Koster had long since been booked into the St. Cloud jail when Whippletree and Sarah climbed into the squad car for the trip back. (That helicopter would sure come in handy, all right.) Sarah was tired, and the sheriff said nothing as he turned onto Main Street and headed back. Behind him, the church tower stood lonely and tragic against the incredible royal-blue sky of Minnesota. Ahead lay the pleasant, peaceful, easily rolling fields that were a joy to drive through when you had no worries and you had the time. Wasn't it all you needed, really? Enough to get by and a little peace?

There was a lot more in the world now, the sheriff was thinking. There was far too much. The hidden quality of goodness in the old days had been the lack of things, but it was not until there was abundance that it was missed. Then you had to work just to live. Now you simply existed, with money, ease, boredom, and aimlessness. Many had been destroyed by the possession of things that were unnecessary and even meaningless. Koster had perished in the desire for things that promised ruin. The corruption was in the desire; the ruin lay already all about.

The poor bastard. He had had everything. And now, forever, his memories would be terror, would be loss, would be the blue flashing reverberation of death.

What was it with man! What was it *in* man?

Whippletree remembered again, remembered the feel of the tiny arms around his neck in the morning, and how it was to walk in the woods in spring, when every flower, every joyful cry of bird or animal was a chorus to his daughter, his wife, himself. *Oh, yes, the past comes with you, but it is up to you to make it what you wish.*

Abruptly, Whippletree swung the patrol car into an illegal

U-turn, right there on Main Street in Lake Eden. Sarah, dropping off into a doze, was surprised.

'Emil . . . what . . . ?"

"We're heading down to Clearwater for a little," he said. He suppressed a happy sob. "There's somebody down there I've got to thank."

THE END